A CHILD WIDOW'S STORY

> *By buying this Katha Book*
> *you give 10% of its jacket price to help educate a child at the*
> *Kathashala*
> *Giving has never been so enjoyable, so affordable.*

OUR RECENT RELEASES

Fiction

Asomiya Handpicked Fictions
   Selected by North East Writers' Forum
Seven Sixes are Forty Three
   By Kiran Nagarkar
   Trans by Shubha Slee
Inspector Matadeen on the Moon
   By Harishankar Parsai
   Trans by C M Naim
Hindi Handpicked Fiction
   Trans and Ed by Sara Rai
Downfall by Degrees
   By Abdullah Hussein
   Trans by Mohammad Umar Memon
The Resthouse
   By Ahmad Nadeem Qasimi
   Trans by Faruq Hassan
Katha Prize Stories 12
   Ed Geeta Dharmarajan
Best of the Nineties:
Katha Prize Stories 11
   Ed Geeta Dharmarajan
The End of Human History
   By Hasan Manzar
Hauntings: Bangla Ghost Stories
   Ed and Trans by
   Suchitra Samanta
Forsaking Paradise: Stories from Ladakh,
   Ed and Trans by
   Ravina Aggarwal
Ayoni and Other Stories
   Ed and Trans by
   Alladi Uma & M Sridhar

Non-Ficton

Links in the Chain
   By Mahadevi Varma
   Trans by Neera Kuckreja Sohoni
Travel Writing and the Empire
   Ed Sachidananda Mohanty

ALT (Approaches to Literatures in Translation)

Ismat: Her Life, Her Times
   Eds Sukrita Paul Kumar &
   Sadique
Translating Partition
   Eds Ravikant & Tarun K Saint
Translating Caste
   Ed Tapan Basu
Translating Desire
   Ed Brinda Bose
Vijay Tendulkar

Trailblazers

Ambai: Two Novellas and a Story
   Trans by C T Indra,
   Prema Seetharam & Uma Narayanan
Paul Zacharia: Two Novellas
   Trans by Gita Krishnankutty
Ashokamitran: Water
   Trans by Lakshmi Holmström
Bhupen Khakhar: Selected Works
   Trans by Bina Srinivasan,
   Ganesh Devy & Naushil Mehta,
Indira Goswami: Pages Stained with Blood
   Trans by Pradip Acharya

Katha Classics

Pudumaippittan
   Ed Lakshmi Holmström
Basheer Ed Vanajam Ravindran
Mauni Ed Lakshmi Holmström
Raja Rao Ed Makarand Paranjape
A Madhaviah: Padmavati
   Trans by Meenakshi Tyagarajan

Katha Novels

Singarevva and the Palace
   By Chandrasekhar Kambar
   Trans by Laxmi Chandrashekar
Listen Girl!
   By Krishna Sobti
   Trans by Shivanath

FORTHCOMING

Rajaji
   By Monica Felton
J J : Some Jottings
   By Sundara Ramaswamy
   Trans by A R Venkatachalapathy

A CHILD WIDOW'S STORY

BY

MONICA FELTON

KATHA

First published by Katha in 2003	KATHA A-3 Sarvodaya Enclave Sri Aurobindo Marg
Copyright © Katha, 2003	New Delhi 110 017 Phone: 2652 4350, 2652 4511 Fax: 2651 4373
	E-mail: kathavilasam@katha.org Internet address: http://www.katha.org

KATHA is a registered nonprofit society devoted to enhancing the pleasures of reading. KATHA VILASAM is its story research and resource centre.

Cover Design: Geeta Dharmarajan
Cover Photograph Courtesy: N Krishnaswamy

In-house Editors: Gita Rajan, Shoma Choudhury
Production Coordinator: Sanjeev Palliwal

Typeset in 12 on 16pt ElegaGarmnd BT at Katha
and Printed at Usha Offset, New Delhi

All rights reserved. No part of this book may be reproduced or utilized in any form or by any means, electronic or mechanical, including photocopying, recording or by any information storage or retrieval system, without the prior written permission of the publisher.

ISBN 81-87649-91-7

2 4 6 8 10 9 7 5 3 1

Contents

Looking Backward
7

The Education of Subbalakshmi
13

The Widows' Home
96

Living in the World
172

Looking Forward
271

Looking Backward

I HAD BEEN living in Madras for more than four years when one of Sister Subbalakshmi's nephews suggested that I should try to persuade her to tell me the story of her life.

I knew that she had an unusual story to tell, but it seemed far from certain that she would be willing to tell it. She was old, almost seventy six, and not in good health. Her eyesight had begun to fail, and she was very deaf.

She was also, I was warned, exceedingly busy. It was doubtful whether she would be able to spare the time to tell me everything I wanted to know.

Still, there seemed no harm in asking. So I made an appointment and went to see her.

Her house was one of five, all of them occupied by members of her family, grouped around a big courtyard tucked away at the end of a lane leading out of the fashionable Edward Elliots Road. It was a hot afternoon in May – the year was 1961 – when I went there for the first time, and the bougainvillaea which climbed over the facade of Sister Subbalakshmi's house were all in bloom, dripping over the veranda roof in cascades of pink and flame and purple. The veranda itself was shadowy, dim and cool looking. As I came near I could see the chains of a swing seat, of the kind to be found in most old fashioned South Indian houses, hanging from the ceiling. Then, just as I reached the veranda wall I saw that Sister, as everybody called her, was sitting in the middle of the swing, swaying gently backwards and forwards, with her bare feet three or four inches from the ground.

Everyone who had talked to me about her had spoken of, indeed emphasized, her goodness. Several people had told me that she was a saint. I had found this rather intimidating. If anyone had thought of mentioning that she was beautiful and charming and gay I should probably have made an effort to meet her much earlier.

As she rose and came towards me, pressing her small, neat hands together in the traditional Indian greeting, I could see at once that she was all these things. I guessed, and people who had known her when she was young afterwards told me that I was right, that she had always been beautiful. She had not always been gay.

She smiled up into my face, and I saw that she was not only beautiful in a classical sense, she was pretty, too, as pretty as a blue Persian kitten.

I was still looking at her with surprise and pleasure as she took my hand and led me into the house. She was very tiny and round and silvery, her plump little body swathed in a sari of pale grey silk that was almost exactly the colour of her thick, rippling hair. I followed her through the square entrance hall, through a sitting room hung with old family photographs, and into what seemed to be a study-bedroom. A divan-bed ran along one wall. Opposite was a businesslike desk. On either side of the door were glass fronted bookcases, crammed with books and files and pamphlets.

Sister motioned me to sit on the divan. Then she came and sat beside me, cross-legged, her little feet hidden in the folds of her sari. "Tell me," she asked in a voice that was sweet and firm, "which do you prefer, sweet things or hot things?"

She was watching me intently, as if the question were a new kind of personality test and my answer would tell her everything she needed to know about me.

I answered, "I like both."

"Oh!" She lifted her right hand and pulled out, from between the front of her blouse and the upper folds of her sari, a small silver box about the size and shape of a cigarette case. "This," she explained waggling it backwards and forwards with impatient distaste, "is the battery of my deaf-aid. Did you say both?"

"Yes."

"Very well. You shall have both."

She clapped her hands. A second or two later the cook, a girl of eighteen or so, appeared in the doorway.

"I didn't," I protested as soon as Sister had finished giving instructions, "come here to eat."

"Of course you didn't. But we must observe the laws of hospitality don't you know." She tossed her head, and gave the battery of her deaf-aid another shake. "Now what would you like me to tell you?"

"Everything."

"Everything!" She knew, of course, why I had come. She would she said at once, do her best to answer my questions. It did not seem to have occurred to her that she would find it hard to spare the many hours that would be needed to tell me her own story and the stories of some of the many hundreds of girls and women whom she had helped to save from what I had often heard called a living death. Instead, she spoke as if she were a little afraid that I might be wasting my time in listening.

She said, "Here in the South, child marriages are very much a thing of the past. They do, of course, still take place, and the average age at which girls marry is still far too young. But nowadays there are not the thousands upon thousands of child widows that there were when I …"

She broke off as the cook came back, carrying sweets and savouries on little stainless steel dishes.

"You must eat everything," Sister told me. She leaned forward, peering through her glasses at the contents of my plate. "Some of my girls used to be very finicky about their food. It wasn't at all easy to make them understand that they could not expect to grow up strong and healthy and able to do useful work in the world if they didn't eat properly. Such a fuss some of them would make because Chitti and I insisted that they should eat greens every day!" Her face, golden pale as sundried bamboo, wrinkled into creases of sarcastic amusement. Then she laughed, also on a sarcastic note. "But what a ridiculous thing it is for me to be talking to you about such trivialities!"

"It isn't," I answered. "I want to hear everything!"
"Very well. Where shall I begin?"
"At the beginning."
"You mean when my calamity happened?"
"No. When you were born."

She laughed again, this time with pure merriment. "You want me to lead my whole life over again? Well, I shall try. But it is going to be a very long story, and it will take weeks to tell it."

In fact, it took months. I visited Sister several times each week. Often I would arrive to find other visitors already there. Many of them were just as eager to talk to me as I was to listen to what they had to say. I learned a lot from them, as well as from some of Sister's former pupils who lived in other parts of the country and whom I was able to visit. I wrote to Miss Prager, who was living in far-off Coventry. She answered all my questions and sent me books and pamphlets and old press cuttings.

As for Sister Subbalakshmi herself, the more she talked about the past, the sharper her memories became. She was so utterly without the egoism of old people that she had destroyed, as worthless, the diaries which she had kept throughout her adult life, but she had preserved what she called a consolidated diary, in which she had noted the principal dates in her own history and the history of her family. She allowed me to read it, and I don't think I ever asked her a question which she refused to answer.

I have tried to tell her story and the stories of some of her pupils as nearly as possible as they were told to me. Sister is now a little less energetic and rather more noticeably fragile than she was when I first visited her, but she still has something new to tell me whenever we meet. She still, too, seems to think that I am wasting my time in writing about her.

"Why don't you," she asked me the other day, "finish your big biography of Rajaji instead of writing about me? He is a very great and important man, and everyone will want to read how he became the first Indian governor general of India. And who am I?" She paused, pulled out the battery case of her deaf-aid and gave it a tentative, disapproving, and then suddenly violent, shake. "Nobody! Whoever heard of me?"

"Then," I answered, "it's time they did."

"No, no. You are wrong. Anyone given my opportunities could have done as much as I have done."

"Possibly. But most people don't use their opportunities. You did. That's what makes you important."

"Important!" She laughed scornfully. "Who cares about being important? Being useful is the only thing that matters."

The Education of Subbalakshmi

SUBRAMANIA IYER WAS twenty two and had been married for almost eight years when, on 18 August, 1886, he first became a father.

His own father, Venkatarama Iyer, was a man of great piety who traced his ancestry back through many generations of poor and learned Brahmins. For more than three hundred years the family had been settled in the village of Rishiyur, a name which means the village of the saints, in Tanjore district. Venkatarama Iyer spent much of his time in the math – the Hindu monastery – in the big town of Kumbakonam. He had sent both his sons to the English school there, and afterwards to the Presidency College in Madras city. Subramania Iyer took a degree in civil engineering, and immediately afterwards obtained an appointment in the Public Works Department of the Government of the Madras Presidency.

His wife, Visalakshi, spent the last months of her pregnancy in the house of her parents, which overlooked the tank of the great Kapaleeswarar temple in Mylapore, on the southern edge of Madras city. In those days there were no trained midwives either in Madras or anywhere else in South India. Instead, it was the custom, as it still is in most villages today, to send for the barber's wife as soon as a woman's labour pains started. Visalakshi, who had been in constant pain for many weeks, was suffering such agony that her parents decided to call in a doctor.

Visalakshi braced herself to protest. She was, she declared, ready to endure anything rather than submit to the degradation of being touched by a man. She was only sixteen, but she was a girl with a very strong character and no amount of persuasion could induce her to change her mind.

Fortunately, there was a European lady in Madras who was a qualified doctor. Her name was Miss Scharleib, and when she was sent for she came at once. She would, she explained, deliver the baby by using forceps.

"Those forceps," Sister Subbalakshmi told me, speaking with such authority that she sounded almost as if she had been an independent witness of her own birth, "were not at all the kind that doctors use now. They were huge, great clumsy things that gripped the baby's head as if its poor little skull were as hard as iron." She lifted her hands, pushing back her hair. "My mother and my aunt – Chitti – used to say that it was the forceps that gave me these two bulges in my forehead."

"Nonsense," I answered. "They were probably made by your brains pushing their way forward."

She laughed. "Brains! Most people have brains, though too

often they don't care to learn to use them." Her hands came down, resting on her lap. "At any rate, I may tell you that it was a very great disappointment to everyone when the doctor did succeed in pulling me out, and after all that pain and worry and trouble I turned out to be a girl."

There was another disappointment a few days later when Visalakshi tried to open her baby's clenched fists. The right fist refused to open. The fingertips were turned inwards against the palm of the child's hand, with a growth of skin attaching the palm to the first joint of each finger.

"Imagine," Sister exclaimed, "if I had had to stay like that all my life! I shouldn't have been able to learn to write. I shouldn't have been able to keep a diary. I shouldn't have ..." She paused for an instant glancing about her as if searching for some glimpse of the unremembered past. Then her tone became brisk. "But it was all right. My mother oiled my hand every day, and the unwanted skin soon disappeared. It was only my character that did not change."

I asked what she meant.

"I was born," she explained, "on the dark side of the moon." It was at an hour between the waning of the old moon and the waxing of the new, and according to Subbalakshmi's aunt, who had a great reputation as an amateur astrologer, children born at that time are endowed with exceptionally obstinate characters. "Well," Sister continued, acknowledging what everyone who knows her recognizes as self-evident truth, "I suppose I am obstinate. And why not? How can anybody get any thing done if they are perpetually taking advice and wondering what other people will think of their actions? You have to be a little bit obstinate if you are to be of any use in this world. Now I shall tell you ..."

"Tell me," I interrupted, "what is your very earliest recollection?"

She answered, without an instant's hesitation, "The sting of a scorpion."

She had just begun to walk, and was toddling from one room to another when, putting her right hand against the jamb of the door to steady herself, she was nipped in the first finger. She remembered her sudden scream and the terribly sharp thrusts of agony as the poison spread. It was the worst physical pain she was ever to know. By next day she was well again, but before her childhood was over she was to suffer pain of another kind, hardly less agonizing and far more enduring.

She was not quite two years old when her father was transferred from Madras to work in the Godavari and Krishna districts, among the Telugu-speaking people of what is now the State of Andhra. The little family travelled north by ship to the port of Vizagapatnam. There, they changed into a small boat which was to be their home as they moved from place to place along the inland waterways while Subramania Iyer made surveys and supervised repairs. The work, he soon found, did not suit his health. He had always suffered from asthma, and as he settled down to his new job the attacks became more frequent and more severe.

Both he and Visalakshi felt themselves to be foreigners among the people of Andhra. The Telugu language, though not difficult for Tamil people to learn, was written in an unfamiliar script. The food was different, disagreeably hot. There were, too, some religious practices among the Telugu brahmins which Visalakshi and her husband found very distasteful.

Subramania's father had died some time earlier, and the young couple found themselves faced with a great difficulty when the time came to perform the shrarddha ceremony, at which prayers were to be said and offerings made for the repose of the souls of the dead. The purohits – the priests – who came to officiate commanded Visalakshi to anoint their heads with oil.

She refused.

They insisted. The ritual, they explained, could not be satisfactorily performed unless she obeyed.

"When a Tamil brahmin performs shrarddha," Sister explained to me, "it is the custom for his wife to present the oil to the purohits. They then go into the bathroom and anoint themselves. That is perfectly correct. No Tamil lady would ever touch a gentleman, and when my poor mother was asked to put oil on the heads of these two strange men she got a most terrible shock. No, no, said my father when the priests still insisted, that won't do at all. We cannot have that. It seemed to him a most disgusting practice."

After this incident, Subramania Iyer's health became very much worse. His letters to his family must have caused a good deal of alarm. Very soon a telegram arrived from his brother, urging him to resign his appointment and come home.

He went, and found that his family had already planned another career for him. A new academic year was about to start. If he took the course for graduate students at the teachers' training college, he would be sure, as soon as the year was over, of getting a job as a teacher of engineering.

The advice seemed sound, and he took it. By this time Visalakshi had become the mother of a second child, Balam, who had caused a further disappointment to the young parents by not being a boy. Subramania and Visalakshi loved their little girls dearly but when, before Balam was a year old, Visalakshi conceived again, they both hoped and prayed that their third child would be a boy. Visalakshi's mother had taught her that the first duty of a Hindu wife was to be the mother of sons. No woman or girl might ever perform the annual shrarddha ceremonies, which were of utmost importance since it was only through their observance that the continued peace of the souls of the dead could be ensured. A man whose wife failed to bear him a son was not merely unfortunate himself. His misfortune would condemn his father, and ancestors as far back as genealogy could reach, to eternal torment.

Visalakshi hoped for the best. Everything else was going well. Her husband, at the end of his year's training, was appointed as a lecturer in the Government Agricultural College. It was a job that suited him perfectly, and he never wished for, or tried to obtain, another.

The college was at Saidapet, about ten miles south of Madras city. Nowadays Saidapet is a rather dreary suburb, bisected by an arterial road along which buses and cars and bullock carts and lorries and motor-scooters roar and rumble all through the day and during most of the night. In 1889, it was a quiet village, and Subramania Iyer had no difficulty in renting a house which exactly suited his family.

As soon as they had settled in, it was decided that Subbalakshmi, who was just three, should go to school.

It was a most astonishing decision to make.

There were, in fact, two schools in the village, a public elementary school for children over the age of five, and a private school for very young children which was situated about halfway between Subramania's house and the college. Most of the pupils in both were boys. Girls from good families did not often go to school, and as a rule they received very little education at home, either. Their mothers and, later, their mothers-in-law taught them the domestic arts, but it was not considered necessary for them to learn to read and write and become familiar with men's affairs.

Of course, there were exceptions. Subbalakshmi's mother and her aunt, Valambal, were learned ladies. Both had a remarkable knowledge of the Sanskrit and Tamil classics, but there were many subjects which the men of the family discussed and about which the two young women were totally ignorant. Subramania's brother was a gifted mathematician who had been nicknamed Euclid by his schoolmates at Kumbakonam. When he came to visit the house at Saidapet most of the talk among the menfolk would be in English.

Sister Subbalakshmi thinks that it was her father who first decided that she should go to school. Other members of her family have guessed that it was more probably her mother or her aunt.

"My parents," Sister told me, conjuring up a picture of herself as she had been seventy three years before, "had bought me a small little umbrella and small little shoes." Until then she had always walked barefooted. Her dress, like that of most little girls in South India today, consisted of a gathered skirt, long enough to cover the ankles, with a long sleeved, waistlength jacket above it.

"Every morning," she went on, "when my father left the house to go to the college, I would trot along beside him until we reached the school. My mother or Chitti …"

"Chitti?"

"My Aunt Valambal, who lived with us. You know that Chitti is our word for aunt? Everyone called her Chitti because – because she was an aunt to everyone."

Chitti or her mother, she went on, would give her, each morning, a handful of roasted chickpeas to put in her pocket in case she got hungry before she came home again. The little girl would gobble up the whole supply long before lessons were over. "I didn't learn anything at that school," she told me, chuckling happily at the recollection. "Eating peas was my only study."

She had been at school for just four months when the new baby was born. Visalakshi and Subramania had, for the third time, to try to overcome their disappointment at not having a son.

Subbalakshmi had been named after her great grandmother. Lakshmi, her mother explained to her as soon as she was old enough to understand, was the goddess of wealth and prosperity and the wife of the great god Vishnu, Lord of Creation. Nobody troubled to explain the first two syllables, and Subbalakshmi thought they were just sounds, without any meanings.

The new baby was named after the goddess Savitri, to whom the most sacred of Hindu prayers, the Gayatri mantram, is addressed. This was the name always given to the third daughter in families in which there were no boys – in the prayerful hope that the god would before long provide the gift of a son.

It was generally believed, as most Hindus still believe today, that a woman who failed to bear sons was punished for the sins which she had committed in a previous existence. One of the ways of expiating these sins was to make a pilgrimage to

Rameshwaram, a shrine of great holiness in the extreme south, to pray for forgiveness and to wash away the evil of the past by bathing in the sea.

Subramania and Visalakshi had some friends who were in a situation similar to their own, and the two families decided to make the pilgrimage together. "The strange things is," Sister went on, "that in the following year my mother actually did give birth to a son. Of course, it was purely a coincidence, and the poor little boy did not live very long. Some time afterwards my mother had another son. He also died while he was still a baby. That is why there was such a big gap in age between we three older sisters and the two younger ones, Swarnum and Nitya."

The two boys did not live long, and the sadness of their death was soon forgotten. Little Lakshmi was a happy child, and she loved going to school. By the time she was five she had learned all that the private school could teach. The elementary school in the village was next door to her home, and it seemed to her natural enough that she should go there.

Her father's friends were rather shocked that she should be allowed to do so. This was not so much because she was a girl as because the headmaster of the school was a nadar Christian. The nadars were regarded as very low caste, hardly better than untouchables, and it seemed to orthodox folk very wrong that a child from a respected brahmin family should be put under the care of such people.

It soon appeared that the headmaster's wife and daughter were very kind, good and well-mannered. Subbalakshmi soon became very much attached to them, though not to the headmaster himself.

"He," Sister recalled, "was the most uncouth, uncivilized brute of a man you ever could meet. His only pleasure was in beating the children. Every morning he would count up those who were present. Then he would start beating the nearest child. The poor little thing, whoever it happened to be, would be given one stroke for each of the absentees. The master would carry on like that for the whole day, and by the time we went home every one of us would have had a beating."

Despite the beatings, the little girl enjoyed school and learned avidly. Before long, she could read and write Tamil, and in the arithmetic lessons she never got a sum wrong. There was not much else to be learned at school, but she was learning a great deal at home almost without knowing that she did so.

Every evening before the children went to bed their mother or Chitti would tell them stories from the great Hindu epics, the Mahabharata and Ramayana. They were exciting tales, crowded with the adventures of gods and goddesses, kings and queens and simple, ordinary people, good and evil spirits, and animals who behaved like people, and people who behaved like animals. Subbalakshmi could never have enough of them.

All these stories had a lesson to teach, which was not always clear at the first telling. The little girl would ask question after question, and her mother and Chitti would answer patiently, trying to develop her understanding.

Subramania, too, would spend as much time as he could with his children. He would often take them for walks down to the river which flows into the sea at Adyar. Nowadays, except in the rainy season, the riverbed at Saidapet is almost dry, shrunk to a veining of shallow streams which trickle erratically among rocks and sandbanks and emerald bright turf. The stretch beneath and on either side of the bridge has become the washermen's paradise and when buses coming into the city from Meenambakkam airport are held up, as they often are, on the narrow bridge, travellers from all over the world stare down with incredulous amusement at the sight of thousands of dhotis and saris, shirts and blouses, sheets and bath towels being beaten against the stones or spread out on the grass to dry.

When Subbalakshmi was a child the river was deeper, and on Sundays and holidays people would drive out from the city in carriages or jutka carts to take a trip in one of the government owned pleasure boats. Subramania and Visalakshi would often take their little girls on these trips, pointing out the landmarks and telling them about the world in which they lived.

When they got home again, her grandmother and Chitti would have a meal waiting for them. The children were taught to believe that it was wicked and cruel to kill living creatures for food, or to eat eggs, which might have the germ of life in them. Instead, there was a great variety of fruit and vegetables to be obtained from the gardens of the Agricultural College, pure, rich milk to be turned into curds and butter and ghee, as well as rice and lentils and other grains which could be prepared in countless different ways. Subbalakshmi loved to eat.

She loved, too, to go into the kitchen to watch her mother performing puja, praying and offering flowers and coconuts and plantains to the small, dark image which stood, surrounded by coloured pictures of the gods, in a recess where a lamp was kept burning all the time. She tried very hard to understand the meaning of the Sanskrit prayers which her mother was teaching her to repeat. Sometimes these mantrams, as they were called, were difficult to follow, although the beauty of the sounds made the words easy to memorize.

"It doesn't matter," her mother told her, "if you don't understand everything now. The meaning will come later, and it will help you very much to know these things and to be able to repeat them to yourself when you get older."

She was still very small when her mother taught her that although there were hundreds, indeed thousands, of gods to whom people prayed, there was really only one God. "The reason why we have all these different names and different stories and images to worship," Visalakshi would say, "is not because there are many gods, but because there are many different kinds of people, and we cannot all satisfy ourselves by calling god by only one name. We learn to express our feelings by saying many different words, and we speak as if there are many gods because it is so hard to find a way of expressing everything in one word. If we add all the different ideas of god together, we can get a little bit of a notion of his greatness. It will still be only a little bit, because this greatness is too much even for the understanding of grown-up people. We must try to understand as much as we can, but nobody can expect to understand everything."

It was not at all difficult for Subbalakshmi to understand that she had been born into the world many times before, and that after she had left the body in which she was living now she would be born into the world again. She learned that people who led wicked lives might be punished by being reborn as untouchables or, if their sins were less grave, by being afflicted with misfortunes of one kind or another. She knew, too, that she was very fortunate to have been born into a brahmin family, even though she was a girl and so could never become, in the full sense, a brahmin.

Her home was wonderfully happy. She had everything she wanted, and although she was forever asking questions she had never, as far as she could remember, asked one that either her parents or Chitti had refused to answer.

Yet there was one question that she could not ask.

It was about Chitti. Chitti was not old like her grandmother, and although nobody had ever called her beautiful she was lovely to look at, with the kindest, merriest eyes imaginable. Yet there was something very strange in the way she dressed. Subbalakshmi's mother wore silk saris in beautiful, bright colours with nicely made blouses underneath, and her hair was fastened in a heavy, shining knot at the back of her head. All the ladies who came to the house dressed in the same way. Only Chitti looked different. She dressed always in a sari of the plainest white cotton, with nothing whatever underneath it, so that when she was busy in the kitchen her arms were bare and her back was not properly covered. The upper edge of the sari was drawn over her head and pulled tightly around it and down behind her ears, as if she had no hair at all underneath it.

Grandmother dressed like that, too. She was old, and perhaps that explained why. But Subbalakshmi simply could not understand why her dear Chitti, so energetic and full of fun, should be dressed in such a horrid way. Somehow, she could not tell how, she began to have a feeling that it would be wrong to ask. She had a feeling, too, that if she did ask nobody would tell her.

She had to know. She simply had to. She was getting to be a big girl. Soon she would be nine years old. And she still could not ask.

Subbalakshmi was turning out to be an exceedingly clever little girl. She was only nine when she sat for the public examination which was open to all the children in the elementary schools of the Madras Presidency who had reached the fourth standard, and she won the first place in the whole of Chingleput District.

Her education, her parents decided, was now finished. It was time to think of finding her a husband. There was no need to hurry, since it was unlikely that she would attain her age, as her parents put it, until she was several years older. Still, it was not easy to find suitable boys for little girls whose parents could not afford to give them big dowries, and it would, Subramania thought, be as well to start looking around and making enquiries.

The long summer vacation from the Agricultural College had just begun. It happened, too, that Visalakshi's young brother was about to be married to a girl whose family lived in one of the villages in Tanjore District. So it was decided that Visalakshi and her husband and the three little girls should all go to the wedding. Then, when the ceremonies were over, they would make another pilgrimage to Rameshwaram, and perhaps afterwards Visalakshi would again be blessed, this time more fortunately, with a son.

The wedding, with its ceremonies and feasts spread over five days, was a boring affair for children. The small bride and bridegroom sat stiff as dolls before the sacred fire, repeating the mantrams after the priests. Although the smoke from the burning ghee sent tears running down their cheeks, they kept obediently still, and when, hand in hand, they circled the fire their eyes were lowered and they did not once turn to give each other a sideways glance. They had never met, and it was unlikely that they would be in each other's company again until the child bride had attained her age. Then, within a week or so of her first menstruation, the nuptial ceremony would take place. Immediately afterwards, the young wife would leave the home in which she had been brought up and go to live with her husband and his parents.

Subbalakshmi could not bear to think that this would someday happen to her. She simply shut the thought out of her mind as if it didn't exist. Nobody ever had to tell her to go out of the room while the grown-ups discussed the avarice of fathers who had marriageable sons and who would make the most exorbitant demands for dowries, and the cruelty of mothers-in-law to the young girls who were trying to learn to be good daughters in their new homes. Long before the conversation got to this point, Subbalakshmi would have slipped away by herself, to wander into the kitchen or to take a book and sit outside on the pial, beneath the shade of the overhanging eaves.

She was rather lonely. The girls and boys in the house where her parents were staying were all either much younger or much older than herself. As she sat on the pial, reading or daydreaming, she sometimes couldn't help feeling a little envious at the sight of the children of the agraharam, the brahmin quarter, playing together in the street.

One day when she was sitting there reading, only half-aware of the shouts and laughter coming from a few yards away, she was aroused by a loud, pitiful scream.

She looked up. Seven or eight big girls were standing in a circle around a tiny tot, a baby who could not have been much more than two years old. The little creature, who had now burst into great, heaving sobs, had nothing on, not even a skirt around her waist, and the older children were laughing and teasing and making fun of her because she was a widow. Most of the other girls, Subbalakshmi could see, wore gold chains around their necks, each with a taali, the symbol of marriage, hanging from it.

"Ha! Ha! Ha!" the big girls were shouting. "Janaki hasn't got a taali!" They danced around her, shouting what Subbalakshmi knew was a bad word which nice people never used. "Widow! Widow! Widow! You wicked, wicked girl not to have a taali!"

The baby cried and cried, struggling to escape, while the dancers moved faster and faster, shouting the same words again and again. Then, at last, baby Janaki managed to slip between the arms of two of the bigger girls and ran into the house opposite.

Subbalakshmi could see, through the unglazed window of the house, the baby's mother rush forward to pick up the child and comfort her. Then, after a minute or so, the mother took off her own taali and fastened it around her little one's neck.

In an instant, Janaki had slipped off her mother's lap and was running out into the street again.

The big girls were waiting. They attacked the child savagely, trying to tear the gold chain off her neck, screaming that she had no right to wear it. Janaki's mother had evidently gone back to her kitchen and was out of earshot. Subbalakshmi, half-petrified with horror, watched helplessly until the baby, still with the taali around her neck, managed to escape once more and ran into the house and disappeared.

Subbalakshmi never saw baby Janaki again. Nor did she

ever tell anyone what she had seen. She tried to put the incident out of her mind, but it kept coming back. Often after she had gone to sleep at nights she would wake up sharply, imagining that she could hear the baby screaming for help, for the help which she had not been able to give.

After this, the village in which the family was staying seemed a horrid place, and Subbalakshmi was delighted when she and her sisters were suddenly whisked off, without their parents, to pay a visit to their father's uncle.

"As soon as we got there," Sister told me, her face wrinkling into a crosshatching of amusement and disgust, "my greatuncle said that we must be given a purgative."

"Because you had all eaten too much at the wedding?"

"No, no. It wasn't that at all. It was because he was so proud of his castor oil plants. The oil had just been pressed, and my greatuncle said that whatever the state of our intestines it would be sure to do us a lot of good." She laughed, briefly and sharply. "I can tell you that it was a most horrible experience."

It was soon over. Within a few days they were staying in the house of another greatuncle, who had very different ideas about how little girls should be treated. They were petted and made much of, and feasted on sweet potatoes stewed with brown sugar and other delicious dishes which they had never tasted before. Then their parents came to take them to stay with their uncle at Kumbakonam and the holiday became even more delightful.

Their uncle had five children, three boys and two girls. One of the girls was about the same age as Subbalakshmi, and she taught her cousins to play games which had been handed down from one generation of South Indian children to another for hundreds, perhaps thousands, of years. Some of these games were played with cowrie shells. Some, like kummi and kolattam, were not really games but traditional dances. They were great fun to perform, and beautiful to watch. Then, almost every day, the children would be taken to bathe in the river, and Subramania decided to teach his children to swim. Subbalakshmi learned quickly, and she loved the water so much that she sometimes wished the holiday would never end.

As the weeks went by, Subbalakshmi's sister, Balam, who was seven, seemed to be spending more and more time with one of the bigger boys, a sixteen year old who had been nicknamed Sandy because he went to a Christian school and the family liked to tease him by pretending that he was a Christian too. Although he was already in the sixth form, he seemed to enjoy talking to little Balam just as much as she enjoyed being with him.

One day, as the visit was coming to an end, Sandy took Balam upstairs to his room and said, "I want to speak to you very seriously."

Balam looked up at him earnestly. "What is it?" she asked.

"I love you. If you love me too, I should like to marry you when you are a little bigger. What do you say?"

"I say yes."

The parents, when they heard about it, said no. Children did not arrange their own marriages. Mothers and fathers knew best what was good for their children. The grown-ups were certain that a marriage between Balam and Sandy would not do at all.

"Don't worry," Sandy told Balam, "Just be patient. In the end they will have to agree."

A few days later they said goodbye. The pilgrimage, the last part of this unforgettable holiday was about to begin.

The train went only as far as Madurai. When Subbalakshmi and her parents and sisters arrived there, three double bullock carts, which had been ordered in advance, were waiting for them outside the railway station. The family climbed into one. The other two were loaded with bedding, boxes of clothing, bags of rice and all the other foodstuffs which would be needed during the next two or three weeks.

There were choultries, hostels for pilgrims, every few miles along the road from Madurai to Rameshwaram, just as there were along all the pilgrim routes in India. Each contained a prayer room, and rooms where the pilgrims, most of whom travelled on foot, could eat and sleep, take their baths and wash their clothes, and prepare their food.

Subbalakshmi and her sisters had been taught that it was sinful to sit down to either of the main meals of the day until they had taken their baths and put on clean clothes. So at nights, when the family had finished unpacking, there was always a big pile of silk and linen to be washed before next morning. When morning came, enough food would be cooked to last throughout the day, and everyone would eat heartily before the bullock carts were reloaded and the little caravan set off again.

There were wonderful sights to be seen along the road. Subbalakshmi loved to watch the patterns of light and shadow made by the trees, all of them so beautiful and so mysteriously different. Giant banyans, their leaves so thick that they seemed almost black, made arches of darkness overhead, and the tendril-like roots which grew downwards from the branches looked like tresses of hair waiting to be combed and plaited.

Here and there were monkeys, sometimes scampering across the road and at other times sitting contemplatively in a patch of shade. Every now and then the bullock carts would pass pilgrims trudging along on foot, swamis in their orange coloured robes and packmen with their bundles. Then they would come to a village, and Subbalakshmi would lean out to try to catch glimpses of coppersmiths and brassfounders hammering away in their dark caverns, weavers at their looms, and ropemakers twisting long coils from coconut fibre. In every village there were small shrines, and in many of them there were, too, great temples, with their outer walls painted in vertical strips of red and white, and with great square tanks where women stood washing their clothes or taking their baths, holding their saris around their shoulders to keep themselves decently covered, and old men sat, talking together gravely, or sitting in peaceful silence.

Subbalakshmi had never been so happy. When, at the end of a week, they reached their destination, she was enchanted by the great temple at Rameshwaram. She was thrilled to listen again, as she had often listened at home, to the story of Lord Rama, who was God Himself in human form, and of his wife, Sita, who had been stolen from him by the wicked king Ravana and carried off to Lanka, the island which was now called Ceylon, and rescued by the monkey god, Hanuman. Here in Rameshwaram the story seemed as real as if it had just happened, and as Subbalakshmi walked with her mother beside the sea she could picture the good and lovely Sita, who was the perfect example of what every wife should be.

Back again in Madurai, where they stayed with relatives, the grown-ups spent many hours closeted together.

Subbalakshmi did not try to hear what they were talking about, but when her mother told her that she was to go and stay for six months with an aunt and uncle who lived in Coimbatore and attend the high school there she was delighted. Nothing could have been better.

The school was rather a disappointment. The teachers were Christian women, rice-Christians as everybody called them, converts from among low caste people and untouchables. They seemed to dislike answering questions, perhaps because they did not know much more than their pupils. They did not look nice, either. Their hair was not oiled, and they wore no jewels. Their saris never seemed to be quite clean and sometimes when a teacher walked down the lines between the desks to watch what the girls were doing, the smell was so bad that Subbalakshmi wanted to hold her nose. None of the girls liked their teacher very much, but Subbalakshmi liked the other girls and they liked her. Although she was glad to go home again at the end of the six months she was sorry, too, to realize that her schooldays had now really come to an end.

When she returned to Saidapet there was another wedding to attend, this time in Madras. Subbalakshmi, much more aware of the world and of what was in store for herself since she had begun to mix with other girls, was fascinated by the ceremony and by the gorgeous saris worn by the lady guests. One of the grandest saris, so stiff with gold thread that it looked as if it could stand by itself, was worn by Lady Sadasiva Iyer, whose husband was a famous lawyer and one of the greatest men in the city. Sir Sadasiva Iyer was, of course, sitting among the gentlemen, and his wife among the ladies. Everyone was either staring at her or else trying, politely and self-consciously, not to look. Her beautiful hair had all gone, and her head was shaven clean, white and smooth as a peeled jackfruit seed.

Subbalakshmi just couldn't take her eyes off that naked head. She knew now that Chitti's head, when she uncovered it, looked just like that, although Chitti didn't wear silk saris or go to weddings. It was very puzzling, and Subbalakshmi simply had to know what it all meant.

This time her courage did not fail. As soon as they got home that evening and mother and daughter found themselves alone together, Subbalakshmi asked, "Why does Chitti have no hair?"

As soon as she had spoken she wished she hadn't. Her mother, who never cried, burst into floods of tears and could not answer.

"My marriage," Sister Subbalakshmi began one day, speaking in a remote and singularly calm voice, "was not even a dream."

It had meant little to her at the time. Afterwards, except for one detail, it had been forgotten almost as completely as if it had never been.

She had been eleven at the time, getting on for twelve. Her husband's family were strangers. Sister did not know how they came to be introduced to her parents. She did know quite certainly that after the calamity the two families never met again.

There must have been the usual haggling over the sums which Subramania Iyer was to spend on the wedding ceremony and to provide for his eldest daughter's dowry. Gifts had to be bought, not only for the bridegroom and his parents, but for many of Visalakshi's and Subramania's relatives as well. Subramania's salary had not yet reached its maximum of rupees hundred a month, which at that time was the equivalent of about eight pounds sterling. With a fair sized household to maintain, and another baby on the way, it was not easy for him to meet all the costs of the marriage.

Horoscopes were, of course, exchanged. The astrologer predicted that the bride would enjoy an unusually happy and fortunate life. Although it soon afterwards appeared that he had been very much mistaken, Sister, looking back over a distance of sixty four years, had no doubt that his prediction had been fulfilled.

When the marriage was celebrated she was perhaps too tired, after all the bustle and fuss of the preparations, to take much interest in the long, elaborate ceremonies. She, like the boy who sat beside her, obediently repeated after the priests the lovely Sanskrit sounds in which, for uncounted centuries, husbands and wives had made their promises of eternal faithfulness. Her head was bent and her eyes modestly downcast when the moment came for her to rise and, hand in hand with her bridegroom, circle seven times around the sacred fire. If the garland around her neck was uncomfortably heavy and made her skin itch, she forgot about it afterwards as completely as she forgot whether her husband was tall or short for his age, fair or dark. The only thing she remembered was the beauty of her wedding sari. It was of rich Benares silk, intricately woven and bordered with a pattern woven in threads of gold. It seemed to her that she had never seen anything so lovely in all her life. She could hardly believe that it was really her own and that she would be able to wear it on festival days and whenever her mother took her to weddings and thread ceremonies. She pinched the stuff between her forefinger and thumb, and for a moment felt the thrill of certain ownership. She was, she knew, an exceedingly lucky little girl.

A house in Mylapore, quite close to Subbalakshmi's birthplace, had been borrowed for the wedding. As soon as the ceremony was over, the whole family returned to Saidapet. They had not been at home many weeks when the new baby was born.

"This child," said her grandmother, coming out of the room in which Visalakshi had been shut away from the family, "is also a girl." Her tone was dry, and harsh with disappointment.

"The baby," Chitti retorted swiftly, "is a god given treasure. Why should we be sad?"

It was decided to name the child after a local deity, a goddess who was worshipped as the spirit of love and compassion. Swarnambal was so sweet tempered that no one could help loving her. Subbalakshmi thought that Swarnum, as the baby was generally called, was quite perfect. Even her grandmother, after that first outburst, was never again heard to bewail the fact that Visalakshi had once again failed to produce a son.

The new baby was still only a few weeks old when the calamity happened.

Subbalakshmi had to be told. Her husband had meant nothing to her, and at first the news of his death meant nothing, either. She felt nothing, because there was nothing to feel. It did not occur to her, when her mother explained what had happened, that there was any reason why she should feel sorry for herself.

It would not have been possible, Subramania and Visalakshi and Chitti had agreed among themselves, to keep Subbalakshmi in ignorance of her husband's death. But they would, they decided, do everything within their power to prevent the little girl from finding out, at least until she was very much older, what it meant to be a widow. They hid their own grief. The life of the household went on as usual. No one in the family ever spoke of the dead boy whom they had never known. Even her grandmother kept silent.

It was impossible to keep visitors away. Friends and neighbours streamed into the house to offer their sympathy, to pity the little widow and to mourn with her parents over the fate that was now in store for her.

She was such a good little girl, so obedient and so respectful to her elders as well as so pretty and charming, that it was very difficult to believe that she could ever, even in her previous birth, have committed any sin grave enough to deserve the lifelong punishment that was now in store for her.

The punishment was inescapable. Since no widow might ever, in any conceivable circumstance, be allowed to remarry, she was cut off forever from the joys of being a woman, of becoming a mother, of managing a household. From now on, most of the simple pleasures of life would be denied to her. She would no longer be allowed to attend weddings or any other kind of festivities. For a year or so, perhaps a little less or possibly a little longer, she would be allowed to dress as she did now. Then, as soon as she attained her age, she would be disfigured. Her head would be shorn. She would have to stop wearing blouses, and the only garment in which she might hide her nakedness would be a sari of plain white or unbleached cotton. She would be allowed to eat only once a day, and never anything but the plainest food. Even such little luxuries as pickles and betel nut would be denied her. She would seldom go out of the house, except occasionally to visit a temple or to perform some errand that nobody else wanted to do. It would be her duty to keep, as far as possible, out of the way of other people, because even the sight of a widow was known to bring bad luck.

She would, of course, have a home for as long as her parents lived. After her father's death her fate, as well as that of her mother and of Chitti, would depend on the attitude of the families into which her sisters eventually married. If Balam and Savitri and baby Swarnum were fortunate in their husbands, Subbalakshmi and her mother and aunt would have homes to go to in which, in return for doing a large share of household work, they would be treated kindly. Chitti had so far been exceptionally fortunate. Most widows who had never really been wives or who had failed to become the mothers of sons were condemned to be mere household drudges, slaving away from morning till night, perpetually on the verge of starvation and with never a kind word from anybody. The most for which they might hope and pray was a happier fate in their next birth.

Subramania and Visalakshi and Chitti succeeded, perhaps much better than they had dared to hope, in saving the little girl from hearing such talk as this. The three of them had already made up their minds that they would, somehow, or other, save Subbalakshmi from her fate. They tried to save her, too, from the prying eyes and easy tears of their sympathizers. She herself, if she caught a glimpse of friends or acquaintances approaching the house, would run and hide in one of the back rooms. Although she could not feel any sadness for herself, the sight of such grief made her almost unbearably miserable.

Sometimes she failed to escape in time. One day a favourite uncle arrived unexpectedly, and walked into the room in which she was sitting. She jumped up to greet him, joyfully certain that he, at least, would be as cheerful and easy as he always was. Instead, he flung his arms around her, hugging her to him tightly, and burst into heaving, uncontrollable sobs. She felt his tears falling on to her face, and struggled wildly, as if he had suddenly become an enemy, to free herself. At last she succeeded, and ran out of the room. Those few minutes had been so terrible that as soon as she was alone she herself burst into agonized tears. She had not known that grown men ever wept, and the sight of her uncle's grief for her was so much more than she could bear that suddenly she, too, was sorry for herself.

Then, at last, it was summer again. Every year, as soon as the college closed, Subramania Iyer would take his wife and children away for a holiday. This year, a friend lent him a house on the banks of the Cauvery river, not far from Trichinopoly. Nothing, it seemed, could have been more delightful. Balam and Savitri played together as they always did, and for the first few days Subbalakshmi spent most of her time on the riverbank, watching the fishes.

The water was so clear and pure that from where she sat she could see right down to the bottom of the riverbed. The fishes, of many different shapes and sizes, were so fascinating that they drove every other thought from her mind. She would have liked to find someone who could tell her the names of all the different kinds of water creatures, but her father had been obliged to go back to Madras to attend a wedding, and there was no one else who could answer her questions.

Besides, it was really better not to have to talk. The villagers here were even more curious than the people at home in

Saidapet, and every time the little girl strolled back from the river to the house some strangers would be sure to pounce upon her and ask questions.

"Is it true that you have lost your husband?" a servant from a neighbouring house would ask. "You poor little thing! You must be feeling very bad yourself just now, isn't it?"

She did feel bad when people talked to her like this. She would answer briefly, because she was a polite little girl, and then run indoors as quickly as she could. Visalakshi would suggest that they should go out together, perhaps to take a short stroll round the garden, or to pay a visit to the temple in the next village, a couple of miles away.

She seemed to understand exactly how her daughter felt. But Subbalakshmi herself could not understand why, when the family returned to Saidapet, her mother should have unpacked the beautiful wedding sari, snipped it in two and made it into skirts for Balam and Savitri to wear.

"How eager I was," Sister told me, "to wear it again! After the calamity, I used to ask if I might put it on, but my mother wouldn't hear of it. Now I realize, don't you know, that she cut it up because she did not want a single thing to be left to remind me of what had happened. I used to feel so resentful when I saw my sisters wearing those skirts, and all the time I would be wondering how my mother could have done such a thing with silk that really belonged to me."

She looked directly at me, smiling with great sweetness. "I have never told this to anybody before, but I was thinking last night that since you are so interested in all these little details there was no reason why I should not tell you how I felt. I did so want to wear that sari again. Of course, I wouldn't have dreamed of telling my mother how I felt, but those bitter feelings lasted for a long, long time."

It is possible that the great decision had already been taken before the summer holiday began. At any rate, the family had been back in Saidapet for only a few weeks when Subbalakshmi learned about it.

"Today," her father told her one morning, "we are really going to commence your education."

She looked at him in astonishment. Her education had been completed twice already. She could not believe that her parents and Chitti would really send her away from home again, and especially just now. Yet what else could her father possibly mean?

He was smiling. Her mother and Chitti, who were both in the room, were smiling, too, looking down at her as expectantly as if they were about to put into her hands some precious and surprising gift.

"This time," her father explained, "you are going to learn many things which most ladies in our country don't know. To begin with, I am going to teach you English."

"English?"

"Yes. It isn't really at all difficult."

If her father said so, she knew it must be true. "How can you teach me," Subbalakshmi asked, "when you are busy at the college all day?"

"I shall," he answered, "give you a lesson each morning before I go. Then you can study by yourself during the day, and when I come back in the evenings we can spend some more time together, and I shall see how much you have managed to learn."

It sounded wonderful. "How long will it take me?" Subbalakshmi asked.

"If you are diligent," her father told her, "you should be able to speak and read and write perfectly well in about a year. After that …"

"What after that?"

He was laughing at her excitement. "Then you will be able to go to school again – to a very much better school, a school for English girls, where all the lessons will be in English."

She could hardly wait. "Will you give me my firsts lesson now?"

"Why not?" he went to the cupboard and brought out an English primer, a dictionary and an exercise book. Then he came and sat on the floor beside her and, while Visalakshi and Chitti went about their household duties, the little girl began, for the first time, to look at the English alphabet.

When Subramania got back from the college that evening, Subbalakshmi was again sitting where he had left her. The daily newspaper, *The Hindu*, had just been delivered, and she had spread it out in front of her, with her primer and dictionary on either side. Her lips were moving as she tried to spell out the words, and she was so absorbed that she did not hear her father enter.

Then he laughed his big, jolly laugh, and she looked up.

"There's no need," he told her, still laughing, but with pride in his voice, too, "to be in such a terrible hurry. You must try to be a little bit patient. Everything will come in time."

The months passed quickly. Before long, Subbalakshmi was studying, besides English, Sanskrit, mathematics, history, geography. She was so happy and absorbed that she scarcely noticed the visitors who came to the house, and when her mother took Balam and Savitri to attend weddings or other festivities, she was perfectly content to stay at home with her grandmother and Chitti and baby Swarnum.

Chitti encouraged her to work hard at her lessons, and it was Chitti, too, who suggested that Subbalakshmi should also learn to cook. A girl cousin who had recently been married came to spend a few months at Saidapet, and she and Subbalakshmi took turns to help Chitti or Visalakshi in the kitchen. By this time, Subbalakshmi was old enough to know why it was that her mother and her aunt each spent several days each month alone in the outhouse, leaving the other to manage the cooking and other domestic affairs with such help as her grandmother and the servant could give. A woman during her menstrual periods was ritually unclean until she had, on the fourth morning, taken a purifying bath. Visalakshi explained to her eldest daughter that she, too, would soon have to learn to follow this observance. But, she had added, although Subbalakshmi might suffer some discomfort and even pain when these periods began, they were a natural part of a woman's life. There was no need, she had added, for Subbalakshmi to worry or feel distressed. Nothing bad would happen to her when her body changed from that of a child into a woman.

Subbalakshmi could not even understand why it should be necessary for her mother to say such a thing. The sad thing that had happened a few months ago was already more than half-forgotten. Her life was crowded, more full of interest than it had ever been. She loved to study, and she enjoyed the hours she spent in the kitchen, listening to Chitti's stories as she learned to make rasam and sambar, idlies and dosai and bajjis, lime rice and coconut rice and chutneys and sweets and pickles.

Subbalakshmi's father often went into the city. One day when he came back he was carrying, tucked under his left arm, a long, strangely shaped parcel. He put it down in front of Subbalakshmi.

"This," he said, giving her one of his wide, loving and slightly amused smiles, "is for you, if you will learn to use it."

She unwrapped the parcel. The box inside was black, rather old and shabby, with brass hinges on one side and a catch on the other. She lifted the catch and saw, to her utter, dazzled astonishment, a violin.

She was speechless with joy. Her grandmother, who was looking on, was silent, too. For a few moments she was too scandalized to speak.

"It cost only five rupees," Subramania said pacifically, "and it really has a most beautiful tone."

It was not, and he knew it, the extravagance of buying such a thing which shocked Grandmother. She had been far from pleased by the decision to give Subbalakshmi an education of a kind that was really only suitable for boys. She had disapproved actively when she had realized that the girl was not to be shorn when she attained her age, or to lead the kind of life that was appropriate to a virgin widow. These things had been bad enough. The violin was really the last straw. Ladies might sometimes sing, though only in the privacy of their own homes. Even that was very unusual, and no lady would ever, in any circumstances whatever, learn to play a musical instrument. Music was for dancing girls, devadasis, as the temple prostitutes were called. Surely Subramania, who came from such a good family, could not really intend to engage a teacher and allow his widowed daughter, of all people, to take lessons?

That was his intention, and he carried it out. Before the summer holidays came round again Subbalakshmi had made such good progress that it was decided that later on she should learn to play the veena as well. By this time she could speak English quite fluently, and the headmistress of the Presidency Secondary and Training School at Egmore, in Madras city, had already agreed to accept her as a pupil at the beginning of the autumn term.

She could not, of course, be allowed to make the long journey from Saidapet to Egmore, which was in the heart of Madras city, all by herself. Fortunately, one of the other professors at the Agricultural College, a Christian, had a daughter about the same age as Subbalakshmi. It had been settled that she, too, was to attend the Presidency Secondary and Training School, the P T School as it was generally called, and that the two girls should travel backwards and forwards together.

A jutka cart was engaged. The driver was an elderly man, sober and trustworthy. There was nothing frisky about his horse either, and as long as the two girls sat well inside the cart, as they could be trusted to do, the roof would shelter them from the eyes of prying strangers. They would be perfectly safe.

Grandmother was not at all happy about the arrangement. Even Subbalakshmi's mother was a little worried, but she and Chitti were both anxious for Subbalakshmi to continue her education, and there seemed to be no other way of getting her to school. Subramania pooh-poohed these fears. Of course it was true that young girls did not usually travel without the protection of some older person, and even ladies seldom went out alone. But there would never be any progress in the world if a few people did not set an example by showing the courage to do things which had never been done before. Besides, Subbalakshmi and Mary were both sensible girls. They could be trusted not to lean out of the cart or to do anything to arouse the attention of strangers.

At last, the longed-for day came. The journey into the city was rather hot, but quite uneventful. When they arrived, Subbalakshmi was at first quite overcome by shyness. Her father had told her that the school was the best in the whole of the Madras Presidency, and that all the teachers and nearly all the pupils were either English or Anglo-Indian. She had known that she would be the only brahmin girl in the school, but she had not realized that although there were a few Hindu students in the Tamil and Telugu Teachers' Training departments, she would be the only Hindu pupil in the whole of the high school.

The teachers and the girls in her class were all so kind and friendly that her shyness had quite worn off before the day was over. She found that she could follow the lessons quite easily, and when she was asked a question she had no difficulty in answering it quickly and correctly. She was almost sorry when the day was over, and by the time the jutka cart was back in Saidapet she and Mary had agreed that school was even more delightful than they had imagined it to be.

When the cart drew up outside Subbalakshmi's house, both her mother and grandmother were sitting outside on the pial. Their faces looked pale and drawn, as if they had just heard some terribly bad news.

Subbalakshmi jumped down quickly and ran towards them.

"This," Grandmother exclaimed, "won't do at all! No! No! We can't have this!"

Subbalakshmi looked at her in astonishment. What could be the matter?

"You have frightened us," Grandmother went on, "almost out of our lives! We have been sitting here, your mother and I, the whole day long, worrying about you and waiting for you to come back. We cannot have you going off like that again. No! No! This going to school just won't do. It will simply have to stop, or our lives will not be worth living. I shall have to speak to your father about it as soon as he comes home."

She did, and Subramania was compelled to yield.

Subbalakshmi's disappointment at not being allowed to go to school again was almost past bearing. She did not show it. She had become very reserved, and when she was hurt or disappointed she bore the pain as best as she could and never talked about it.

Her father still taught her. Soon it appeared that although he had been obliged to yield to Grandmother's insistence he had not really given up his intention of sending Subbalakshmi to the P T School. He talked things over with his wife and Chitti, and during the next few weeks he went in to Madras more often than usual. Subbalakshmi was not told the reason for these visits, and she did not hear the talk that went on among the grown-up people when he came home again. So when everything was at last happily settled, her surprise was tremendous. The autumn term at the P T School was not yet over, and she was to go back and join the class in which she had been enrolled.

This time, though, she was not to travel backwards and

forwards every day. Her father had succeeded in renting a house which was situated almost exactly opposite the school. Chitti and Subbalakshmi were to go and live there together during the working days of each week, and at weekends they would either come home to Saidapet or the rest of the family would go and spend a few days in Madras.

Subbalakshmi adored Chitti, and it seemed to her that no arrangement could possibly have been better. Her mother seemed quite delighted with the idea, and so did Chitti herself. Grandmother seemed to acquiesce, though she didn't say a word.

Peepal Tree House, Subbalakshmi's father explained, had been given its name because of the two fine trees which grew in front of it. It was quite big, two storeys high, so that there would be plenty of room for all the family when they came to stay. And, he added with a glance at Grandmother, the rent was very reasonable, only fourteen rupees a month.

"How soon can we go?" Subbalakshmi asked.

"Very soon," Chitti told her, "but not quite at once. First, the house will have to be got ready. Then, of course, we shall have to choose an auspicious day."

The day, when it came, was one on which Subramania had to be at the College all morning and until fairly late in the afternoon. So it was settled that Chitti and Subbalakshmi should wait until he was free. Then he would accompany them to Madras and see that they were comfortably settled in before he returned to Saidapet.

The family took their morning meal together as usual. Only Grandmother, who habitually ate alone, was not present. This morning she was sitting by herself, as she often did, in a small room at the front of the house. When the meal was finished and Subramania was about to leave the house, Grandmother called him.

He went into the room where she sat. The door was closed, and they were shut up together for so long that Visalakshi was afraid that her husband would be late for his first lecture.

When he came out, the bad news could be read on his face. Grandmother had once more put her foot down. It was not right, she had said, that two virgin-widows should live together all by themselves, and without anyone to protect them. Chitti and Subbalakshmi must remain at home.

Nothing that Subramania had been able to say to her had had the least effect. Once more he had been obliged to yield.

"Don't worry," he told Subbalakshmi. "And don't give up hope. We shall find a way."

"How?" she whispered, blinking and turning her head so that he should not see her tears.

"Never mind how. Just try to be patient."

She tried. Weeks went by. Lessons continued as usual.

Then Uncle Euclid came to Saidapet. This great, good mathematics man, as Sister often calls him, possessed tact as well as intellectual ability. He could handle Grandmother as nobody else could. Before he left he had proposed a new plan and had induced the old lady to accept it. The whole family should go and stay at Peepal Tree House for a week. If Grandmother did not approve of what she saw during that time, the whole family should return to Saidapet. If she did approve, then Chitti and Subbalakshmi should be allowed to remain at Egmore.

Once more it was necessary to wait for an auspicious day.

Before long it came. That night grandmother, father and mother, aunt and the four girls all slept at Egmore. Next morning Grandmother seated herself behind a window at the front of the house to watch Subbalakshmi cross the road, and when the young girl took her place in a classroom, her grandmother was still sitting there. She did not move all day.

She was still at the window when Subbalakshmi returned in the afternoon. At last, the old lady was smiling. "I have seen everybody who came and went," she announced. "There are no men there. I have seen only ladies. Now I am satisfied. Everything will be perfectly all right."

Subbalakshmi was very happy at the Presidency Secondary and Training School. She settled down to the new routine as easily and naturally as if she had never known any other life, and she did not feel at all lonely or distressed when, at the end of the first week, the rest of the family returned to Saidapet and she and Chitti were left alone together. Chitti was a wonderful companion. Her face, with the edge of her white sari drawn as tight and close across her forehead as the coif of a nun, was so intensely and yet serenely alive that nobody could ever get tired of looking at it. She had the brightest eyes imaginable, but she wasn't hasty and excitable and quick tempered, as bright eyed people so often are. Whatever she did seemed to be done effortlessly, so that she always had time to do anything she was asked, to answer Subbalakshmi's questions, or to help her, if she needed help, with her homework. Subbalakshmi herself had so much to do that there was scarcely a moment between the beginning and the end of each week to think about how much she was missing her mother and father and her three little sisters.

They missed her terribly. At the end of a month Subramania and Visalakshi decided that the brief weekend visits between Egmore and Saidapet were not enough. Besides, it was not easy to meet the cost of maintaining two households. So the whole family came back to Egmore and settled down in Peepal Tree House.

Ever since he had begun to educate his widowed daughter, Subramania Iyer had lived under a constant fire of criticism from his orthodox friends and acquaintances. His conduct seemed to them to go for beyond the bounds of mere eccentricity. It was a defiance not simply of an ancient custom, but of what they declared was the will of god. The humiliation and sufferings which widows were expected to endure were divinely ordained. Punishment, bravely borne, was also a form of penance through which the soul could be absolved for past sins and acquire the merit which would entitle it to a more fortunate existence in its next birth.

Surbramania Iyer was a religious man. He accepted the belief that every child was born into the world with an immortal soul, and that these souls had passed through many previous existences. Although they did not carry with them any memory of their past lives, they brought with them the qualities which they had hammered out for themselves through good and evil deeds, noble and ignoble thoughts. This was the doctrine of karma, of fate. Fate was not, as most foreigners and even many Hindus believed, capricious and imposed from outside. Fate was the destiny which each soul earned for itself through its obedience, or disobedience, to the Divine Will. Subramania Iyer could not believe, nor could his wife and nor could Chitti, that the god he worshipped could really desire that a healthy and exceptionally intelligent girl should be immolated in the kitchen for the rest of her life because she had been so unfortunate as to lose her husband. On the contrary, no one could shake his conviction that it must surely be the will of god that his child's talents should be developed and used to the best advantage.

If educating Subbalakshmi, and at the same time continuing a happy and united home life, meant sacrifice, then the sacrifice would have to be made.

He made it. He had to be at the Agricultural College every morning at six o'clock. He bought a bicycle. "My father," Sister told me, her eyes flashing behind her glasses with the clear, golden rays that lit them whenever a long forgotten memory came rushing back, "was rather a constipated man, and getting up and out in the mornings was not easy for him. Sometimes when I woke and looked out of my window, I would see him down below, pacing up and down, perhaps for the sake of the exercise, or perhaps because he was waiting until the last moment before getting on to the bicycle and riding off. In those days there were no pneumatic tyres. The roads were not very good, either, and those rides to and from the station on that solid tyred bicycle were a great strain on him. Generally, he would come home at eleven to take his food, and then go back to the College again in the afternoon."

She herself rose every morning at five. By the time she had washed her face and hands the music teacher would have arrived. There were two music teachers now, and they came on alternate days, one to give violin lessons and the other to teach her to play the veena, the big stringed instrument which lies flat on the ground when it is played, and which is plucked with the fingers to produce the delicately balanced tones and half-tones and quarter-tones of classical South Indian music – Carnatic music, as it is generally called.

Then when the lesson was over she would settle down to learn five slokas, verses, of the Bhagavadgita, the Song Celestial, which is regarded by many people as the most sacred of the Hindu scriptures. The Gita has seven hundred slokas altogether, and at first it was enough to be able to repeat the beautiful, soft-vowelled Sanskrit sounds and to understand the literal meaning of the words that the warrior-prince Arjuna and Lord Krishna, who was the incarnation of Vishnu, Lord of Creation, spoke to each other. By the time Subbalakshmi knew them all, she was beginning to realize that these words had deeper meaning than she had at first realized. Sometimes her mother or Chitti would explain these meanings to her, and sometimes she would puzzle them out for herself.

During her schooldays the next task was, of course, to prepare her lessons. One morning when she was sitting in her room, poring over them with her usual intentness, she chanced to look out. Through the window she could see, downstairs in the courtyard, the cook, seated on a stool. Cook was a middle aged woman who always dressed like Chitti, with her head covered closely by her sari. Now she had removed the covering. There was a short, thick stubble of greyish black hair all over her head. A man whom Subbalakshmi knew by sight, though of course not to speak to, the barber who came to shave her father, was standing near by, holding his razor so that the blade glittered in the sunlight.

She watched with fascinated horror, sick with disgust yet unable to turn her head away from the sight, as the man stepped forward. Barbers, she knew, were filthy, low caste people. Their touch was polluting, even to a man, and her father always took a bath and changed his clothes as soon as he had been shaved. Yet now, though no gentleman, not even a close relative, would ever touch the hands of a lady or allow his fingers to come into contact with her garments, this dirty fellow was taking the cook's head in his hands and leaning over her as if – as if she were not a human being at all. Subbalakshmi had never seen anything so horrible in her life. Did the same thing, she wondered, happen to Chitti and to other ladies who had been disfigured and who kept their heads covered? She couldn't ask. She didn't want to know.

That morning, when she had taken her bath and changed into a fresh blouse and sari, ready to go to school, she could not eat even a mouthful of the morning meal. She said that she felt sick in her stomach, though she would not explain why. She had never guessed or imagined that anything so degrading could happen to any woman. She did not suspect, even then, that it was the quiet courage of her parents and Chitti that had saved her from a similar fate. But for days she could think of nothing else.

She herself always wore pretty, brightly coloured saris. Her weekly oil bath kept her long hair thick and glossy. She wore it parted at the centre, drawn back behind her ears, and then fastened in a plait. She did not wear a taali or silver toe-rings, or the nose jewels which married ladies liked to wear and which Europeans thought rather ridiculous, but she had a pair of diamond earstuds which suited her small, delicately shaped ears. Although she wasn't vain, she couldn't help knowing that she was very pretty.

There were only two respects in which her life seemed to be different from that of the daughters of her parents' friends. The big difference, of course, was that she went to school. The other, which was far less important, was that she did not attend weddings or thread ceremonies or any kind of festivity.

In the year 1900, a few months before Subbalakshmi's fourteenth birthday, the two sisters who were nearest to her in age, Balam and Savitri, were married. Balam was twelve, and Savitri not quite eleven. The attachment between Sandy and Balam had come to be recognized by the whole family as something so out of the common that it would have been wrong to force either of them into marrying anyone else, and everybody was delighted when it was decided that there should be a double wedding, and that Savitri should marry Sandy's younger brother, Dorasami.

"This morning you will go to school as usual," Subbalakshmi's mother said on the day when the ceremonies were to begin. "Marriages are not for you. You have something better. Education is for you."

The big sister was perfectly satisfied. Going to school was much more enjoyable than sitting at long, tedious marriage ceremonies where the loud music made people's heads ache, and many of the ladies, and perhaps the gentlemen, too, repeated all kinds of unkind scandals to each other while the purohits chanted and whispered the holy, ancient mantrams.

School was endlessly interesting. Miss Chatterton, who taught English, was an Anglo-Indian lady. Both Sister herself, and generations of girls who came after her, were taught by Miss Chatterton to write and speak with impeccable accuracy. She was, everybody says, a born teacher, and she made the girls love English literature so intensely that they would stretch their imaginations to the utmost limits to try to picture scenes and to visualize the beauties of landscapes and trees and flowers that they could never hope to see.

Subbalakshmi thought that English was a beautiful language, but she wished that the English and English-speaking girls and teachers in the school could realize that Tamil was a beautiful language too, and that there had been great Tamil poets – poets whose verses could still be understood quite easily – hundreds of years before Chaucer wrote his *Canterbury Tales*. As more Hindu parents began to follow her father's example and send their daughters to study in the English section of the P T School, it seemed to her very wrong that they should be scolded and even punished if they were caught talking to each other in their mother tongue.

Her favourite subject was still mathematics. The subjects she liked least were sewing and knitting. She learned, because all the girls in her class did, to cut out and sew a chemise, an article of clothing which she could never possibly wear, and to knit babies' woollen booties which, in the climate of Madras, would certainly cause prickly heat to break out on the skin of any child who wore them. She kept her criticisms, as she kept most of her thoughts, to herself. But when the time came to sit for a public examination – the lower secondary examination, as it was called – she was so nervous during the afternoon set aside for practical tests in domestic subjects that the first sewing needle she threaded snapped in two between her fingers. So did the next and the next, and she broke ten needles altogether before she managed to keep her fingers steady enough to sew a seam.

It didn't matter. When the results came, everyone in the family, even her grandmother, was intensely proud to read that Subbalakshmi had won the third place in the whole of the Madras Presidency, and was to be presented with a silver medal.

By this time both Balam and Savitri had entered the P T School. They were cheerful, contented little girls, and very proud to be attending the same school as their big sister. They got on well until one day when Balam came home crying bitterly.

"Whatever is the matter?" her mother asked. She had never seen the child so distressed about anything in all her life.

Balam sobbed and sobbed. She was a very tiny child, smaller for her age even than Subbalakshmi, with a face that seemed to have been made for laughter. Now she buried her head in her mother's lap, her whole body shaking with grief.

"What is it?" her mother asked gently.

Balam looked up. "It was the head ..."

She broke off, nuzzling against the folds of her mother's sari.

She had meant, Visalakshi guessed, the headmistress. Yet what could Miss Patterson, who was an English lady, have said, or what could Balam herself have done, to cause such agony?

"What happened?" her mother insisted. "Did you do something bad and have to go to her room for punishment?"

"No. No. It was worse than that." Balam released herself, and stood facing her mother. Her face was angry as well as hurt. "She ... she called Subbalakshmi by a bad name."

"Surely not!"

"Yes. Truly."

The headmistress had been showing a lady visitor, a foreigner, around the school. During the mid morning break they had been strolling through the playground, and Miss Patterson had led the visitor to the spot where Subbalakshmi and Balam were chatting together.

"This," the headmistress had said, pointing to Subbalakshmi, "is the little widow."

"Amma," Balam cried, "Sister isn't a widow, is she? It was wicked ... wicked! ... to say such a thing! How could anyone call Sister by such a bad word?"

It was a very bad word, a word which no lady would ever use. Yet, Miss Patterson, when she had used it, had looked pleased and proud, and had smiled as if it gave her all the pleasure in the world to speak in such a dreadful way about Sister, who was so good and clever and who herself had never been heard to say an unkind word about anyone.

Subbalakshmi herself was beginning to discover, without ever being explicitly told, what it meant to be a widow. Although her own life was so happy and sheltered, she was becoming aware that there were many girls among her family's circle of friends and acquaintances whose husbands had died. She did not often meet them. They lived like ghosts, haunting the kitchens and backyards of their parents' house – pale, undernourished, hard-worked. Subbalakshmi had always accepted as a matter of course whatever plans her parents had made for her. Nobody had ever told her that she was exceptionally fortunate. Now, with a growing awareness of the world in which she lived, it was not necessary for anyone to tell her. She was beginning to realize it for herself.

Many of the girls at the P T School either left altogether after passing the lower secondary examination, or else moved across to the training section, to begin the course which would enable them, after another two years, to become schoolteachers. It was only those who were exceptionally clever, or whose parents were very well-to-do, who stayed on at the school to study for matriculation.

Subbalakshmi stayed. In the following year, 1993, when Subbalakshmi was almost seventeen, another child was born to Visalakshi. By this time the hope that she might someday have a boy had receded so far that nobody expressed any particular disappointment when this baby, too, turned out to be a girl. She was named Nityananda, and grew up, everyone says, to be the most gifted of all the five sisters, and her death, during the Second World War, was a tragedy of which they still find it difficult to speak.

At Peepal Tree House a special puja was performed every Friday morning, when Visalakshi herself prepared the food that was to be offered to the gods, and would not take even a cup of coffee until all the prayers had been said and the ceremonies, which lasted for about three quarters of an hour, were over. However much homework Subbalakshmi had to do before she crossed the road to go to school, she would never miss a minute of these ceremonies.

"I was," she remarked one day, "a devotedly religious person, and when I was in my sixteenth year I was initiated into the Siva mantram by my father's uncle, a very learned and devout man." She asked, "You have heard of the sacred syllable Om?"

"Yes, of course." Om had been regarded since the most ancient times as a syllable of great holiness, filled with utmost power and mystery, and containing the whole essence of the Vedas, the ancient Aryan scriptures and hymns to the gods.

"My greatuncle," Sister continued, "when he taught me this said, Women must never utter that Om. Never. It is too sacred for them. Women must, instead, only say Um." She tossed her head scornfully, and again I could picture the young girl, proud, obstinate, outwardly obedient yet, with all her devoutness, refusing to swerve from her own conception of her rights as a human being. Then she laughed. "All the time I was repeating to myself Om Om Om. I could see no reason why women should be less than men in the eyes of god."

She was trying to understand the Advaita philosophy, the belief which she had been taught as a child, but which not all Hindus share, that there is but one Supreme Reality. "Advaita," she observed, "cannot easily be understood by all. For many people it is too abstract, too far from the experiences of their daily lives. It is also very difficult to grasp the doctrine of maya. It is not everyone who can understand that the world as we know it is based upon illusions." She paused, leaning forward as if by looking at me closely she could decide whether I was really grasping her meaning. "How real our dreams are! How hard it is to understand that ultimately we shall be one with god when we realize that everything here is all a dream ..."

Her dreams were vivid. Sometimes she daydreamed, too. Generally, though, there was not much time for daydreaming. She studied European history, geography, physics and chemistry as well as English and mathematics. The matriculation examination took place in December, and in the summer of 1905, the year in which she was to sit for the examination, Subbalakshmi took her notebooks and textbooks with her when the family travelled south for their holiday.

At Ernakulam they stayed as guests in the house of one of Subramania Iyer's acquaintances who was a professor of mathematics. His mother was a widow. She didn't keep to the kitchen, but moved freely among the guests, dressed always in a sari of shining whiteness. She talked a good deal about her grandchildren and the plans which were being made for their future. One of them was a girl of about eight or nine, called Ammukutty, and her grandmother and her parents were trying to find a family in which there was a boy who could make a suitable husband for her. It was difficult for them to do so, the grandmother explained, because people were demanding such big dowries for their sons, and professors of mathematics were not very well paid.

Subbalakshmi did not, of course, join in these conversations. She listened and remembered and wondered and thought.

Then they went home again, and for the next few months Subbalakshmi could think of nothing but the forthcoming examinations.

That year, there were not many candidates from the schools in the area – just one other girl in addition to herself, and twelve boys. Subbalakshmi was not nervous, and when the examination was over she waited for the results patiently, and with calm confidence.

The news came during the Pongal holiday, the harvest festival of South India which is celebrated in mid January. Subbalakshmi had not merely passed. She had gained honours in every subject. Of the boys, only one had managed to obtain pass marks.

When the results were published in the newspapers there was a great scandal.

"How," people asked each other, "could a girl be awarded honours when eleven boys fail? It just isn't possible! How could it have happened?"

They answered their own question. "Subramania Iyer," they declared, "must have bribed the examiners. There is no other possible explanation."

Sister was laughing when she told me this. At the time when it happened it had seemed anything but funny. "My father," she continued, "was terribly upset. He had made such great sacrifices for me, and he was so very proud of my success. Really, it was a most cruel and wicked thing to say!"

Subbalakshmi was nineteen and a half.

"Now," her mother said to her, "you may leave school. Your education is finished."

Subbalakshmi, who had always been so docile, disagreed. There was nothing more to be learned at the P T School, but she wanted to continue her studies.

"Why should you?" Visalakshi asked. "When girls go to college it is only so that they may become teachers."

Subbalakshmi nodded. She said, "I should like to be a teacher."

Her mother looked at her in astonishment. Such a possibility had never been mentioned. No brahmin lady, much less a widow, had ever become a teacher.

"We did not educate you," Visalakshi answered, "so that you might go out and earn your bread. We educated you so that you should not weep. Now you may stay at home and read books."

Subbalakshmi appealed to her father and to Chitti. Both of them supported and even encouraged her. If she wanted to go on studying and to make a life for herself, then it was, they agreed, the duty of her family to help her to do so.

But where was she to study?

The government inspector, an English lady who had often visited the P T School in the course of her duties, came to call at Peepal Tree House and had a long talk with Subbalakshmi's father. She had come out to India, she told him, fired with one ambition. The future of every country, she believed, depended on the level of education of its girls and the status of its women. India could only become happy and prosperous and, eventually, free if the mothers of future generations were educated as well as Western women, not in the same way, but within the framework of their own traditions.

That meant that there must be Indian women educators. She herself, all through the years she had spent in the Madras Presidency, had been on the watch for girls who could benefit by being given the best education that it was in England's power to give, and who would return to India to take a lead in educating the women and girls of their own country. She had searched in vain. Now, at last, her hopes could be realized. Subbalakshmi, she knew, had the character as well as the intelligence to benefit from all that she could learn in an English university. If her parents would allow her to go to England to study, the government would pay her fare each way and give her an allowance of three hundred pounds a year to cover her expenses.

It was a wonderful opportunity, but one which it was utterly impossible for Subramania Iyer and his wife to accept. It was not simply that a girl, a young lady, who had been so carefully protected all her life that in the city she never went out, except to cross the road to go to school, could not possibly be allowed to make the seven thousand mile journey alone. There was an even bigger obstacle. For a brahmin to go abroad, to cross the black waters as it was called, meant defilement, and to be defiled in this way meant being outcasted. Some brahmins, it was true, did go abroad, and when they returned underwent a ritual purification before being accepted again into their families and their caste. It was unthinkable that a girl from a brahmin family should make such a breach with tradition. Her family had broken many conventions for her sake, but there was a limit beyond which they could not be expected to go.

So the question remained – What was she to do?

There were no women's colleges anywhere in the Madras Presidency. The only institution in which a girl could work for a university degree was the Presidency College. A few girls, not many, did go there. Those who did were almost all Europeans or Anglo-Indians. Subbalakshmi quailed at the very idea. "I couldn't bear," she told me, "the prospect of going there and sitting in class with so many strange boys."

She would, someone suggested, perhaps continue her education at the Presentation Convent in George Town, Black Town as it was then called, in the heart of the city. The notion seemed worth trying, so Subramania Iyer went to the convent and asked for an interview with the Superior. Certainly, Mother Xavier agreed, she would be glad to accept Subbalakshmi as a student, but there was no possibility of her working for a university degree. Instead, she could study for the Faculty of Arts examination, for which one of the girls in the convent already intended to prepare.

It was the best that could be managed. Visalakshi was still not convinced that it was right to allow Subbalakshmi to continue her studies, but she did not protest. Chitti was delighted.

"We shall never be able to get our tongues around that huge great long name of yours," said Mother Patrick in her rich Irish voice. "So what are we going to call you?" She paused, in a way which seemed to suggest that the question had occurred to her for the first time at that very moment. Then, as Subbalakshmi was about to reply, the nun exclaimed, "I have it! We shall call you Sybil. How do you like that?"

Subbalakshmi did not like it at all, but this was only her second day at the convent, and it would have seemed impolite to disagree with her teachers before she had even begun to learn anything. So she acquiesced, and soon grew accustomed to her new name.

All the same, the change aroused a suspicion. Most Hindu converts to Christianity adopted Christian names. Subbalakshmi guessed that the nun was trying to do things in reverse order and was hoping that by giving her a Christian name she would be taking the first step towards turning her into a Christian.

Mother Paul, her other teacher, seemed concerned only that the new pupil should do her work well. In fact, both Mother Paul and Mother Patrick were excellent teachers, and before long Sybil-Subbalakshmi was just as happy at the convent as she had been at P T School.

In one way she was happier. The convent was three miles from Peepal Tree House and the daily journey, for a girl who scarcely went anywhere between one summer and another, was almost as exciting as a trip to another world.

Subramania Iyer had hired a steady, elderly man who knew

how to drive a horse and wanted to own a jutka cart and to ply it for hire. It was arranged between them that Subramania should pay for the cart, and that driver, who would be free to make what use of it he pleased during the hours when it was not needed, should repay him by monthly instalments.

It seemed an excellent arrangement. The only difficulty was the horse. He, Sister declared, was the most obstinate and self-willed animal that ever walked on four legs. The creature evidently enjoyed wandering through the Madras streets, and was never in a hurry to get to Black Town. Subbalakshmi liked to be punctual, but she liked to see the city, too, and it didn't seem to matter much that the poor driver didn't seem to be able to control his animal.

They would set off early, and presently the quiet, tree shaded roads of Egmore would be left behind. Subbalakshmi, sitting so far back in the shadows of the arched roof that passersby hardly noticed that she was there, would stare out at the carriage and rickshas and bullock carts that went up and down Poonamallee High Road, to and from the Central Station. Then, if the horse remembered to take the proper turning, she would be able to have a good look at the shops in China Bazaar, the busiest shopping street of the city. When the shutters were taken down in the mornings the goods would be piled up outside, so that it was impossible to be sure where the pavement ended and the shops began. There were rugs and carpets from Kashmir and from Kidderminster in England, and exquisitely thin straw mats from Muslim villages in the far south, all spread out for customers to look at. In front of the hardware shops were pagoda like towers made by brass and copper vessels piled accurately on top of each other. The cloth shops were festooned with Manchester cottons and Japanese cottons hung over high railings like many coloured banners, and it was possible to peep inside at the shelves stacked with saris from Conjeevaram and Benares and Lucknow and Kollegal and Bangalore.

After that, if the horse took a wrong turning, Subbalakshmi would find herself in the street of the ironworkers and locksmiths, or the street of the glasscutters, where looking glasses made countless reflections of everyone who passed. Sometimes the horse wandered into the fruit market, where bananas of every imaginable size hung from the roofs, over stalls crammed with guavas, melons, suppotas, and mangoes and oranges and grapes and custard apples and mangosteens and papaya. Then there was the street of the jewellers, whose dark caves glimmered with gold and silver vessels, gold chains and taalis and bangles, and the sudden flashing gleam of diamonds and rubies and sapphires and emeralds. Subbalakshmi, during the long, protected years of growing up, had never realized how full the world was of beautiful things.

She saw squalor, too. Homeless families camped in the streets. Women in filthy rags, with naked babies crawling in the rubbish around them, sat on the pavement outside the walls of the High Court, lighting fires of dried leaves and waste paper, cooking evil smelling messes in vessels of sunbaked clay which looked as if they were never cleaned from one year's end to another. Lepers thrust out their mutilated hands, begging for a copper coin. Young widows crept along the streets, their saris pulled tightly over their heads to hide their disfigurement, hardly daring to show themselves, yet unable to refuse to perform whatever domestic errand had brought them out into the glaring light of day. Their saris were often torn and dirty, their bodies emaciated by perpetual hunger. They were not perhaps the poorest of the poor, since there were many people in the city who could not count on getting even one meal a day, but to Subbalakshmi, so happily conscious of her own good fortune, they were the saddest sight of all. Even when the horse had at last drawn up before the convent and she had climbed the stairs to her classroom on the top floor she could not get these poor creatures out of her mind. It needed all her willpower to settle down to her books.

She had been at the convent only a few weeks when Mother Patrick gave her a Bible. "Read it," the nun said. "You will find that it will help you to improve your English very much."

Subbalakshmi accepted the gift, though not quite happily because she was sure that it had been prompted by another motive. She took it home and asked her father, a little doubtfully, "Shall I read it?"

"Certainly," he answered. "It is written in the purest and best English you can ever find. Besides, there are many excellent things in the Christian teaching. You are not a child any more, and it is right that you should know about all religions and decide for yourself what you believe."

A few days later, Uncle Euclid came to the house. "What are you reading now?" he asked, when he went upstairs and found Subbalakshmi sitting alone in her room.

"The Bible," she answered.

"It is beautiful, isn't it?" Then, after a moment, he added, "There is another book that you should also read. I shall bring it to you next time I come. It is by an American, Colonel Robert Ingersoll."

When Sister had got to this point in her story we were interrupted by the arrival of a shoal of nieces and nephews. They wanted to hear what she was telling me, but she refused to go on. "No," she said, in a tone so decided that it would evidently have been useless to try to persuade her to change her mind, "that is quite enough for one day, don't you know. I shall tell you the rest next time you come."

She was very busy at that time, and it was not until a week later that I visited her again. When I arrived she was sitting at her desk, writing. I sat down on the divan, staring around the room as I waited for her to finish. On the wall beside her desk was a coloured picture, which I had often seen but never really looked at, of Lord Krishna, the god-king who had been born in a cowherd's cottage. The picture, about half-lifesize, showed him as a boy, with a flute between his fingers and a curious smile on his face, at the same time both dreamy and provocative, rather feminine.

After a few minutes, Sister came and tucked herself up beside me, with her legs crossed and the silvery folds of her silk sari hiding her bare feet. She asked, "I was speaking of Robert Ingersoll last time you came, wasn't I?"

"Yes."

"What a wonderful book he wrote! Have you read it?"

"No, only a few passages here and there."

"You should read it all. It begins, Did god make man or did man make god? What a splendid question! I found it a most absorbing book."

I enquired, "Did the nuns know that you were reading it?"

"Certainly. Why not? Mother Patrick – Mother Paul never troubled me even once – was really a most bigoted Christian. It was the way that Mother Patrick talked, don't you know, that made me realize how much intolerance there was in the Christian religion. She would say to the Protestants, I would rather have these Hindus than you Proddies!"

She pulled the battery case of her deaf-aid from the upper folds of her sari, waving it backwards and forwards between us, as if to give emphasis to the unusual note of indignation in her voice. "Yes! Proddies, she called them! What an offensive way to talk! She would have done so much better to show some respect for beliefs that were different from her own. I used to argue with her. I repeated some of the things I had read in Colonel Robert Ingersoll's book – about the creation of the world, and the Flood, et cetera, et cetera. She said, I have never heard of that book. Will you bring it?"

Sybil-Subbalakshmi took the book with her to the convent next morning and gave it to Mother Patrick. A day or two later she was called to Mother Patrick's room. "This is a very wicked book," the nun said. "I shall have to burn it."

Subbalakshmi gazed at her in astonishment. People's ideas of right and wrong might vary. Often, indeed, it was a good thing that they should. Her own life had already demonstrated that it was through these differences that progress was made. Nevertheless, to burn a book, however wrong one might believe its author to be, could never be right.

She said so.

Mother Patrick disagreed. The book would have to be burned. It would corrupt the mind of anyone who read it.

If that was the nun's opinion, it was probably useless to try to persuade her to think differently. Subbalakshmi said, "The book belongs to my uncle. I must return it to him. Please give it to me."

Mother Patrick was silent for a few moments. Her head was bowed, her face invisible beneath the starched coif. Then she looked up and said, "I will give it back to you on one condition."

"What is it?"

"That you promise not to read it again."

It was Subbalakshmi's turn to reflect. "I promise," she replied, "that I will not read it again as long as I am studying in the convent."

Since that was the most that could reasonably be exacted, Mother Patrick returned the book and Subbalakshmi, of course, kept her promise.

Months went by. Mother Patrick was still as determined as ever to save the soul of her brightest pupil. She was not always very tactful.

"Your Hindu customs," Sister remembered hearing her say on one occasion, "are so repulsive!"

"Which customs?"

"Taking a bath every day and refusing to eat meat."

Sister, when she told me this, was bubbling with indignation, her battery case waving backwards and forwards so fast that it almost seemed to have taken on a life of its own. "What customs to choose for criticism! I answered her. Is there any saying of Christ that people should not wash their bodies every day or that they must eat meat? I told her that in this climate it is better for the health not to eat meat, and that it is absolutely necessary to take a bath not just once a day, but twice at least." She tucked the battery case back into its place, between the front of her blouse and the upper folds of her sari. Then she continued in a milder tone, "These were the sort of ideas which very many Europeans – though of course not all – had in those days. Once, some years ago, I was visiting a boys' school" – she named it – "and the headmaster said to me in a very proud voice, We see that all the boarders here take a bath once a week. I was so shocked! Look here, I said to him, Do you mean once a week or once a day? No, he answered, Not once a day, but weekly as people do in England –"

"Even in England," I interrupted, "many people take a bath every day."

"No doubt. Of course, not everybody who goes to England has the opportunity to learn how gentlefolk live. And many low caste converts to Christianity adopt the customs of those whom they imagine to be their betters, without ever considering whether they are suitable for our life here or not."

The Christians in South India were not all of low caste origin. The Syrian Christians on the West Coast, who date the foundation of their church to the early centuries of the Christian era, might not unfairly have been described as the brahmins of the Christian community were it not for the fact that in the eastern part of the Madras Presidency there were brahmin Christians who really were brahmins.

Many of them lived at Trichinopoly, where they adhered to many of the traditional customs of their caste and were not troubled by uncomfortably literal interpretations of the doctrine of the brotherhood of man. Hindus retained the usual caste distinctions and untouchables remained untouchable. Nearly twenty five years after Subbalakshmi left Presentation Convent, Gandhi, Vallabhbhai Patel and Mahadev Desai, who were in prison together, received news of the trouble that these distinctions were then causing. Desai, who was Gandhi's secretary, recorded in his diary on 30 December, 1932 that some of the Christians in Trichinopoly had warned the Bishop of Madras that they would fast unto death unless the barrier in the church which divided the brahmins from the lower caste people and the untouchables was taken down. "Gandhi," Desai added, was "very amused," and Vallabhbhai Patel, in his practical way, asked why the non-brahmins did not simply remove the barrier instead of fasting to compel others to do so.

Perhaps Mother Patrick thought that a brahmin Christian might be able to succeed where she had failed. At any rate, one day she said to Subbalakshmi, "I want you to stay a little late tomorrow evening. Please ask the permission of your parents, and tell them that there will be no cause for them to worry."

Subbalakshmi obeyed. Next day, when classes were over, she was taken to a room in which a lady was sitting alone. The stranger was dressed as a smartha brahmin lady should be, with her sari folded correctly around her legs, and then drawn over her shoulders, and with the pallav end pulled forward across her stomach like an apron. She wore, too, a red tilak, the happiness mark of the married woman, painted on her forehead. She was, she explained, Mrs Natesa Iyer from Trichinopoly, and Mother Patrick had invited her to come to Madras to have a talk with Subbalakshmi and, she added frankly, to try to persuade her of the truth of the Christian faith.

Subbalakshmi was not to be persuaded. She took Mrs Natesa Iyer back to Peepal Tree House. That evening there was much agreeable conversation, though not of the kind which Mother Patrick had intended.

"I may also tell you," Sister continued with a victorious smile, "that in the end things happened in quite the opposite way, and both Mr and Mrs Natesa Iyer became reconverted to Hinduism. That was an event of real historical importance, because until that time converts to Christianity who regained their original faith were not accepted back into the Hindu fold. Mr Natesa Iyer succeeded in convincing our religious authorities that they were wrong. Since then all those who have wanted to return to their old religion have been allowed to do so. I can remember hearing Mr Natesa Iyer tell my father that he had been very much shocked by the intolerance of the Christian sects, and I believe that this was the chief reason why he decided to give up Christianity."

By the end of Subbalakshmi's first year at the convent it was becoming evident, though Mother Patrick could still not bring herself to acknowledge it, that no one would ever succeed in persuading her to give up the religion in which she had believed all her life. She never became a Christian. Yet the two years she spent studying for the Faculty of Arts examination were crucial. Although she could not accept the faith of the women and girls in whose company she spent her days, their example was to determine the course which she has followed throughout the rest of her life.

Visalakshi had always hoped to be able to take a bath in the waters of the most sacred of all rivers, the holy Ganges, before she died. Now it was decided that she and her husband and Subbalakshmi should make a pilgrimage together to the north, visiting Calcutta on the way and then going to Benares, Allahabad and Gaya.

Subbalakshmi and her parents travelled by train, though in 1906 many pilgrims still made their journeys on foot. It was quite a common thing to see a man tramping along with a rope slung over his left shoulder and the bundles containing his clothes and cooking pots tied at either end. Benares was the first important stopping place for those going north. "Everyone who got so far," Sister went on, "would also visit Allahabad and Gaya. After that, those with strength in their bodies would go on to Hardwar. Some – a few – would go further, all the way to Badrinath. That was a difficult and dangerous journey, as it still is even now."

Even the shorter pilgrimage made on foot could scarcely last for less than six months, and it was quite common for pilgrims to remain away from their homes for a year or even two years, and sometimes much longer.

Sister, when she had told me this, suddenly began to laugh. "What is funny?" I asked.

She said, "I have just remembered that when I was a girl there was a man from a village in Tanjore district who went away and simply didn't come back. There was no word from him, not so much as a postcard, and when five years had passed he was given up for dead. His wife, who was a thoroughly orthodox lady, had herself disfigured and put on a white sari. Then the very next year her husband came back!" Sister laughed again. "He had thought nothing of staying away for so long, and he was so astonished to see his wife looking like that!"

When a pilgrim from the south returned home his pilgrimage was not yet completed. The final stage was a journey to

Rameshwaram. Each pilgrim carried with him a bottle of holy water from the Ganges. This was presented to the idol in the inner sanctum of the Rameshwaram temple, who was then bathed in it. Afterwards the pilgrim, back home at last, completed his duties by feasting a number of poor brahmins.

There were two holy rivers to be crossed on the way from Madras to the north, first the Krishna, and then the Godavari, which is the younger sister of the Ganges. Subbalakshmi's parents decided that they would stop at each of them in order to take a bath.

When they left the train at Bezwada, they went to spend the night in a choultry near the banks of the Krishna river. The choultry was crowded with pilgrims, sanyasis and other holy men, and ordinary folk from many different parts of the country. There were tall, angular men from the north and plump Bengalis with bodies as round as the soft, sweet rasagolas which they loved to eat. There were slant eyed Assamese and fair skinned Punjabis and Maharashtrian ladies whose saris were fastened in such a peculiar way that they looked from the back almost like the breeches which Europeans wore when they went riding on horseback. The strangest sight of all, which Subbalakshmi simply could not take her eyes off, was a man from the Telugu country who was drawing water from the choultry's well in a small vessel, no bigger than a drinking cup, and pouring it over his naked torso and dirty cotton dhoti. He poured and poured, but even after ten minutes he had still not managed to wet himself properly, and the river, where he could have taken a good bath, was two minutes' walk away.

Subbalakshmi went on staring. Other people were watching the spectacle, too. Presently the man opened his bundle and pulled out a silk dhoti, which he wound around himself, allowing the filthy cotton beneath it to fall to the ground. The silk dhoti was dirty too, stained with food and sandal paste.

"Why hasn't he washed it?" somebody muttered.

There was no need for such a question because everyone, even the man who asked it, must have known the answer. Silk was madi, ritually pure, because it had never been washed. The fellow, whoever he was, evidently didn't want to take the trouble of washing it after each wearing, as he would have to do if it was to maintain its purity when once it had been in the water.

Subbalakshmi smiled to herself with an amusement that had in it, perhaps for the first time in her life, a sharp twist of irony. There were, the girl acknowledged to herself, many customs and habits and superstitions which foreigners in India could legitimately criticize. It was unfortunate that they should so often pick on the wrong things.

Next day, the travellers moved on. When they got down from the train at the railway station at Rajamundry, on the banks of the Godavari, they were invited by the stationmaster to be his guests. He and his wife were Telugu brahmins, and the invitation was accepted with pleasure.

Their hostess was delighted to entertain visitors, and especially ladies, who she hoped might be able to answer questions which had been puzzling her for many years.

"Do you," she began by asking them as soon as the gentlemen were safely out of the way, "come into contact with any European ladies in Madras city?"

Yes, Visalakshi and her daughter acknowledged, they did.

The stationmaster's wife had never spoken to a European

lady in her life, nor had she ever before met anyone of her own sex who had. She asked, "Do they come straight down from heaven?"

Subbalakshmi and her mother avoided each other's glances. Even so, they were both finding it almost impossible not to laugh.

"No," Visalakshi managed to answer without smiling, "they come from Europe, generally from England."

"Yes," their hostess agreed, "I know that, of course. But how do they come into the world? Surely they cannot be born as we are?"

"Certainly they are."

"They go through all those things and suffer as we do?"

"Yes, indeed!"

"How can that be? They are so soft and white and beautiful, not like us with our hard brown skins. They look so like goddesses that I always imagined that it was the gods who sent them down to earth, and that he sent their children down to them in the same way. It is really so hard to believe that it is not so!"

She went on questioning, still not wholly convinced. "And really," Sister commented, "it is not so very surprising. You know yourself how much importance our people attach to the colour of their skins, and how very much easier it is to get a husband for a girl who is fair complexioned. I suppose you know, too, that although some of the gods were born, most of them were not. Even the saints were generally found under trees or gooseberry bushes or other plants. This poor woman had naturally grown up with the idea that superior beings – and most people in those days thought of Europeans as superior beings – were spared from having to undergo the sort of sufferings that common people did."

After that, there was a long, hot journey to Calcutta. By the end of a week Subbalakshmi was so tired that when she and her parents got in the train for Benares it needed all her willpower to look out at the scenery instead of falling asleep. Then, as soon as they arrived she went to bed.

She woke next morning to find herself in a delightful house. The window of her room looked out onto the Ganges, and when she went downstairs she found that there was a big puja room, decorated with beautiful pictures and images of the gods, and with fresh flowers and fruits ready to be offered in worship.

Best of all, she learned that among the worshippers were two uncles of the young Tamil poet, Subramania Bharathi. Although he was only four years older than Subbalakshmi, his poems had already made him famous throughout South India. Unlike most of the gifted young men of his generation, he did not write his poems in English and copy English models. Instead, he wrote in his mother tongue, and many of his poems were about the freedom which he dreamed of for his own people, and which he believed it was in their power to win.

When Bharathi used the word Freedom he meant, in the first place freedom from British rule. He also meant much more. Real freedom he believed could only come if the Tamil people were roused to liberate themselves from superstition, ignorance and the restriction imposed by ancient, outworn customs. Subbalakshmi, who at Courtallam had learned to dance the traditional kummi dance with other little girls, had read the poem which Bharathi had entitled "The Kummi, of Women's Freedom."

The poem was a vision of the future, of the time when,

> ... gone are they who say to the women, "Thou
> shalt not open the Book of Knowledge."
> and the strange ones who boasted, saying
> "We will immure these women in our homes."
> Today they hang down their heads.
> Dance the Kummi! Beat the measure!
> Let this land of the Tamils ring with our dance,
> For now we are rid of all evil shades.
> We have seen the good.

It was far more beautiful in Tamil than it could ever be made to sound in any English rendering. It described, as precisely as if he had had her in mind when he wrote it, the liberation which had been won for Subbalakshmi, not through her own efforts, but through the patience and determination of her parents and Chitti. For thousands, indeed millions of other girls, those who had or would have husbands as well as young widows, such a liberation was not even a dream.

Subbalakshmi sat in her room, looking out at the turbid, filthy, beautiful and sacred river, gazing upstream and then downstream, thinking back over the years, the months, the last few weeks, and then forward, to a future which would not be made for her but which, she had already begun to realize, she would have to decide for herself. She could not, as her mother still wished, stay at home and read books when her second, and final year at the convent was over. Such a life, with her two youngest sisters still to be educated, and her older sisters' babies to look forward to, would be neither empty nor useless. Yet it would not be enough. She had to think not only of the future that might be in store for herself and the rest of her family, but of the future of others, of many, many others.

She pictured again, as she had done so often since she began to grow up, the baby widow whom she had seen so long ago and whose cries still haunted her dreams. There were, she knew now, countless little girls all over India who were just as unfortunate as little Janaki. And, as her thoughts moved forward again, she seemed to see, almost as if they were passing in front of her, the bent heads and meagre, half-starved bodies of the young widows whom she had passed on her way to and from the Presentation Convent. In contrast, the girls who were studying in the convent were radiant creatures, shining with health and joy and hope.

One of these girls, whom Subbalakshmi had met when she first went to the convent and who was about the same age as herself, was unforgettably lovely, a goddess like creature such as the stationmaster's wife at Rajamundry imagined all European ladies to be. She was slender and very fair, with a complexion as delicately textured as a pearl and long golden hair that rippled down her back with the soft brightness of clouds at sunrise. She was, Subbalakshmi soon learned, not English but French, and came from a wealthy and aristocratic family to which she would, after a year or two, return and eventually make a suitable marriage.

As the months passed, Subbalakshmi had seen less and less of this lovely creature. Presently she learned why. The girl had found her vocation and was to become a nun. She would probably never return home and never again meet anyone who belonged to her own family. When her noviciate was over, the golden clouds of hair would be shorn off, not cruelly and against her own will, but with glad acceptance of every action which belonged to the life she had chosen for herself. Thenceforwards, her life would be spent among girls and women to whom she owed nothing, but to whom she would give everything that was in her power to give. Subbalakshmi knew that she would never be able to accept the religious doctrines in which the French girl believed. Yet if she, and Mother Xavier and Mother Paul and Mother Patrick could dedicate their lives to the education of Indian girls, surely theirs was an example to be followed?

It was not the first time that she had begun to think like this. Perhaps, too, Chitti, in her quiet, tactful way, had helped to put such thoughts into her mind. At any rate, from now on they recurred more and more often.

Benares seemed a strange place in which to be thinking about the future. Many of those who came to the holy city were not visitors or pilgrims who would move on again after a few days or a few weeks, but old people who had come there to die, perhaps soon, perhaps after a few months or even years. Every day the dead, citizens and strangers, were carried to the ghats for their bodies to be burned and their ashes thrown into the river. There were, Subbalakshmi could see from her window, too many bodies to be disposed of. While groups of mourners stood around their dead, waiting for the ceremonies to begin, the priests who were officiating would hurry over the rites which they were performing for those at the head of the queue. Then, when the essential formalities had been completed but before the fire had had time to do its work, they would fling the half-burned corpse into the river. After that, the next body would be carried forward, a fresh pyre lighted, and after a short time another corpse, not yet turned to ashes, would be flung into the water to sink or to drift downstream among the city's sewage, vegetable refuse, dead flowers and dead animals.

"They say so much about Ganges water," Sister observed when she had described this scene to me. "It is said to be so sacred and so pure. With all those bodies and all that filth floating in it, how can it be pure?" She paused and glanced about her. The bougainvillaea was in flower, and at the far end of the big courtyard small boys and girls, greatnieces and nephews, were playing together, their shouts and laughter the only sounds in the afternoon quietness. Sister was not looking at them but beyond, into the far, far distance. Then, after a moment or so, her attention came back to me. "Yet all the same," she continued, "Ganges water is pure. There must be something in it – antibodies – or should I say antibiotics? – which neutralizes all these poisons. I have a bottle of Ganges water here in the house now, and it seems to be keeping very well."

From Benares, Subbalakshmi and her parents went on to Allahabad, a city of especial holiness because of its location at the junction of the Ganges, the Jamuna and the underground flowing Saraswati. There were always pilgrims coming and going from the Triveni, as the meeting place of the waters was called. They would take holy baths on the riverbanks and then get into boats to go to the most sacred place of all to take a dip and wash away their sins.

It was popularly believed that women of outstandingly good

character were marked out by the gods for special favours, and were carried off to heaven while they bathed. Since only their spirits could go to heaven, their bodies would sometimes be seen floating below the Triveni, down the broad main stream of the Ganges. It was sometimes noticed, too, that although these corpses were still fully clothed there were no jewels or gold ornaments to be seen on them. Subbalakshmi, who had been taught by her father to seek rational explanations and to be sceptical of superstitious beliefs, was not surprised to be told that there were men in Allahabad who had learned, as she herself had learned in childhood, to swim under water. It was they, and not the gods, who carried off pious, believing women to be drowned and robbed.

"Be careful!" someone called to Subbalakshmi one day when she was out swimming. She hurried back to the shore, convinced that she had had a narrow escape. After that, she continued to swim, even though her mother would sometimes be unable to hide her fear that Subbalakshmi was taking too many risks. Subbalakshmi knew that she could trust herself to be careful.

Meanwhile their host, a purohit, was frightening Visalakshi very much by the stories he told her. Or perhaps it was not so much the purohit himself as Subramania Iyer's refusal to act as every husband who came to Allahabad with his wife was expected to do, which scared Visalakshi almost beyond endurance.

It was customary, as everybody knew, for married couples who visited Allahabad to make a special journey to the Triveni in the company of their purohit. As soon as they got into the boat, the wife would seat herself on her husband's lap. Then, as the boatmen began to row, she would let down her hair, and her husband would fasten it in a long plait. As they reached the meeting of the waters, the husband would cut off the last inch of the plait and present it to the purohit, along with a gift of money which would vary with the means of the husband.

"My father," Sister said, "had no belief in such things. He couldn't tolerate them at all."

Her mother was different. She was terribly distressed when her husband refused to perform this ritual.

"Some time ago," the priest told Visalakshi and her daughter "there was another couple here who disagreed about this question. For a long time the wife was unable to persuade the husband to perform his religious duty. She was a very good woman and she persisted in her pleadings until at last her husband was obliged to yield. We went to the Triveni together. The thing was done and I was given a respectable sum. They then went to Gaya. As they reached that city a most terrible storm broke out. Very many pilgrims were drowned. Because of what this couple had done, the gods in their mercy chose to spare their lives and they were able to return home happily."

Visalakshi repeated this to her husband. He answered by reminding her of what had happened when Sri Sadasiva Iyer and his wife had visited Allahabad some years earlier. Lady Sadasiva Iyer had wanted the rite to be performed. Her husband had been unwilling. The purohit had insisted that it would be a great virtue on the part of the husband to sacrifice an inch of his wife's hair.

"If it is virtue to cut off one inch," Sir Sadasiva, the eminent lawyer had enquired, "will it be more virtuous if I cut off two inches?"

"Certainly," the purohit had replied.

"And three inches will be better still?"

"Yes."

"So it will be even more virtuous if I cut off four inches?"

"Well, yes."

"And if I cut off all my wife's hair and her head is shaven that will be the most virtuous action of all?"

There was, of course, only one possible answer which the purohit could give without entangling himself. He gave it and this, Subbalakshmi's parents told her, was the reason why she had, as a little girl, seen Lady Sadasiva Iyer at a wedding with her head shorn.

Perhaps the recollection of this incident made Visalakshi begin to wonder whether, after all, her husband might be right. The purohit, however, had not finished with her yet.

"There was another lady," he told her, "whose husband most obstinately refused to perform this rite. Although his wife tried to persuade him, he finally succeeded in convincing her that it should not be performed. They went away. When they came to the Godavari river which, as you know, is the younger sister of our holy Mother Ganges, there was an accident to the train in which they were travelling. The husband was killed. His wife was obliged to stay in the place to perform the death ceremonies. The river came to her in a dream and spoke, saying, "You refused to sacrifice even one inch of your hair to my elder sister, the holy Ganges. Now the tenth day is coming when I shall punish you for your disrespect by taking away all your hair." And the wife who had come so happily to this holy city returned to her own place as a shorn widow, to spend the rest of her days in tears and bitterness."

Visalakshi had never felt so frightened. She tried not to show it. At Gaya, she and her husband and daughter prayed, as all pilgrims did, for the souls of their ancestors. Then, at last, they began their return journey. Visalakshi was still trying not to show her nervousness, though she had not forgotten a word of the stories which the purohit at Allahabad had told her. Her husband, she knew, would merely laugh at her fears, and Subbalakshmi did not share them, either.

The train crossed the Godavari and Krishna rivers. All seemed to be well. In another day they would all be back safely in Madras. That night Subbalakshmi slept soundly, as she always did. When she awoke, the train was standing at a wayside station.

"Where are we?" she asked.

"I don't know," her mother answered. Her voice was quivering. "The train has been standing in this place for more than two hours."

Passengers were strolling up and down the platform. Villagers had arrived from their homes near by, offering curds and milk for sale. Subbalakshmi's father, who had been sleeping in the opposite berth, sat up. "You had better get down to the platform," he said to his wife, "and light that little stove of yours and make us all a cup of coffee."

Visalakshi, calmed by his tone, got up and was soon busying herself outside. Soon the stationmaster appeared. A goods train, he said, had been derailed a few miles ahead. The accident was not serious, but it would take another hour or so to clear the line.

A friend strolled down the platform from another coach. "Ah!" he sniffed, "I haven't smelled such good coffee since I left Madras. Do you think you could spare me a little?"

They were delighted. It was wonderful to think that they were almost home again. Visalakshi became her natural, cheerful self. Her daughter, looking forward, was taking another glance back, back to a street in Gaya through which she and her parents had driven on their way to bathe in the Ganges.

"I have never been able to forget that sight," Sister told me. "There was an old woman lying there dying, right in the middle of the road. She was dressed in rags and her poor old bones were sticking through her skin, and there were flies – thousands upon thousands of flies – crawling all over her. All the time people were going past, some walking, some in their carriages and carts, and not one of them paid the slightest attention. We wanted to help her, but what could we do? We couldn't even speak the language. We didn't know of any place where we could take her so that she could die in peace. Whenever anyone speaks of the holy city of Gaya, I think of that poor old woman, lying there with no one to move her, to help her, to ease her sufferings." Then she asked, not of me, nor of the visitor who had just arrived and was sitting at the other end of the veranda, but addressing the empty spaces of the long courtyard with the sky, paling towards evening, arching above, "What is religion? What is this thing? Where is kindliness? How can people treat each other so?"

Subbalakshmi returned to the convent to finish her studies for the Faculty of Arts examination. She had no doubt that for the rest of her life she would have to be as single minded in her dedication as Mother Xavier and Mother Patrick and Mother Paul. Once her decision had been made it was as if she had never really had any choice. She would, she promised herself solemnly, strive to liberate all child widows, to help them to become useful and happy, valuable to the world and valued by it.

Chitti encouraged her resolution. Visalakshi acquiesced. As time went on, she became enthusiastic. It was she, no less than Chitti, who eventually made it possible to start the Brahmin Widows' Home.

Subbalakshmi's resolve led, inevitably, to another decision. In order to qualify herself to educate others, she would need a university degree. That meant that when her second year at the convent came to an end, she would have to brace herself to endure the embarrassments and discomforts which she would inevitably meet at the Presidency College.

She tried not to worry. At home, and at the convent, she worked harder than ever. There were still occasional difficulties. The jutka cart driver and his horse could still hardly ever agree as to where they wanted to go, and as often as not it was the horse who got his own way. So Subbalakshmi decided that a special effort would have to be made when, one evening, Mother Patrick asked her to be sure to arrive half an hour before the usual time on the following morning, because government inspectors were coming to examine the pupils.

When morning came, Subbalakshmi set off a whole hour before the usual time. The horse responded by taking it into its head to make a tour of the whole city. "The poor driver," Sister told me, "kept on getting down to try to persuade the horse to go to George Town. The creature most obstinately refused. People kept coming up to try to help, but it was no use. We went right along the Marina, and then the horse turned round and went into Triplicane. The result was that instead of being half an hour early, I was half an hour late. It didn't matter. My classroom, as I told you, was at the top of the building, and I was sitting in my place before the inspectors got up there."

Of course, she satisfied them. Later, when the results of the Faculty of Arts examination were announced, nobody was greatly surprised, though of course everyone was delighted, to learn that Subbalakshmi had won two gold medals.

Then a difficulty arose.

"Mother Xavier," she told me, "particularly wanted me to wear a white sari and white shoes and stocking for the prize giving ceremony. At first, my mother simply wouldn't hear of it. All the other girls, the Christians and Europeans and Anglo-Indians, were to wear white dresses. According to our custom, as you know, white is the colour for widows, and for that reason my mother had never allowed me to wear it." She paused briefly, and then went on, "The nuns had been so good to me, and for them white meant something quite different from what it meant to us. So in the end my mother was persuaded, and I took my medals and prizes dressed all in white so that they should not be disappointed."

After this, it was time to say goodbye to Mother Xavier and Mother Paul and Mother Patrick. Subbalakshmi was truly sorry to leave them all. They never forgot her. Today, when they are no longer alive, the nuns' affectionate relationship with the young brahmin widow is still remembered by their successors. To them, she is still Sybil.

By this time, a few brahmin parents in Madras city and other parts of South India, though still not many, had begun to educate their daughters in the European fashion. In far-off Poona, Dr

Karve had begun to pioneer in the education of widows, but among the brahmins of the south, who were known all over India for their extreme conservatism, no one had yet followed the example which Subramania Iyer had set. But although Subbalakshmi would be the only widow among the students at the Presidency College, there would, it seemed reasonable to hope, be several other young ladies who would help to ease the difficulties which she would have to face.

Her cousin Krishnaswami offered to take care of her, and protect her from the curiosity of the other boys. Chitti didn't say a great deal, but the calm way in which she seemed to take it as a matter of course that Subbalakshmi should do something which no girl like her had ever done before was better than any words. Visalakshi, who was now spending much of her time with her husband at Coimbatore and leaving Chitti in charge of Peepal Tree House, was equally confident that whatever difficulties there might be, her eldest daughter would succeed in overcoming them.

The jutka cart was given up. Instead, Subbalakshmi was to travel from Egmore to the Marina by ricksha.

That was the first ordeal. No young lady ever travelled alone in a ricksha. When Subbalakshmi climbed in for the first time, the hood was pulled up, and as soon as she had seated herself she opened her big black umbrella, holding it straight out in front of her like an enormous shield. In this way she managed to conceal herself completely, and all that passersby were able to see was the wide, brightly coloured border of her sari.

Even that attracted attention. Passersby stopped, transfixed by the sight. Men and women who were standing on their doorsteps or sitting on the pials outside their houses called to those who were inside to come out and look. Subbalakshmi could hear their rude comments and their vulgar laughter. She felt herself shrinking, yet she didn't get any smaller. She didn't dare to lower the umbrella for an instant to look out and make sure that the rickshawala was going the right way. It was dreadfully hot. Between the canvas hood of the ricksha on one side and the tightly woven silk of the umbrella on the other not a breath of air seemed to move. She felt as if she would suffocate.

When the ricksha stopped at last under the great red brick portico of the college and Subbalakshmi jumped down, there were scores – it seemed to her hundreds – of boys and young men standing about. They gaped with astonishment as they moved back, making comments, laughing, calling out to others not to miss the sight of the new lady student, who would now have to join the queue of those who were waiting in the corridor to enter the secretary's office and pay their fees.

It had been arranged beforehand that Krishnaswami would stand in the queue for her and pay her fees and she had brought the money to give to him. She had caught a glimpse of him as she went up the steps. Next time she looked, he had disappeared. Then she saw that he hadn't really gone, but had shrunk into the background and was pretending not to see her.

She climbed the great staircase, hoping to find some older person who could help her. Coming out of one of the lecture rooms was a servant in uniform, one of the college peons. She gave him the money, and walked down the stairs behind him to point out Krishnaswami. Then she went to the room which had been set apart for the use of lady students. Several other young ladies were already sitting there. They greeted her politely, but their manner was cool and aloof. She did not belong to their world.

When lectures began, her situation became still more difficult. The students clapped and jeered and cheered when she entered the room. The professors seemed to find her presence embarrassing. They would mumble over their notes, their faces turned away from the corner in which she sat, so that it was difficult to catch what they were saying. When the lecture was over, some of the boys would go up to the dais to ask questions about the points which they had not understood. Subbalakshmi couldn't bring herself to do that. If she had, the poor professor would probably have been too confused to answer.

She couldn't believe that a time would come when she would be perfectly at ease in the company of men and boys. She hoped, though, that as time went on and the novelty of her presence wore off, things would quieten down and the boys would stop pestering her.

They did not. She was not quite alone. Three other brahmin girls, belonging to families who were acquainted with her parents, had joined the college. They, of course, were married, but they were teased and tormented almost as much as Subbalakshmi. The teasing was a little easier for them to bear because they were all studying the same subjects, so that none of them had to sit, as Subbalakshmi generally did, all alone in a roomful of young men.

Subbalakshmi didn't want her family to know how much she was suffering. They found out, and in the most humiliating way imaginable. In the examinations that were held at the end of her first year, she failed in mathematics, her favourite subject.

It was the first failure she had ever had in her life, and she wept bitterly.

Her father comforted her. "It isn't your fault," he said. "Everybody knows that mathematical ability runs in our family. You haven't had a fair chance. When the new term starts, you had better change over to another course. If you find out what the other girls are studying, you can put your name down along with theirs, and when you are all together you will find that there won't be nearly so many embarrassments – or, if there are, you will be able to bear them much more easily."

She was sure he was right. When the next academic year began, the first thing she did when she entered the college building was to scan the lists of subjects under which students intending to study them had put their names. Most girls, she found, had chosen botany as their honours subject. She was laughing a little as she told me, "And I didn't even know what botany was! I had never even heard the word. But I put my name down. I was so glad that I did. I had always been interested in the behaviour of plants and trees, and although at the time I was sorry to give up mathematics, it was really a very good thing that I made the change."

There were still difficulties. The daily journeys became even more troublesome as time went on. It became a regular thing for the boys from other colleges to stand on the pavements to catch a glimpse of the border of her sari as she went past.

I asked, "Did they fancy themselves in love with you?"

"Certainly not." Her tone made it evident that she found the mere suggestion disgusting. "They were mostly young men who had come up from mofussil – country – places. In the villages and small towns girls were not allowed to go out after their coming-of-age, and these boys had probably never seen a girl outside of their own families. It was mere curiosity which made them behave as they did.

"They were," she said, "always thinking of some new trick to make me and my friends uncomfortable. They would write our names on the walls and carve it into the woodwork of the desks. When we found out, we were terrified in case there should be some scandal." She looked at me with sudden apprehension. "You won't put this in your book when you write about me, will you?"

"Not if you say I mustn't. But why shouldn't I?"

"Well," she conceded after a moment's thought, "if you don't mention anybody's names – the names of any of my friends – I suppose it will be perfectly all right."

The boys played so many tricks that the young brahmin girls were in perpetual dread of what would be awaiting them when they entered a classroom. They would linger in the corridors until all the boys had taken their places. Then, when a professor appeared, they would file in after him, and move quickly to their places. This did not save them. One day, as Subbalakshmi was about to sit down she realized, just in time, that one of the legs of her chair had been sawn off. Somehow, she managed to keep seated without losing her balance, though she could scarcely take in a word of what the professor was saying. The girls then decided to club together to pay one of the peons to go into each classroom and inspect their seats before they took their places. After that, there was no more trouble.

The Widows' Home

WHEN SUBBALAKSHMI ENTERED her second year at the Presidency College, her father was no longer teaching at Saidapet. The Government Agricultural College had moved into new premises at Coimbatore, more than three hundred miles away.

Peepal Tree House was not given up. Visalakshi spent as much time as she could with her husband, while Chitti managed affairs at Egmore. Both parents tried to spend their holidays with their daughters. This was not always possible, and during the Christmas holidays of 1909, Subramania Iyer's duties obliged him to remain at the college.

A day or two after Christmas, a party of young women teachers who were attending a vacation course in Coimbatore came to picnic in the college grounds. They were, of course,

Indians, but the leader of the party, who had been inspector of female education in the district for the past four years or so, was an Irishwoman – tall, blonde, formidably handsome, an ardent feminist who was passionately in love with India. This was Christina Lynch.

She accepted, with unaffected pleasure, Professor Subramania Iyer's offer to show her over the college building. She found him a delightful companion, well informed, serious minded, good humoured and with a refreshingly astringent wit. By the time the two of them reached the flat roof and were leaning over the parapet, gazing at the great plain spread out in front of them with the Nilgiri Hills rising in the distance, Miss Lynch had begun to feel that here was someone in whom she could really confide.

She had realized, she said, before she came to India that there were far, far too few educational opportunities for Indian women and girls. But it was not until August 1905, when she took up her appointment and went to inspect the Government Secondary and Training School at Coimbatore, that she discovered how altogether inadequate most Indian women teachers were. She had observed that they were recruited from much lower castes than the majority of their pupils, and lacked the cultural background of the society in which these pupils were growing up. Most of the teachers were rice-Christians, converts from among the untouchables, imitators of European ways, disliking, even hating, Hindu traditions and quite incapable of understanding the importance of preserving all that was best in India's ancient culture. If Indian girls were to be helped to take what was useful in Western education while at the same time remaining essentially themselves, they would have to be taught by women who came from backgrounds like their own, who shared the same values and who had inherited the same beliefs.

Miss Lynch had, she went on, cogitated for a long time over the problem of where, in a society in which all girls married, such teachers were to be found. Then, before her first year in India was over, the solution had flashed upon her. She had consulted the census returns, and found her guess confirmed. In the year 1901 there had been, in the Madras Presidency alone, 22,395 brahmin widows between the ages of five and fifteen. If even a small fraction of these could be rescued from their surroundings, educated and trained to become teachers, a new educational era could really begin.

Professor Subramania Iyer listened in silence, but with an air of absorbed interest, as Miss Lynch told him how she had worked out a scheme for a small, government managed home for young brahmin widows who were willing to be trained for the teaching profession. Her plan had aroused the interest of some of the more progressive among the brahmin elders in Coimbatore. They had warned her that the plan would meet with intense opposition from the more orthodox members of their community, but they themselves had not only approved of her idea but had helped her to frame proposals for submission to the Madras government.

The scheme had been submitted nearly two years ago, in February 1908. No decision had yet been made. Miss Lynch knew, as everybody did, that it took a long time to get anything done in India. She had tried to be patient. She was still trying. She was not ambitious for herself. But she was very ambitious for the young girls of India who were growing up and whose chances of becoming educated, useful women would, once lost, soon have gone forever.

It was then that her host, smiling quietly, gave her the biggest and pleasantest surprise of her life. At first, Miss Lynch could hardly believe him when he told her that he had a widowed daughter whose ambition was the same as her own and who was at present studying in the B A class at the Presidency College. Yet, she could not doubt him. She realized that he had, so she afterwards wrote, taken a very great risk on his daughter's behalf. A step so revolutionary would, in the ordinary way, have led to excommunication from the caste not only of the young widow's father but of the whole family. Professor Subramania Iyer was obviously a man of great courage, firm enough to command the respect of even those who disagreed with him most strongly.

Miss Lynch was overjoyed, and for more reasons than one. There had been, ever since the plan had first occurred to her, one doubt in her mind. How, she had asked herself, could a mere foreigner hope to work such a scheme without a very decided assurance that help would be coming from the brahmin community itself, who might very well be expected to give one of their educated widows, who would be willing to throw herself into the work and practically regard it as her life's mission?

Now the question was answered. As soon as Subbalakshmi graduated the two of them would meet. By that time the government would, Miss Lynch could scarcely doubt, have given its approval, and she and her young collaborator would be able to go forward together.

The start was, in fact, made during Subbalakshmi's last year at the Presidency College, and without either Miss Lynch's help or the assistance of the government of the Madras Presidency. It was a very small beginning and might, if the idea had not already been so firmly fixed in everybody's mind, have been considered almost accidental.

One morning Visalakshi, staying with her husband at Coimbatore, was busying herself about the house when a stranger, a gentleman, arrived and asked to see her. When she went into the room into which he had been shown she had, at first, no recollection of ever having seen him before. Then she recalled, as he pressed his palms together and murmured a namaskaram, that he was the professor of mathematics in whose house she and her husband and Subbalakshmi had been guests when they had visited Ernakulam almost eight years ago.

He seemed to have aged very much, and his manner, as he accepted Visalakshi's invitation to sit down and take a cup of coffee, was tense, as if he were suffering from some nervous illness. They had hardly begun to exchange a few courtesies when he asked abruptly, "Do you remember my little daughter, Ammukutty?"

"Indeed I do," Visalakshi answered cordially. She recalled that there had been some difficulty in finding a husband for the child. "I do hope," she added, "that she is well and happy."

"She is," the father answered, "as well as can be expected. But she is far, far from happy." He glanced about him for an instant before he added, "I have brought her to you, and I do so much hope that you may be able to help her."

Suddenly the girl was standing beside him, materializing out of nothing, like a ghost. No doubt she had been just outside the door, waiting for her father's signal before she entered.

Visalakshi would not have recognized her. Ammukutty was eighteen now, rather tall and pitifully thin. She was dressed in a white sari, with no blouse underneath it. Her eyes were red with weeping, and her cheeks hollowed like those of a very old woman. Her hair had not been shorn, and it hung around her head in dry, untidy wisps, as if it were months since she had had an oil bath.

"Yes," the professor said sadly, "she has indeed lost her husband, and she is in even greater trouble than most young widows. She has a child, a little daughter. The husband's parents agreed to keep the infant. They sent Ammukutty back to me, saying that now that her husband is dead they have no more use for her. As you know, I am a poor man. I was obliged to borrow far more than I could afford for my daughter's dowry. The debt is still not paid. I have not the means to keep her, so I have brought her to you in the hope that you may find some work for her in your house. It would be a great kindness if you would employ her as your cook."

Visalakshi was overwhelmed with pity. There was only one answer that she could give. She was quite certain that her husband, when he returned from the college, would tell her that she had been right to say yes.

A week later, she took Ammukutty to Madras. The girl was wearing a blouse. Her hair was neatly dressed, and she had already begun to put on a little weight. She was so evidently intelligent that there could really be no thought of allowing her to spend the rest of her life as a cook. She could, it was decided, help Chitti in the house while she studied. Then, if she made good progress, she might eventually be trained to be a teacher.

Subbalakshmi herself was working very hard for the final examination for her Bachelor of Arts degree. She was not at all nervous. She was sure that she would do well.

She fared better than she had dared to expect. In May 1911, newspapers all over India reported the success of the young brahmin widow in Madras who had won first class honours and had outshone all the men of her year. Subbalakshmi, to her intense surprise, was, for the moment, famous.

Her parents had pioneered for her. Now she herself was invited to do pioneer work elsewhere. The maharaja of Travancore invited her to go to his state to help in developing educational facilities for women and girls. A similar offer came from the maharaja of Mysore. The government of Ceylon offered a salary of rupees three hundred per month – just three times as much as her father was earning – if she would go there to teach.

These invitations seemed to offer much bigger opportunities than any job which she was likely to find in Madras. She loved to travel, to see new places, to meet people whose lives were different from her own. Except among the young men of her own generation, she did not feel particularly shy, and she knew that such shyness as she felt could be, without too great an effort, overcome. But she knew that she could not leave Madras. "It is good for a man," Lord Krishna had said to the warrior-hero, Arjuna, "to do his own duty. Though he may do it unsatisfactorily, it is better than even the satisfactory performance of another man's duty. Even death is glorious if it comes in the performance of one's own task."

Her own duty was clear. Nothing, she resolved, should ever tempt her away from it.

Her mother still hoped that Subbalakshmi might be persuaded to stay at home. There was no necessity for her to earn money. Indeed, that was something which young ladies never did. The house was roomy, and it would be possible to find space for two or three more young widows. The main entrance was at the side, screened by shrubs and trees, so that the girls would be perfectly secluded. There could be no criticism from any quarter if a group of young widows stayed together in a place which was, as Sister herself afterwards expressed it, free from men.

Subbalakshmi was eager to find more girls whose parents would allow them to join Ammukutty. With Chitti in the house all the time, there was no reason why she herself should stay at home to look after them. She needed to be trained to be a teacher.

Madras had only one training college for secondary school teachers, and most of the students were men. Subbalakshmi couldn't bring herself to face the prospect of joining them. She would have to find some other way of qualifying for her teacher's degree.

She went across to the P T School. Her old headmistress, Miss Patterson, was delighted to offer her a post on the staff. The salary was small, only fifty rupees a month. However, Subbalakshmi would be able to study for the Licentiate of Teaching in her spare time. The headmistress was certain that the authorities would, for once, agree to waive the regulations and, at the end of a year, allow the young teacher to sit for the examination as a private student.

Everybody says that Subbalakshmi did not really need any paper qualifications to make her an excellent teacher. The qualifications were useful, of course, for filling up forms, and the textbooks on psychology were fascinating. When she wasn't teaching she was as busy as ever with her studies, learning a lot of things which, she realized, she needed to know.

It was at this time, too, that she learned the meaning of the first two syllables of her name. One day when she was climbing the stairs in the school building, she passed two lady visitors who had come from Andhra. She noticed that they were staring at her rudely and that they drew to one side as she passed them. Then, when she was only a step's distance away, she heard one of them remark to the other in a sarcastic tone, "Well, let us hope that it is subba to have seen her."

It was the first time she had heard it pronounced like that. Sub-ha, which was what everybody at home still said, meant nothing. Subba was an adjective which meant auspicious or fortunate. She knew that. She knew, too, and indeed had known for a long time now, that the sight of a widow was considered to be extremely inauspicious, so much so that both men and women who were going out of their houses on some morning errand would retrace their steps and go indoors again if they saw a widow as they stepped into the street. Widows and black cats were equally unlucky.

The two women were standing still, halfway down the stairs, turning to watch her. It was horrible to be started at like that, to know that it was not because she was the only Indian lady teacher in the English section of the school, but because she was a widow. At the same time, it was wonderful to know that her name, the name of Lakshmi, the goddess of fortune, was made doubly fortunate by its prefix. She lifted her head proudly. To have been given such a name must, she told herself, surely mean that she would bring great good fortune to others. For herself, she wanted nothing but to be allowed to continue as she had begun.

Three more young widows had come to live at Peepal Tree House.

Two of them were big girls, almost grown-up. The youngest, who was about eleven, was already studying at the P T School.

Her name was Parvathi. Her father, T S Muthuswami Iyer, was a teacher at a school in the big inland town of Salem, high up on the Deccan Plateau. The brahmins of Salem had the reputation of being very orthodox people. There were also rebels among them, young men who had become notorious for their defiance of conventions and for their advocacy of new ideas. The most outstanding of these social reformers, as they called themselves, was Chakravarti Rajagopalachari, a brilliant young lawyer who was one day to become Governor General of India. He and his friends had outraged orthodox Hindus' opinions by inviting untouchables to their houses and sitting down to meals with them, and by advocating such unpopular and daring innovations as the remarriage of widows and marriages between people of different castes.

Among these friends was a young science teacher called Seshu Iyer. It was Seshu who had suggested that Parvathi should be sent to school in the town. He did not propose to Muthuswami Iyer and his wife that they should postpone their daughter's marriage, which took place soon after her ninth birthday. But he convinced them that she should stay at school until she was old enough to join her husband's family.

Parvathi loved school. Other girls liked to have an excuse to stay away now and then, to nurse a cold or to attend a wedding or some other festivity. Not Parvathi. To her, school was the most fascinating of all places, and it seemed that nothing could keep her away.

Because of this, her parents were very much surprised when, one morning a few months after her wedding, she said, "I am not going to school today."

"Why not?" her mother asked.

Parvathi couldn't answer. She didn't know why she felt as she did. She was not feverish. In fact, she felt quite well. She simply wanted to be allowed to stay at home for once.

She was usually a very obedient child. She was also the baby of the family, accustomed to being allowed to do as she liked. Her parents did not try to force her against her will. Since she wanted to stay at home, she stayed.

Parvathi never forgot that morning. Ever afterwards, it seemed to her that she must have received some instinctive or telepathic warning of the news that reached her parents later in the day.

Her mother was weeping bitterly as she told the little girl that her boy-husband was dead. Parvathi wept, too. She had not known the boy, and she could not feel any sorrow at what had happened to him. She felt sad because everyone around her was so miserable, and it was for their sakes that she cried.

Friends and relatives arrived to offer their sympathies. It was not long before the child realized that the tears and the wailing, the pitying glances, the endless talk among her mother's friends, concerned herself and all the dreadful things that must happen to her in the future. Her parents were not able to save her, even to the extent that Subbalakshmi had been saved, from the tormenting sympathy of the people who crowded into the house day after day, and who kept the flow of tears running so incessantly that it seemed to the child that she would never see dry eyes and smiles or hear laughter and cheerful talk.

After this, Parvathi couldn't even bear to think of going back to school. She knew that she would never be able to endure the pitying curiosity of her schoolmates and teachers.

Her parents did not try to persuade her to change her mind. Instead, her father suggested that she should spend the daytime hours in his upstairs room, out of sight and hearing of grown-up talk. He would, he proposed, set her lessons to do every morning before he himself went to school. In the evening he could mark what she had done and help her to go on learning.

Parvathi got on fast. Her older brothers were studying in Madras. It was one of them who suggested to their mother that she should come to the city for a year or two and bring their little sister with her. There, where Parvathi's history was not known, it would be easy for her to start going to school again.

Muthuswami Iyer arranged for a relative to come and keep house for him during the absence of his wife and children. Then, when the family had settled down in Madras, they found, to their dismay, that there was no girls' school in their neighbourhood. They made enquiries. At first, nobody could help them. It was only after some months that they learned of the existence of the Presidency Secondary and Training School at Egmore, still the only girls' high school in the city.

Parvathi could not travel all the way to Egmore by herself, and there was nobody who could take her to school and bring her home again each day. She would either have to give up the idea of continuing her education, or the family would have to move again.

Her brothers, like her parents, felt that no sacrifice was too big to make for the little girl's sake. Soon, they moved to Egmore. Parvathi then became the second brahmin widow – the first after Subbalakshmi herself – to be enrolled in the English section of the P T School.

She had been there only a short time when Muthuswami Iyer's housekeeper died, and his wife was obliged to return to Salem. The boys went back into lodgings. Subbalakshmi invited Parvathi to come and stay with the three older widows who were under Chitti's care, and the offer was gratefully accepted.

Balam and Savitri, who were both expecting babies, were staying in the house too. The two of them, it was decided, should teach the older girls while Subbalakshmi and little Parvathi were at school and while Chitti was busy with the affairs of the house.

The plan worked well. The young widows kept their hair, or, if it had already been shorn before they came to Peepal Tree House, were encouraged to let it grow again. They wore cheerfully coloured saris and neat blouses. Except that they did not often go out visiting, their lives were not very different from those of most young girls of their age. They settled down easily. Even Parvathi, who was still only eleven, soon forgot to feel homesick. She doted on Chitti, slept beside her every night, and when school finished in the afternoons was always in a hurry to run across the road and be with her again.

The older girls were eager to learn, and never seemed to be tired of doing their lessons. Subbalakshmi was certain that if they kept on as they had begun there would eventually be no difficulty in getting them admitted to the P T School.

Then the time came for Balam's baby to be born. Visalakshi arrived from Coimbatore, and the whole household waited anxiously, scarcely able to think of anything else.

Balam's labour was prolonged and agonizing. She cried and screamed, suffering so much that her mother, her sisters and the four young widows all felt that they were suffering with her.

Only Chitti, who was so proud of her skill as an amateur astrologer, seemed undisturbed. While the others bustled about, trying to make themselves useful, she sat quietly in a corner, poring over an astrological chart, calculating what would be the most auspicious moment for the baby to be born. The English lady doctor came and went. When Balam had been in labour for two days and almost two nights, she could bear it no longer. The doctor had left the house only a few minutes earlier, promising to return after an hour or two.

"Call the doctor back!" Balam whimpered. "I cannot – I simply cannot – bear it any longer. Tell her she must use forceps to pull the baby out!"

The doctor returned.

Chitti intervened. "Doctor," she said, "I have just worked out what will be the most auspicious moment for the child to be born. Don't use your forceps for another half-hour. If you can persuade Balam to endure for so long, the child who is on the way will have an exceptionally happy and fortunate life."

Chitti's word was law. Even the doctor had to obey. At last, at the precise moment that Chitti had planned, the child was born.

In a day or two the household had settled back to its normal routine. Everyone was happy, Chitti's face glowed with satisfaction. Little Subramaniam, named after his grandfather Subramania, would, she declared, grow up to be famous. Perhaps he would, like his father, became a doctor. Whatever career he chose, his success was certain. She had guaranteed it.

"Many years later," Sister added when she had finished telling me all this, "when I was at Cuddalore, the two maharanis of Kollegal became friends of mine. Once when I was visiting them it happened that the astrologer to the royal family of Cochin was staying in the house. We discussed with him when the horoscope of a child should be taken. I knew that there were two opinions on this question. One was that the time to cast the horoscope was at the instant that the head appeared. The other was that the calculation should be made on the assumption that the instant of birth was the moment when the whole body appeared. This great astrologer said that both views were wrong, and that the correct time from which the horoscope should be taken was the moment of conception. Imagine! How can anyone ever possibly know the moment of conception? When he said that I simply laughed and went out of the room. So, I said when I told this to my family afterwards, if that man was right poor Balam need not have waited that extra half an hour. Mani would have been a famous doctor just the same."

The first meeting between Subbalakshmi and Miss Lynch took place in the autumn of 1911.

Subbalakshmi was extremely nervous. Her visiting cards had just come back from the engraver. She could feel her fingers shaking as she handed one to the clerk in the outer office.

The hour that seemed to pass as she waited was really no more than a minute. The clock ticked, and she was summoned in.

Miss Lynch, very stately behind the big desk, did not look at Subbalakshmi as she invited her to sit down. She was studying the visiting card, and her lips were tightly compressed as if she were angry. But, why, Subbalakshmi asked herself, should she be? Surely she had not expected to find Subbalakshmi's father's name on the card? She had been in South India long enough to know that people used their given name in the place of surnames, with the initials either of their father or their native village, or both. Subbalakshmi's card had both initials – R for Rishiyur, the ancestral village, and S for Subramania, so that it read *Sister R S Subbalakshmi*.

Miss Lynch looked up. Her eyes were icily blue, her voice stern. "Why," she asked, "do you call yourself Sister?"

The answer was so obvious that Subbalakshmi almost smiled. "My two younger sisters," she answered, "are in a class I teach. They call me Sister, so the other girls have taken to doing the same." Then she gathered her courage to add, "I want to be a sister to all young widows."

"Ah! I see." Miss Lynch unfroze. In an instant she was transformed, human, talking to the young stranger almost as if they were equals. She explained that she had been transferred to work in the eastern part of the Presidency, with Madras city as her headquarters. Then she went on to describe how she had been struggling for three and a half years to get her scheme approved by the government.

"Now," she continued, "we shall have to take some drastic

action. We must raise enough money to rent a house and to maintain some poor girls whose families cannot afford to pay for their maintenance. Then, when the authorities see what we can do they will be shamed into giving official sanction – and into giving the money we shall need to continue. Do you agree?"

Years afterwards, Miss Lynch, who by then had become Mrs Drysdale, recalled the solemnity of the discussion which followed. Although Sister Subbalakshmi was so young and inexperienced, she seemed to the older woman to carry on her shoulders years of innate wisdom. There would, she pointed out, be many difficulties. No doubt they could be overcome.

The first difficulty, both of them recognized, was that until Subbalakshmi had passed the Licentiate of Teaching Examination she would have no time to spare. Only after that was safely behind her could she busy herself with raising money, searching for a house, inducing more parents to put their daughters under her care. In the meantime, the girls who were already living at Peepal Tree House could continue with their studies and, if necessity arose, one or two more might be squeezed in.

Subbalakshmi passed the examination in April 1912. By July, she had, miraculously, succeeded in raising nearly two thousand rupees.

Some of the money had come in response to appeals made in the newspapers. Much of it had been given by members of the Sarada Ladies' Union and their friends.

The Sarada Ladies' Union had been formed only a few months earlier, in January 1912. For several years before that it had been customary for the ladies of the neighbourhood to visit Peepal Tree House in the afternoons, to listen to Chitti as she read and explained episodes from the Mahabharata, the Ramayana and other sacred books. Her comments were so apt and at the same time so stimulating that often when she had finished the ladies would find themselves discussing ideas and topics which they had never even thought about before. Talk which started with some simple question about morality or religion would lead on to philosophy, history, archaeology and art, and even to problems of current politics.

It was difficult to crowd into the house all the ladies who wanted to attend. Everyone was welcome, and the discussions ranged so widely, and were guided by Chitti with such broadminded tolerance, that Christian, Muslim and Parsi ladies were delighted to join in. When the time came to form a regular organization, everyone agreed that the Ladies' Union should be named after the goddess of wisdom, Sarada, who was also called Saraswati, and that Miss Patterson should be the first president. Subbalakshmi had been elected as secretary, and the meetings were held every Saturday afternoon at the P T School.

The members were eager to see the establishment of a home for young brahmin widows. The choice of a house was restricted, since it was essential that the girls should live within walking distance of P T School. Luckily, Adi Cottage was to let, and seemed perfectly suitable.

When I persuaded Sister to take me to see it, we drove slowly along Egmore High Road, while Sister peered out of the window of the car, making little exclamations of astonishment at the changes which had come about during the past fifty years. She remembered the street for its quietness.

Now many of the houses had been replaced by shops, and the narrow thoroughfare was crowded with bicycles, cars, lorries, bullock carts. We were beginning to doubt whether Adi Cottage could still be standing when suddenly Sister exclaimed, "I think that must be it!"

On our right was a narrow gap between a dilapidated house and a vegetable stall. Within, a short flight of steps led upwards to a paved courtyard. The house, which looked on to this courtyard, was at right angles to the street and completely hidden from it. The yard was bright with potted plants and flowering creepers, and the cottage itself neatly picturesque, with a window on either side of the porch, and three more windows above, set behind a narrow, wooden balustraded balcony.

We knocked, a little hesitantly, at the massive door. After a minute or so it was opened by a young girl. Behind her stood an old lady dressed in a sari of dark toned silk, twisted around her legs in the style of orthodox smartha brahmins. At the sound of Sister's name she hurried forward. Her hands, as she pressed them together, quivered with pleasure.

She invited us in. The house was built around a square living hall, its central portion a few inches lower than the level of the surrounding floor. On one side of the hall was a staircase, and on the other were several doors leading to other parts of the house. As in most houses where people still live in traditional style, there was almost no furniture. The light was a little dim, the air pleasantly cool.

The girl, we found out when we had been chatting for a short time, was studying in one of the women's colleges affiliated to the Madras University. There was nothing extraordinary in that, since nowadays many thousands of middle class girls in Madras go from school to college almost as a matter of course. It was not very surprising either that the girl's grandmother should, when her first shock of delighted surprise was over, have claimed to be related to Sister's family. The cousinship, it turned out, was rather remote, but it was evidently enough to make the old lady who lived in Adi Cottage feel intensely proud. Sister, I could see, was rather amused. I thought I knew why. She was, I guessed, remembering how bitterly the brahmin grandmothers of fifty years ago had criticized everything that she and Miss Lynch attempted to do.

In those days, the rent of the cottage was twenty five rupees a month, less than two pounds sterling. It was settled that, as soon as the summer holidays of 1912 were over, Chitti and Subbalakshmi and the young widows who were living at Peepal Tree House would move in together, and two more girls were to come and join them.

Subbalakshmi and her youngest sisters were to spend the summer with their parents at Coimbatore. Visalakshi, who was still in Madras, was packing their clothes when an incident happened which, if Subbalakshmi had not been as wise as Miss Lynch believed her to be, might have wrecked the whole project.

The postman arrived, bringing a letter for Subbalakshmi from Burma. The three older widows, who were left in Chitti's care, were sitting in the room, poring over their books. Naturally, too, all of them listened while Subbalakshmi read the letter aloud to her mother.

The writer began by introducing himself as a fellow countryman, a South Indian brahmin who had settled in

Rangoon and owned a successful business. He was a widower, and childless. He had read in the newspapers that Sister Subbalakshmi and an English lady were opening a home for young widows. For some years now social reformers had been urging that virgin widows should be allowed to remarry. He agreed with their views, and wished to marry again. Could Sister Subbalakshmi please find, among the young widows who were in her charge, a suitable girl who might be willing to marry him?

"Well! Well!" Subbalakshmi exclaimed. It was absurd, not even worth discussing. She still had to pack her books, and she hurried upstairs, carrying the letter with her.

The young widows watched her go. They were all a little in awe of Sister, who was so clever that somehow it seemed a little improper to talk to her about trivial, everyday things. Her mother and Chitti, although they were so much older, were far easier to talk to, and they never seemed to be shocked or displeased at anything that anybody said.

Subbakka, who was sixteen, had been widowed when she was still a very small child. For the first month after she had come to Peepal Tree House she had made rapid progress with her studies, but during the last few weeks she had seemed to be growing restless. Often, when she should have been learning her lessons, she would sit moping or daydreaming. The circumstances from which she had been rescued were so unhappy that it was impossible that she should be homesick, and if she were asked if she felt unwell she would shake her head and then make a fresh effort to get on with her lessons.

Sister had been out of the room for perhaps ten or fifteen minutes when Subbakka rose from her corner and went across the room to Visalakshi. "May I speak to you, please?"

"Of course."

Visalakshi led her into another room. Subbakka, looking at her with the utmost frankness, said, "I should like to marry that man."

Visalakshi was flabbergasted. So, when she was told, was Subbalakshmi. Yet there was, mother and daughter realized as they talked it over, nothing unnatural in Subbakka's wish to have a husband and to lead a normal life. The man seemed respectable, and had given references. The real obstacle was that orthodox people regarded the remarriage of widows, even of virgin widows who had scarcely spoken to their husbands, as a grave sin. Marriage was the continuation of a relationship which had subsisted during the partners' previous births and would be resumed again in their next lives. Not everyone accepted this view. As the writer of the letter had said, social reformers believed and argued publicly that it was right that virgin widows should be given a second chance of happiness in this world, but orthodox people regarded their views as altogether deplorable. Subbalakshmi wanted Subbakka to be happy, and to be happy in what seemed to the young girl the best way, but she knew that it was not going to be easy to persuade brahmin parents to send their widowed daughters to Adi Cottage. If they learned that she had arranged a second marriage for Subbakka it would be impossible.

She was aiming to produce a most fundamental social reform, but on no account must she run the risk of being identified with the social reformers. There was only one thing to do. She would have to find a man among her father's circle of friends whose discretion could be trusted, and who would arrange the remarriage in such a way as to make it appear that neither Subbalakshmi nor her parents had had anything to do with it.

She enjoyed the little intrigue. The would-be bridegroom came to Madras, and Subbakka was married. Subbalakshmi did not, of course, attend the wedding, and nobody ever learned that she had been responsible for it. Many years later, when she visited Burma, she met Subbakka and her husband. No couple, it seemed, could possibly have been happier or better suited to each other.

The move to Adi Cottage, which everyone had looked forward to with so much pleasurable excitement, was overshadowed by tragedy. The oldest of the young widows, a girl of about twenty, had been suffering from tuberculosis when she came to Peepal Tree House. Chitti had nursed her with great care, but she did not recover. The girl's parents were with her when she died. They at once sent for the purohits to prepare the body for cremation and to perform the last rites.

As soon as the purohits arrived they were shown into the room where the dead girl lay. There were flowers at her feet. Her hair was parted at the centre, framing her face and falling in long plaits which reached almost to her knees. Her eyes were closed, and she seemed dreamily at peace.

"I understood," said one of the purohits, addressing the father, "that your daughter was a widow?"

"Yes," the father assented, "that is so."

"Her head must be shaved. We cannot perform the rites for a widow who was attained her age and who is nevertheless unshorn."

The girl's mother, weeping bitterly, ran into the next room and flung herself down beside Sister Subbalakshmi to repeat, between sobs, what the purohit had said. She had hardly finished when the father came in to ask that a servant should be sent to fetch the barber.

"What wicked nonsense!" Sister exclaimed.

"Wicked!" the girl's mother echoed. "Wicked and cruel!"

"Why don't you defy them?" Sister asked of the father.

"We cannot. Religion decrees that we must obey."

It was also the custom, as it still is today, for the women and girls among the mourners to sit beside the dead while the body was prepared for the journey to the burning-ground. So, when the barber arrived, Sister and the young widows, along with the dead girl's mother, sat watching between their tears as he set to work with his scissors and razor. The sight was one which they all hoped that they might some day forget, but which none of them ever could.

The girls had not been long in their new home when the Madras government agreed to pay the rent of Adi Cottage and to grant three scholarships to young widows who were willing to be trained to become teachers. Miss Lynch's temerity in acting without the approval of her superiors was, as she afterwards recorded, "officially noticed." She was not distressed, since she had attained her object. Official recognition and a financial grant, however meagre, meant that the scheme could now go forward with the possibility of future expansion.

Each of the six girls who made up Chitti's new family had more than her share of painful memories. They must, the grown-ups agreed, be discouraged from talking about the past, and, as far as could be managed, they must have no time to think about it. Their days were planned, and they were kept constantly busy.

Several of the girls had come from good homes, and had already learned to observe all the customs laid down for them by their religion. Others had been so neglected that they had forgotten what little they had ever been taught about good behaviour. One of these had been a widow for as long as she could remember. She arrived at Adi Cottage dressed in rags, and the bundle she had brought with her was so filthy that Chitti was obliged to throw it away. Some of the other girls did not trouble to hide their disgust. It was not easy to make them understand that they ought to be specially kind, and to help the stranger as if she were their own sister.

Chitti, of course, was everybody's aunt. She was so good humoured and so impartially affectionate that it was impossible not to love her. It did not take her very long to make the girls feel as much at home as if they were really all members of the same family.

Except for Parvathi, not one of them was sufficiently well educated to join even the lowest class in the English section of the P T School. Some were quite illiterate. Others, though they knew no English, were able to read and write in Tamil and to do simple sums in arithmetic. To outsiders, even those who were sympathetic, it seemed as if it would take years for these ignorant young widows to catch up with the more fortunate girls of their own age.

Subbalakshmi did not accept this view. The girls were intelligent and eager to learn. They had already suffered so many humiliations in their short lives that it would not be right to force them to suffer the shame and embarrassment of sitting in classes with children years younger than themselves. Nor, Sister was convinced, would it be necessary. Instead, they should be coached until they had caught up with those in their own age groups, and only then should they begin to go to school.

It was impossible for Sister herself to give much time to helping them in their studies, since she was responsible for the teaching of both Tamil and botany in all classes at the P T School. She left for school early in the mornings, and when she got back to Adi Cottage at the end of the day she had exercises to mark and lessons to prepare. She spent all the time she could with the girls, but somebody else had to be found to teach them.

An English lady, Mrs Briggs, volunteered to do so. Miss Lynch provided copies of English primers. The first book, which was intended to cover a year's syllabus, contained thirty lessons. Instead of learning one lesson a week, the girls promised Sister that they would try to learn two lessons every day.

Somehow they did it. They managed to learn other subjects as well. At the end of a fortnight, every girl was ready to start on the second year course in English. Within six months, all of them were able to enter the English section of the P T School.

They were – some of them for the first time they could remember – enjoying themselves. They were neatly dressed. Chitti taught them how to take their weekly oil baths, and would massage their scalps for them, and afterwards help them to braid the heavy shining plaits. Then they would look at each other, laughing and making little exclamations of delight, as if they would never get over the surprise of being allowed to be pretty again.

Every night before they went to bed Chitti would tell them a story. She could, often it seemed without even a moment's reflection, find a legend or a scrap of history to illustrate whatever subjects the girls wanted to talk about. Her descriptions were so vivid that she could make happenings which had occurred hundreds and even thousands of years ago seem as real as yesterday. If a girl were unwell, or perhaps feeling a little homesick, Chitti, however busy she might be with her household duties, would always find time to talk to her, to tell her something comical or exciting or to describe some incident which seemed to shed a different light on the small troubles of everyday life.

On Sundays and holidays, Sister would spend the whole day with the girls. She would take them for walks, or to visit ladies who lived in the neighbourhood.

They walked modestly, with downcast eyes. Everybody in Egmore knew who the girls were, and by no means everyone was well disposed towards them. There were many people in Madras city who thought it very wrong that girl widows should have been taken away from households in which they rightfully belonged and should now have opportunities such as very few young wives enjoyed. It was bad enough that they should be learning many things which it was really quite unnecessary, and not even desirable, for ladies to know. It was worse, far, far worse, that widows who had come of age should have been allowed to keep, or to grow, their hair, deck themselves in bright clothes and go out visiting. It was perfectly scandalous.

Scandal, once breathed, spread like a sea fog.

Miss Lynch sent for Subbalakshmi. A letter was lying on her desk. Miss Lynch read it aloud. The public of Madras, the writer stated, had been very much shocked to learn that the young lady who was known as Sister R S Subbalakshmi had taken the widows who were entrusted to her care to attend a marriage ceremony.

Sister felt herself flushing, hardly able to contain her anger at such an accusation. "Do you think," she asked, as Miss Lynch put the letter down again, "that I would really do anything so improper?"

No, Miss Lynch answered, she did not really think so. The writer of the letter had not even signed his name, and she knew what anonymous letters were worth.

Subbalakshmi could not guess who had written the letter, but she could understand quite easily why people wrote such things. They were motivated not only by hatred and malice, but by deep rooted, superstitious fear. Only last week, she reminded Miss Lynch, a marriage had been celebrated in one of the houses just across the road from the P T School. The astrologers had, as usual, fixed the auspicious time for the ceremony to begin. Then the hour had been readjusted so as to make sure that the young widows would be safely inside the school and out of sight before the first of the wedding guests arrived.

She knew, and Miss Lynch knew, too, that to send six young widows to school was no more than a preliminary skirmish in the long, hard battle which they still had in front of them. They could not hope to win this battle by themselves.

Fortunately, the membership of the Sarada Ladies' Union was growing steadily. A reading room had been established, and was kept open every day. It was stocked with books and magazines and newspapers, so that ladies who were literate could keep themselves well informed without having to endure the embarrassment of sitting in the company of men, as they would have been obliged to do if they had been bold enough to go to public libraries.

The Saturday afternoon meetings at the P T School were always crowded. Besides lectures, the programmes included concerts and other entertainment, and for the schoolgirls there were debates, to which older ladies came to listen, as well as oratorical competitions and competitions in singing.

The schoolgirls who performed were often far less shy than the grown-up people. They loved to have a chance to make speeches and to display their talents. They were sometimes thrilled, and sometimes rather condescendingly amused, when they listened to the performances of the adults. Some of the ladies who did not know English were, like Chitti, learned in both Sanskrit and Tamil, and several of them were gifted and powerful speakers whose voices could thrill huge gatherings. But most of the members of the Ladies' Union were so shy and inexperienced that they could not speak even a few impromptu words. The schoolgirls used to smile and try to suppress their giggles when some great lady got up to preside at a meeting and, pulling out the sheet of paper on which her speech had been written, hesitated and stumbled so that it seemed that she hardly even knew how to read.

It was now six years since Subbalakshmi herself had left school. In the interval, the number of Indian pupils in the English section had increased rapidly. Nevertheless, the school had not become Indianized in any other way. On the contrary, the atmosphere was, if possible, more English than ever.

Each day started with a march to the assembly hall. Since

the pupils did not all share the same religious beliefs, there were no morning prayers. Instead, the whole school would join in singing British patriotic songs.

Some of the Indian girls, who had become aware of the first stirrings of the national liberation movement, were inclined to rebel against this practice. They knew that even if they had been brave enough to protest, it would be useless to do so. So they defied authority by changing the words, and would sing at the top of their voices, half-hoping to be punished for their daring,

Rule Britannia, Britannia rules the waves,
Britons Ever, Ever, Ever shall be slaves.

"By sheer insistence on such loyalties," wrote one of Sister Subbalakshmi's pupils, Mrs Nallamuthu Ramamurthy, who in later life was to become a member of the upper house of the Indian parliament, "the authorities ironically enough aroused the opposite reaction in our young minds. Even our dances and drills were European, like the waltz, cakewalk and Swedish drill, and our music was English music. It was our young Tamil teacher, Sister, who introduced the national kummi and kolattam, and dramas and songs in our own language, and made these part of our school entertainment."

Sister also, wrote Mrs Ramamurthy, gave her Indian pupils a new sense of pride in the beauty of their mother tongue and the splendour of its ancient literature. It was a rule throughout the English section of the school that anyone who was caught talking in Tamil was made to pay a small fine. Sister herself thought that this was as it should be. It was the right way to ensure that girls who did not speak English at home would learn to use the language with ease. But she wanted them to understand that although English was an important and useful and, indeed, beautiful language, it was not superior to Tamil, merely different. Tamil, the girls learned from her, could express exact shades of thoughts and feeling for which English had no words. The great Tamil poet Thiruvalluvar had written his Kural nearly two thousand years ago, many centuries before England had anything that could be called literature or even a language like modern English. Yet Thiruvalluvar could still be read and understood, and his verses still had important lessons to teach.

The bigger girls in the school were thrilled and astonished. It was their first experience of intellectual excitement. When Sister suggested to them that they should study Tamil as one of the optional subjects for the secondary school leaving certificate, they agreed eagerly.

Miss Patterson welcomed Sister's innovations. So did Miss Lynch. Sometimes other teachers showed signs of jealousy because the inspectress sent for Subbalakshmi so often. The two of them always had a great deal to talk about. It was proving just as difficult as Subbalakshmi had anticipated, to persuade parents to break with tradition and give their widowed daughters the chance of a new start in life. Sometimes Miss Lynch would be perfectly enraged by the conduct of fathers who had promised to bring their girls to Adi Cottage and afterwards changed their minds for fear of what their friends and relatives would say. Then, because they had given their word, she would try to frighten them into submission.

"Am I not a person to frighten people?" she asked one day when both of them were feeling disappointed that another parent had broken his promise.

"Yes, you are," Subbalakshmi agreed, "but fear and anger are bad weapons, and I think we should do much better if you did not use them."

Miss Lynch stared. No one at the P T School would ever have dreamed of addressing a superior officer as an equal. "You are very bold," she said, "to tell me that to my face."

"No," Subbalakshmi answered modestly, her eyes lowered, "it is not boldness. It is the simple truth. The right way to succeed is by winning respect and affection. Nothing good can ever be done by those who rule through fear."

Miss Lynch was not sure that this was entirely true, but she was delighted that the younger woman should show signs of becoming as frank in expressing her opinions as she was herself. She had met far too many people who had agreed with her because it seemed politic to do so, and whose actions belied most of the opinions they expressed.

Subbalakshmi's frankness made the older woman franker still.

"The Irish and the Indians," she told Subbalakshmi, who had been brought up to regard hatred as one of the deadliest of sins, "are really very much alike. It is only because the English are such cold blooded, materialistic people that they have succeeded in conquering both our countries. Such conquests cannot last. Our peoples are beginning to bestir themselves, and someday we shall all become free."

Now that Chitti had moved to Adi Cottage, it was no longer possible for Visalakshi to spend the college terms with her husband at Coimbatore. She was needed in Madras.

Her two youngest daughters, Swarnum and Nitya, were

growing into big girls. Although Subramania Iyer was not in a position to give her a large dowry, he was approached by many parents who were anxious to have Swarnum as a bride for their sons. Prospective mothers-in-law would often remind Visalakshi that it would be unwise to delay, since there was no knowing when the girl might become a woman.

"In those days," Sister told me, "there was practically no chance for a girl in a brahmin family to get a husband when once she had attained her age. The parents of boys, who were in no such hurry, would make the most exorbitant demands for dowries, knowing that they could get almost anything they chose to ask. Really, it was a form of blackmail, don't you know, and terribly hard on people who had more than one or two daughters."

"What happened to girls," I asked, "if they did not get married in time?"

"The parents would practise deception. The mothers would keep it a secret when their unmarried daughters – these poor young girls – attained their age." She pulled out the battery case of her deaf-aid and gave it a good shake, smiling as she did so. "You know," she went on, "people are so ridiculous! Someone – don't mention the name – came to me in 1916 and was speaking about her daughter, who was then eighteen. This girl, the mother remarked, had not yet attained her age. I asked how such a thing could be possible. The mother answered, "As you know, my daughter is not yet married. No girl can attain her age until after marriage," Sister laughed suddenly, but on a note of disgust rather than amusement. "Fancy saying such a thing!"

Swarnum was absorbed in her studies. She and Nitya had

made up their minds that they were going to follow Sister's example and become teachers.

Marriage, Visalakshi pointed out, need not prevent the fulfilment of this ambition. There were men among her husband's friends who wanted their sons to have educated wives and who would not object if the girls still wished, after they grew up, to enter a profession. But Swarnum wanted to be free, to make her own life. She was already thirteen and her mother was growing more and more anxious. "Don't you realize," she demanded, "what will happen to you if you won't marry? When you get to be old and your father and I have gone and your sisters are busy with their children and grandchildren, you will be all by yourself in the world."

Swarnum looked into her mother's face and asked, "And Sister? What will happen to her?"

Visalakshi's own eyes filled with tears. After that, no one in the family ever again tried to persuade Swarnum to marry.

Visalakshi still hoped that Swarnum would one day change her mind. In the meantime, she decided, the girl should be given, as far as possible, all the pleasures which traditionally relieved the pains of coming-of-age. So, on the day when Swarnum's first menstruation began, Visalakshi went to call on the orthodox ladies of Egmore and invited them and their daughters to come to Peepal Tree House to take part in the festivities of the next few days.

Nobody refused. The Egmore matrons could hardly contain their curiosity.

As they approached the house they could hear the music of pipers. Indoor, Swarnum was seated, as a young bride might have been, on a chair in the middle of the hall. Many of her friends were already sitting on the floor, making a circle around her. As the morning went on, they chatted and laughed a great deal and sang the songs they had learned in school, and then broke off to eat the delicious dishes which were brought in from the kitchen. After everyone had had a short rest, the songs and chatter and laughter began again and continued, with more intervals for eating and drinking, until it was time for the guests to go home for the night.

Next day, the fun was repeated. On the third day, all the guests were served with a special sweet, of the kind that was normally served to young wives whose marriages were soon to be consummated.

On the fourth day, when the festivities reached their climax, Swarnum was given a purifying bath, and all the young girls who had come to rejoice with her were given oil baths to mark the occasion. Then Swarnum was dressed in a new sari and seven matrons – ladies whose husbands were still living – gathered around her to perform the final ceremonies and to give their blessings.

Afterwards, when everything was over and the guests had gone, the local purohits arrived.

"This time," said Sister, "they had not come to criticize. We are grateful to you, I remember them saying, for having shown such courage. We priests are poor men, and we have often had to borrow at exorbitant rates so as to find the money to get our little daughters married before they came of age. Now that you have set an example, others will be sure to follow."

At first, only a very few people followed Visalakshi's example. Within her own circle of acquaintances there were many parents who would have liked, and not only for financial reasons, to postpone their daughter's marriages. Very few dared to do so. They might agree with the social reformers that it was ruinous to the health of young girls to allow them to become mothers before their own bodies were fully developed, but child marriages had been practised among the brahmins for many hundreds, if not thousands, of years, and if once time honoured conventions were defied, there was no knowing what the end might be.

It was true that there were learned pandits who declared that child marriage was not enjoined by the sastras, and that no sanction for the custom was to be found anywhere in holy writ. Their arguments were much criticized by old fashioned orthodox people who claimed to be equally learned, and who declared that the very foundations of society would be destroyed if child marriage were to disappear.

Subbalakshmi had already formed strong views on the subject. None of the heroines of the Hindu religious epics, she reflected, had been married in childhood. Sita, Draupadi and the rest had been young women before they took husbands, capable of choosing their own partners and of assuming the full responsibilities of married life. That, Subbalakshmi was sure, was as it should be. But to say so now would be the greatest possible mistake. People would suspect her of being unorthodox.

Nothing, she was convinced, could be further from the truth. She was still as deeply religious as she had been as a young girl, and she did not doubt that the essential tenets of her faith provided the best possible foundation for a good life. She wanted the girls in her care to learn to be tolerant to all opinions which were honestly held, and to be patient and sympathetic towards those who were too weak in mind to be able to reach intelligent and just conclusions. She wanted them to understand the scriptures, to follow the observances which their ancestors had practised in their daily lives, and to familiarize themselves with the ancient and beautiful rituals through which men and women had, for countless generations, made sacrifices and paid homage to the Supreme Being.

No one could have been a better instructor than Chitti. Many of the customs which the brahmins habitually observed, she explained to the girls, had been adopted for hygienic reasons, and while some might be modified in certain circumstances it was important that most of the rules of daily life should be strictly observed. The parents of the girls at Adi Cottage could be certain that no non-brahmin would ever be allowed to step inside the kitchen and that their daughters would never be allowed to take their meals in the company of anyone of a lower caste.

Although everything possible was done to make these facts known, the prejudice against the Brahmin Widows' Home showed no sign of lessening. At the end of six months there were only ten girls in residence at Adi Cottage.

This was all the more disappointing because the government had by now increased the number of scholarships. The value of each was only fifteen rupees a month, but Chitti was such a skilful and economical housekeeper that this small sum was enough to keep a girl in food and clothing and to leave enough besides to provide her with pocket money and pay her fare home in the summer.

Miss Lynch's duties as an inspectress took her on frequent tours through the eastern parts of the Presidency. She would, she decided, use these journeys to obtain recruits.

At first, she had almost no success. She seemed not to have guessed, either then or later, how much she alarmed people by her fervour.

In most of the small towns and villages to which she went, a white woman was an unusual sight. A woman with the powers of a government official was a phenomenon almost beyond belief. Miss Lynch, with her towering presence and her pale face crowned with great masses of straw coloured hair, looked positively terrifying as she seated herself behind the desk of the sub divisional assistant and asked that some of the leading brahmins should be brought to see her.

When several of them had assembled she would demand in her deep, powerful voice, "Are there any young widows among the brahmin families in this town?"

She did not lower her eyes, as a lady should. She looked at the men boldly, as if challenging them to deny what she knew to be true.

"No, no," the leader, the oldest man present, would often answer, "we are very fortunate in this place. There are no young widows here."

Why did she want to know? She must have a motive. Motives, as everyone knew, were almost always bad. She probably wanted to carry off the prettiest of the young girls to what men who could read and write English had learned to call a fate worse than death. It was useless for her to describe the Widows' Home and to explain that two brahmin widows of the utmost respectability were in charge of the girls. Either her listeners did not believe her, or, if they did, they needed their daughters at home. A girl who did not have to be bought saris and jewels and flowers to put in her hair, who ate only once a day and did whatever work was required of her, could not easily be spared.

Miss Lynch's tone would grow colder and colder as she pointed out how wrong it was to deprive innocent children of all hope of happiness and of being able to do anything useful in the world. At this, the father would become resentful. He would answer rudely. Miss Lynch, who confessed to having a thoroughly Irish temper, would flare up, and there would be hot words on both sides. After that, the Irishwoman would go away defeated.

Back in Madras, she would send for Subbalakshmi, who advised her to be more patient. In the long run, the girls at Adi Cottage would be the best possible propagandists for the Widows' Home. When they went home to their villages for the long summer holidays and, later, when they went out into the world, their conduct would be the best possible proof of the orthodoxy in which they had been brought up, and doubt and opposition would begin to wither away.

All this would take time. Miss Lynch, true to herself, was in a hurry.

"It was then," Sister Subbalakshmi told me, "that Miss Lynch took it into her head that Egmore was a much too cosmopolitan kind of place, and that we would do much better if we moved the home to a more orthodox neighbourhood."

Egmore was the most fashionable quarter of the city, and although a number of brahmin families lived there, so too did many Europeans. The orthodox districts of which Miss Lynch was thinking were Mylapore and Triplicane, whose great temples had been centres of religious learning for many hundreds of years before Madras became a city and swallowed them into its maw.

Adi Cottage would not have room for more than two or three newcomers. Another girls' high school was badly needed. The P T School's section for training Tamil-speaking teachers could be attached to it, and a new model elementary school opened for student-teachers to practise in. The government would certainly look askance at any big scheme, but, if a building could be found and a start made in a small way, the future, it seemed reasonable to hope, would take care of itself.

A group of philanthropists who had opened an elementary school for girls in Mylapore were, it soon appeared, willing to hand their institution over to the government on the understanding that its status would be raised to that of a high school. Negotiations had not got very far when a snag appeared. The philanthropists of Mylapore, who were pious brahmins, suddenly woke to the possibility that when the school came under government control their daughters might find themselves sitting in class with untouchables. They demanded an undertaking that no girl who was not a caste-Hindu should ever be admitted as a pupil.

This was a request to which the government could not possibly accede. Then, just as it seemed that hope of starting a new school would have to be abandoned, Miss Lynch was approached by two gentlemen from Triplicane who were managing a charity school for girls which had been founded by the maharaja of Vijianagaram. The maharaja, they said, would be willing to hand over the institution provided only that its status was raised to that of a high school. They themselves would do their best to help to find the additional accommodation which would be needed.

The offer was accepted. Triplicane was not an attractive neighbourhood. Most of it was densely crowded, with the houses packed so closely together in the narrow streets that there was scarcely a tree or a blade of grass to be seen. But it had two advantages. The Triplicane brahmins were known all over South India for their unswerving orthodoxy. If their approval could be won, the future of the Widows' Home would be secure. Besides, the sea was not far away, and although the girls would have to live and work in rather dismal surroundings, it would be possible to ensure that they got plenty of exercise and fresh air.

Subbalakshmi did her best to hide the distress she felt at going to live so far away from her family. She felt sad, too, at the prospect of leaving the P T School. For that there would be compensations. She was to be promoted and, besides being superintendent of the new Widows' Hostel, would be in charge of the training department for Tamil-speaking teachers. Best of all, Miss Prager was to be superintendent of the new institution.

Mildred Prager was an ardent redhead who had been teaching in a convent in the Nilgiris when she was seized on by Miss Lynch and appointed as a junior inspector in the Madras Education Service. She was only a little older than Subbalakshmi, and the two young women had first met at a party given at the P T School to congratulate Subbalakshmi on her appointment as a fully fledged government servant. Subbalakshmi had liked Mildred Prager at first sight, and Mildred, in turn, had been altogether enchanted by the dignity and grace of the lovely stranger and almost overwhelmed by admiration for her purposefulness. "To me," she wrote many years later, "it seemed a page of vedic history come to life as Sister told how she planned to give and not count the cost in the cause of the child widows of the Presidency."

The new school was opened in March 1913, but it was not until October that Sister and the young widows moved to Triplicane.

"The girls at the P T School," Sister recalled, "gave me a great send off. They all wept profusely because I was leaving them." She paused for a moment or two before adding dryly, "Later I realized that they were not so very sincere. After I got to be a bit more experienced I found out that girls thought it was the right thing to shed a lot of tears whenever a teacher left them. Such tears mean nothing."

According to her pupils, she was wrong about this. She had not only been an inspiring teacher, she had stirred the ambition of the older girls, and some of them had already made up their minds to follow her example. They could not imagine how they would get on without her help.

They did get on. A few months after Sister had moved to Triplicane, the girls in the sixth form at the P T School were asked to write essays about what they thought should be the next step forward in the education of Indian girls and women. Nallamuthu Ramamurthy, so she herself told me, wanted a women's college in Madras.

Her essay won a prize. She was invited to read it in the presence of a member of the Governor's Executive Council who came one day to visit the school.

"A very bold and interesting suggestion," the visitor commented, "but the expense of starting a college for ladies would be very great, and I doubt very much whether we should find that there were enough students to justify the outlay."

There were murmurs of dissent. The visitor asked, "Will those girls who are leaving school this summer and who wish to spend the next three or four years working for a degree please raise their hands?"

The seventeen girls in Nallamuthu's class all raised their hands.

"I have never been able to find out," Mrs Nallamuthu Ramamurthy said, "whether at that time the government had already decided to open a women's college, or whether it was the enthusiasm we showed that influenced them to make a start. In the summer of 1914, just before the First World War broke out, Queen Mary's College was opened, and I and most of the girls in my class joined it."

It was not much of a place. The government had acquired a magnificent site on the seafront, not far from the Presidency College. They were not yet ready to build on it, and the girls were housed and attended lectures in a ramshackle old house which had been used until then as a hostel for sailors. But at least it was a start.

The Triplicane Government Secondary and Training School was an immediate, and indeed embarrassing, success. Within a few months the building was uncomfortably crowded. Applicants for admission had to be turned away and told that they must wait until a bigger building could be found. This time Miss Lynch did not have to search for very long. By the time Sister and Chitti and the girls at Egmore had begun to pack in preparation for their own move, the government had already agreed to the terms on which they were to acquire a building which had just fallen vacant.

It was a large mansion, situated in Tholasingaperumal Koil Street, T P Koil Street as it was generally called, and, by a great stroke of luck, just across the road from the house which Miss Lynch had managed to rent for the Brahmin Widows' Hostel. The house opposite, which had been rented for sixty rupees per month, was also very big, so big that when the young widows entered it for the first time they could not imagine how they would ever manage to feel at home in such a place.

There were twelve widows now. Ammukutty was the oldest, and Parvathi, studying in the same form as the cleverest of the senior girls, was still the baby of the family. Ammukutty laughed and joked as the girls followed Sister and Miss Prager into the dark hall and up the stairs. She had a knack of seeing the funny side of things, and she spoke as if living in this huge, dreary barn of a place was going to be the most comically delightful experience imaginable.

Most of the other girls didn't agree. The house, built straight on to the street and with only a tiny square of yard at the back, seemed a horrid place. There were so few windows and so many dark corners and half-hidden recesses where ghosts might lurk, that it was frightening, too. It needed all Chitti's cheerfulness to convince the girls that they were going to be just as happy here as they had been at Adi Cottage.

The new school, too, was a disappointment. The carvings over the doorway were magnificent, and inside was a big, square shaped hall which went right up to the roof so that the rooms on the upper floor were galleried around it. But the classrooms were small and dingy and, with their high, barred windows, looked just like prison cells. There was no electric light, nor was there any means of cooling the rooms, which in the steamy heat of summer would no doubt be just like the baking ovens which Europeans were said to use for their cooking. There was no playground, and not even a little bit of garden in which plants could be grown to illustrate Sister Subbalakshmi's botany lessons. Sister could not help sympathizing with the girls when she overheard them telling each other that they wished they had never left Egmore.

They soon settled down. Chitti was a natural homemaker, and before long the great, bare house was pleasantly arranged. Sister and Chitti would rise at five every morning. The girls, if they wished, were allowed to go on sleeping until the prayer bell rang at precisely six o'clock. Then they would troop into the puja room which Sister had arranged, and which was always full of fresh flowers. After prayers, they would run downstairs for coffee, and then hurry back to their dormitories to roll up their sleeping mats and tidy things up before they settled down to their studies. An hour or so later, the little ones would go downstairs once more to take their baths, leaving the older girls to work a little longer. Girls who had already attained their age were not sent out of the house during their menstrual periods. It was quite enough, Sister and Chitti agreed, that they should sit a little apart from the others until, on the fourth morning, they had taken their baths and were free to mix with other people.

By the time everybody had bathed, the morning meal would be ready. As soon as it was eaten it would be time to go to school.

T P Koil Street was a busy thoroughfare, and the people

who thronged the pavements and the roadway would stop dead in their tracks to stare at the young widows. Often those who should have known better, respectable men and women, would make rude and unkind remarks. Many of them were brahmins, who no doubt had young widowed relatives, and quite possibly daughters of their own who had lost their husbands. They would gape with horror and prophesy that the most dreadful punishments were in store for those who dared to defy both sacred tradition and the Divine Will.

As soon as the girls stepped inside the school building they could be happy again. There was no distinction between the girls who lived in the hostel across the road and those who went home to their parents every evening. They worked and played together and soon became friends.

The hostel did not fill up. The people of Triplicane did not welcome the presence of the widows in their midst. Many of them regarded the hostel as an affront to their own orthodoxy, and some of them said so in public as well as in private. Criticism of Subbalakshmi and her aunt was much more general and very much sharper than it had been in Egmore.

Miss Lynch's tours became, more frankly than ever, recruiting campaigns. She was still, more often than not, unsuccessful. But she was winning allies. The Collector of Nellore District, Mr R Ramachandra Rao, became a keen sympathizer, and Miss Lynch wrote later, spared neither time nor money in his efforts to persuade conservative parents to send their widowed daughters to the Triplicane hostel. "The prejudices of one parent," Miss Lynch continued, "were quickly overcome when Mr Ramachandra Rao offered to pay him a monthly dole of five rupees if he allowed his young widowed daughter of twelve years of age to join the home, and the money was readily paid for two whole years until Mr Ramachandra Rao was transferred to Madras." By that time the parents were convinced of the value of the education which their daughter was getting and did not require any more bribes to persuade them to allow her to continue. "I may mention," Miss Lynch confessed, "that my own attempts to obtain this widow resulted in very strong language and definite refusal to comply with my request."

The Triplicane Hostel had been opened only a few weeks when Miss Lynch summoned Subbalakshmi to meet her at Kumbakonam. There, the two ladies were invited by a leading brahmin, Mr V K Ramanujachariar, to address a meeting of the Theosophical Society. It was the first time that Subbalakshmi had ever been asked to address an audience of gentlemen, and when the meeting was over she and Miss Lynch were presented with a large donation, to be spent in whatever way would best help their efforts.

A few months later the governor of the Madras Presidency, Lord Pentland, visited the school. By this time Subbalakshmi and Lady Pentland, who were to be friends for the rest of their joint lives, had already become acquainted.

"It all started," Sister told me when I walked in one day to find her examining some pressed flowers which had just arrived from Lady Pentland's Surrey garden, "because of the worms."

I stared down, much mystified, at the dried pansies.

"Which worms?"

Sister laughed gaily. "Silkworms." She put the flowers carefully back into the envelope in which they had come and then went on, "I never believed in teaching out of books. I always thought that the right way for girls to learn about practical things was by seeing and doing. I had just started teaching at the P T School when I came across an article about the habits of silkworms. They sounded so fascinating that I got somebody to give me a few worms and took them to school. We put them in glass cases on the windowsills, with perforated paper at the back of the cases so that the little creatures could breathe, and the girls used to bring leaves to feed them. Then the first worm died just when it should have been making its cocoon."

"Had it been eating the wrong sort of leaves?"

"It didn't seem to be that. I got hold of a book on silkworm rearing, and I found that they have to make their cocoons underground. So I put a layer of sand into the glass case, so as to give them something to burrow into." She was waving the battery case of her deaf-aid like a conductor's baton as she went on, "It was so fascinating! They would burrow into the sand, until the whole of their bodies had disappeared. Their bodies, I may tell you, are covered with tiny hairs, which they use to hold the cocoon together, in exactly the way engineers use metal rods for reinforced concrete. After the moths came out, I would scrape away the sand, and we would all look to see how the cocoon had been made, with its top shaped like a roof to prevent the sand from getting inside. Beautiful!"

She broke off.

"Go on," I said.

"Those first worms were not enough for us, so I wrote to the Government Agricultural Research Station near Delhi and asked them to send me some. The people there were very good. They sent more than a hundred. It was quite a job to feed so many, and I had people scouring the whole of Madras for mulberry leaves and castor oil leaves. Then I found a new way of keeping the worms. You know those palmyra umbrellas which people wear in the rain?"

They are not really umbrellas, but circular trays, a little more than two feet in diameter, made from dried leaves and with a wide rim of dried branches.

"I tried," Sister went on, "keeping the worms in them, of course with a cover over the rim to prevent them from running away. They flourished amazingly, and when Lord Pentland paid an official visit to the P T School, he seemed very much taken with them. Soon afterwards, I got an invitation to a garden party at Government House. I was terribly nervous of going among all those grand people. Of course I had to accept, and I had not been there very long when Lady Pentland came up to me and said, "It must be you who keeps the worms. I should so much like to see them." So she came, and after that she would often bring her foreign guests to visit the Widows' Home, and would always help us in any way she could."

The interest which the governor and his wife showed assisted, if not as much as might have been hoped, in winning public approval for the Home. The decision of Subramania Iyer and his wife to move to Triplicane helped too, probably much more.

The family moved into their new home almost in June 1914, and Visalakshi was again able to spend all her free time helping Chitti in whatever ways she could. Then Chitti suggested that any brahmin lady who wished to inspect the hostel, whether she happened to have young widowed relatives or not, should be invited to do so. Once visitors had examined the kitchen and had had a chance to question the girls and learn how correctly everything was managed, they could hardly fail to report to their friends and associates about what they saw.

The number of girls in the hostel increased steadily, though still not very fast. That, everybody agreed, was probably just as well. If the homelike atmosphere could be maintained now that there were more than twenty girls in the hostel, traditions would be established firmly enough to provide a sure foundation for future developments. Miss Lynch, who was taking six months' leave in England, had the satisfaction of knowing before she left that all the scholarships which had been offered by the government had been taken up, and that more were to be granted. There seemed to be nothing for her to worry about.

She had not been away very long when the landlord of the hostel announced that he had sold it. The purchaser was coming to Madras in three months' time and would, as soon as he arrived, require the place for his own occupation.

This was dreadful.

Big houses were hard to find, and when the autumn term opened there would probably be at least thirty girls to be housed. Miss Lynch had succeeded before she left for England in finding two empty houses, one to be used as a hostel for non-brahmin Hindu girls whose parents were not living in the district, and the other for Christians. Most parents took their daughters away from school soon after their twelfth birthday, so the demand for hostel accommodation for Christians and non-brahmins was not very great. A really big house, such as the widows needed, would be much harder to find.

Subbalakshmi and Mildred Prager had just begun to search when war broke out in Europe. At first, it seemed that the terrible events which were happening halfway across the world would make little, if any, difference to peaceful Madras. Suddenly, it did. During the third week of September, Madras harbour was bombarded by the German battleship *Emden*. At once, many people ran away from the city, fearing that worse was to come.

They soon returned. The bombardment had not made it any easier to find an empty house but it did perhaps make people in other parts of the Presidency a little less eager to come to the capital. At any rate, the new owner of the Widows' Hostel wrote to say that he was willing to allow the present tenants to remain for another three months.

The high school was overflowing, and senior girls had to go from one building to another to attend classes. When the war was over it might perhaps be possible to persuade the government that a new school would have to be provided, designed for the purpose it was to serve. Meanwhile, since there were so many more applicants for admission than the old mansion in T P Koil Street could accommodate, some method of restricting entry would have to be found.

It was done by putting up the fees. This, everyone agreed, was a deplorable thing to do, but little girls who knew next to nothing, and who spoke a diversity of mother tongues, could not be expected to sit for a competitive entrance examination, and reliable intelligence tests had still to be devised. The young widows, for whose especial benefit the Triplicane school had been opened, would all continue to be eligible for scholarships and maintenance stipends and could stay at school until they obtained secondary school leaving certificates and were ready to go to the university. Not all of them would do that, but those with less academic ability could be transferred to the training department and eventually become elementary school teachers.

Miss Lynch encouraged the girls to have other ambitions. Dr Muthulakshmi Reddy, the only woman among the Indian doctors in Madras, had been appointed as medical officer to the Widows' Hostel. She and her husband, who was a doctor too, campaigned tirelessly against the worn out customs which, they were convinced, were responsible for the poor physique of many of their patients. All the candidates for admission to the Widows' Home were, of course, examined by Dr Reddy. Even when there was no one in need of attention the doctor's visits to T P Koil Street were always welcome.

It was after one of these visits that Miss Lynch startled the girls by demanding, with characteristic abruptness, "Hands up those who would like to become doctors!"

Among the South Indian brahmins there were not many families who were prepared to allow their sons to depart so far from tradition as to study medicine. A doctor, by the nature of his work, would be constantly exposed to pollution, unable to avoid people and substances which were ritually unclean. Dr Reddy, whose father was a brahmin, seemed not to mind this at all. But the young widows had learned, in their very earliest childhood, that if their parents happened to touch anyone who was ritually unclean, even a member of their own family, they would at once take a purifying bath and change into clean clothes. The older girls, since they had come to the Widows' Home, had begun to realize that, as Chitti sometimes said, ancient customs were not all equally sacred.

It had certainly not been the intention of the rishis, the ancient sages, that any rule of good conduct should cause unnecessary suffering. The seniors knew, some from what they themselves had witnessed and some from what Dr Reddy had been heard to say, that it was both stupid and wicked to allow babies to be delivered into the world by the filthy hands of barbers' wives. This was one of the reasons, though not the only one, why so many children died during the first few weeks of life and why so many girls, when once they had become mothers, remained weak and sickly for months and even years afterwards.

So, when Miss Lynch asked her question, six or seven of the bigger girls put up their hands. Little Balambal, who was only eleven and had been brought to the home just a few weeks ago, raised her hand, too.

"What made you do it?" I asked Dr Balambal when I met her in the spring of 1962, soon after she had returned from a three months' journey during which she had visited hospitals in London and Moscow and many of the other capital cities of Europe.

She answered, "The idea that I might someday become a doctor had never even entered my head until that moment. But as soon as Miss Lynch spoke, I realized that it would be a most exciting thing to do. It was the only ambition I ever had."

It would not, Miss Lynch realized, be easily fulfilled. Even if the girls' parents gave their consent there was no certainty that the money needed could be found. All the same, she thought it could be. Everything that she and Subbalakshmi had done so far had cost an immense effort, but both of them were prepared to go on struggling.

Subbalakshmi and Miss Prager were still spending all their spare time house hunting. Many house owners who were looking for tenants would close their doors immediately when the two ladies explained that the premises were needed for the Widows' Home. A few had, at least to some extent, overcome their prejudices, and would invite the visitors in.

Miss Prager would behave on these visits with the utmost circumspection. She would, just as if she were an Indian, leave her shoes on the doorstep. She never embarrassed anybody by attempting to shake hands, but would press her palms together in a respectful namaskaram. Her manner was easy and pleasant. Even the most orthodox householders could not help liking her.

At last, she and Sister found a house which looked as if it might possibly be suitable. The owner led them from room to room.

"At first," Sister told me, "he seemed quite happy. Then I noticed, when we had seen almost everything and were moving towards the kitchen, that he was getting more and more nervous. He very much wanted to let the house, so he was afraid of saying anything that he thought might offend Miss Prager – and at the same time he was simply terrified that she would step into the kitchen. Because I knew her so well, I could guess exactly what she was thinking. We were just getting to the kitchen door when she turned to the man and said in her sweetest voice, It's perfectly all right. I'm a brahmin, too." Sister threw back her head, laughing happily at the recollection. "And the funny thing, you know," she went on, "is that she really was. She didn't behave like a European at all. She was completely one of us in all her ways."

I asked, "And what about the house? Did you take it?"

"No. It was too small."

The six months' notice to quit the house in T P Koil Street had almost expired, and they had been quite unable to find another. Sister, almost desperate, wrote to the landlord asking for at least one more month's grace. He was, he replied, very sorry to be compelled to refuse. He and his family were leaving for Madras almost immediately, and would require the house as soon as they arrived.

There was only one thing to be done. Sister and Chitti and the girls would have to carry their possessions across the road and camp in the school buildings.

The school was so overcrowded that it was impossible to set aside even one room for Sister and Chitti and the young widows. The girls' boxes and sleeping-mats were stacked wherever space could be found. At night several of the classrooms were used as dormitories, and in the mornings everyone had to help to put things in order again before the other pupils arrived.

At the back of the building was an old, long-disused kitchen. There was no proper bathroom, and water for both washing and drinking had to be drawn from the murky well in the backyard. Chitti, who suffered from elephantiasis and whose swollen legs caused her perpetual discomfort and sometimes acute pain, laughed and joked about the difficulties of housekeeping in such makeshift surroundings. Nobody ever heard her complain.

Some of the bigger girls were inclined to grumble, but the younger children were perfectly happy. They were not at all sorry to have their morning hours of study cut short and to have to eat hurriedly in the school hall and help to tidy up afterwards. The food was as plentiful and wholesome as it had been in the house across the road, and Chitti still indulged the whims of the girls who fancied that they couldn't eat greens or who, like Parvathi, had a passion for fried appalams.

Everyone was healthy. An epidemic of typhoid had broken out in Triplicane, but not a single girl caught the disease. This, Sister was convinced, was not simply because the girls were isolated from close contact with anyone outside the school. It was also because they got plenty of exercise and fresh air. Sister and Miss Prager had long ago agreed that it would be worth braving the stares and vulgar comments of the crowds in the Triplicane streets in order to give the girls a walk on the beach in the evenings.

The Marina beach was scarcely more than ten minutes' walk away. The girls would march in a double line, their heads slightly bent and their eyes lowered, ignoring the people around them as completely as if they themselves were sleepwalkers in an empty dreamland.

In those days few people went to the beach except on newmoon days, fullmoon days and holidays, or when it had been announced that some famous man would address a public meeting. So, as soon as the girls had crossed the road and stepped on to the sands, they were allowed to lift their heads and move about freely.

At that instant, when they stood facing the far horizon where the great curving arc of the sea joined the fading blue of the eastern sky, it seemed that the whole world, so various, so beautiful, so new, was not, as the poet had said, a place of sadness, but was full of light, joy and the certainty of future happiness.

Some of the older girls, whose favourite poet was Matthew Arnold, would, after running down to the edge of the tidemark, squat in a circle on the sands, listening to the roar of the breakers and fancying that they could hear the voice of the Forsaken Merman. Others would wander right down to the water's edge to search for the treasures that were washed ashore, tiny seahorses, small conches and other beautifully shaped shells. Some of them would stand chatting and laughing and gazing at the fishermen who were riding the breakers in their catamarans, or lowering or hoisting those dark copper coloured sails which, outlined against the sky, were the colour and shape of moths' wings.

The braver girls were longing to learn to swim. Sister would have liked to teach them, but there was no shelter on the beach where it would have been possible for them to change into dry clothes when they came out of the water, and it would have been dangerous as well as ridiculous to march all the way back to T P Koil Street in sodden, bedraggled skirts or saris.

"Sister," one of the younger girls asked one evening. "why can we not come and live *here*?"

The others crowded round, waiting to hear what Sister would reply.

"Here?" she repeated. She was laughing. The question was really too ridiculous to call for any other answer.

"Yes, here!" several girls repeated. Some of them were jumping up and down with excitement. "What a lovely idea! Oh, Sister, do let us come and live here always!"

Away on the north, the red brick of the Presidency College was darkening against the last beams from the setting sun. Not far off was the sailors' hostel which had been turned into Queen Mary's College. There were a few other buildings in sight, but not many, and none that was unoccupied. Sister turned again, this time towards the cluster of thatched huts, mud walled and windowless, where the fishermen lived. "Surely, girls," Sister asked, "you don't want to live in that fashion?"

"No! No! Of course not. But ..."

"But what?"

Afterwards, she could never be sure who it was who had asked the next question.

"Sister," a voice demanded, "why don't we all go and live in the Ice House?"

"The Ice House?" Sister was startled that any of her girls should be capable of imagining anything so fantastic. "Pray, girls, don't talk such nonsense!"

"Why is it nonsense?" one of the little ones enquired, staring up at the great building which stood, high above the shelving beach, facing them from the other side of the broad road.

"Because," Sister answered, "palaces are not for us. Come along now. It's time we were getting back to the school."

The Ice House was not really a palace. Seen from the beach, and with the afterglow of sunset frosting the stucco of walls and cornices and pediments, it looked like nothing so much as a gargantuan three tiered wedding cake, round and sugary, enticingly absurd.

When it was built, more than two hundred years ago, there had been only a narrow width of beach in front of it instead of the broad band of gold which now stretched from its walls down towards the sea. That was before the harbour, several miles away to the north, had been constructed, and ships bringing ice from the Americas had been beached and unloaded within shouting distance of the Ice House doors. For many years the Ice House had housed nothing but ice. When Sister was a child, it had been purchased by a gentleman from

Mysore who had turned the place into a hostel for students from his native district. Swami Vivekananda had stayed there on his way back to Calcutta from his triumphal tour of America and Europe, in 1897. Subbalakshmi knew that during the stifling Madras summers the mansion was usually occupied by rajas or wealthy zamindars who were said to prefer the softness of the sea breezes to the bracing chilliness of fashionable hill stations. She had been perfectly right to tell her girls that such a place was not for them.

So she was very much surprised when, a week or two later, a strange gentleman called at the school and introduced himself as the agent to the zamindar who was the present owner of the Ice House. He had heard, he said, that Sister Subbalakshmi was looking for a suitable home for the young widows who were under her care. If, after inspecting the Ice House, she thought the building would meet her needs, he was sure that the zamindar would be willing to rent it to the government for a term of years and even, quite possibly, to sell it.

Sister, listening with her usual quiet attentiveness, could scarcely believe her ears. When the gentleman finished, she sat perfectly still, trying to regain her self-command before she spoke.

The stranger, misunderstanding her silence, went on to explain that the building, though in need of some repairs, was peculiarly well adapted to the purposes for which he was offering it. The present owner had bought it just before his marriage, and had surrounded the extensive compound with a high wall so that his bride could enjoy exercise and fresh air in the utmost privacy. The marriage, the zamindar's agent continued, had been singularly happy. But it had come to a most unfortunate end when the bride's parents discovered that the zamindar's family were of a lower caste than their own. The zamindar, who had married in the hope that his deception would never be discovered, had at once retired to his zamindari, where he was now living in solitude. It was as certain as anything could be that he would never wish to return to the house in which he had enjoyed so much happiness and suffered so great a misfortune.

Perhaps, the stranger concluded, Sister Subbalakshmi would like to see the place for herself before she committed herself to an opinion.

She and Miss Lynch and Miss Prager and Chitti all went.

Although the Ice House was only a short walk from the crowded, noisy streets of Triplicane, its situation appeared almost too isolated. If Sister and Chitti and the girls moved in, their only neighbours would be fisherfolk who lived in the slum on the south side of the compound wall. The huge compound, with its row of servants' quarters and outhouses running along one side, was overgrown with weeds, and probably infested with snakes. The house itself, with its great pillared portico sheltering a broad flight of steps, had been skilfully designed for the purpose which it had originally been intended to serve, with an enormous cellar down below and, on the upper floors, double walls, partitioned into small rooms, insulating the big storage halls. From the top floor a flight of stairs led up to the flat roof with its magnificent prospect of sky and sea and city and green countryside, all fresh and shining after the autumn rains.

Altogether, it was the oddest place that any of them had ever seen. But it was charming, too, and, all things considered, really quite surprisingly suitable.

For once Miss Lynch succeeded in persuading her superiors

to act expeditiously. The house was rented for one hundred and sixty rupees a month, pending the completion of negotiations for its purchase. Within a few weeks the essential repairs had been carried out, the building cleaned from top to bottom and the walls, inside and out, given a fresh coat of whitewash. By mid January the place would be ready for occupation.

The more old fashioned among the orthodox brahmin ladies of Triplicane were extremely angry when they learned what was afoot. By this time the Sarada Ladies' Union had begun holding regular weekly meetings in the district. The members of the Union often discussed social problems, and invited speakers to address them on such questions as the education of girls and the future of child marriage. Their own opinions were slowly beginning to change, though in the face of the opposition of older people it was often difficult for them to express their ideas freely. Their elders, on the other hand, were monstrously frank. "I wish," more than one old lady was heard to say during the month of December, 1914, "that when those creatures shift into the Ice House a tidal wave would come in and drown them all."

Disquieting rumours were flying around. The Ice House, people in Triplicane said, had a curse upon it. A respectable man, a vaishnavite brahmin, was known to have committed suicide within its walls. His ghost still haunted the rooms. Something terrible would happen when the young widows began to live there.

"I'll come and sleep there, too, for the first week," Miss Prager offered gaily, "and then if there is any trouble we can all deal with it."

"There won't be any trouble," one of the girls said. Everybody knew that Chitti was one of the bravest women alive.

When the red letter day came, Miss Prager and Sister both felt, as they and Chitti supervised the move, that their feet were perpetually getting caught in red tape. Clerks from the finance and education departments were scurrying in and out of the school with forms that had to be signed and countersigned before anyone left the building. When the girls were at last installed in their new home, there were more forms to be filled in while the removal men were busy with their work and Chitti, in the basement, was trying to get the kitchen organized in preparation for the evening meal.

At last, everything was in order. The girls, who had been exploring the jungly compound, trooped into the house. Their new study-dormitories were ready for them, and they stood about, their faces glowing with excitement as they prepared to go upstairs to unpack their possessions before supper.

It was then that someone noticed that two of the youngest girls were missing. Nobody could remember when they had last been seen. The house was searched. Every room was empty. The children were not in the garden.

They could not have slipped away during the march from the school, but the Ice House gates had been open during most of the afternoon, and it was only too possible that some ill-intentioned stranger might have kidnapped the girls.

Miss Prager decided that she herself must make a search. She ran up to the top floor. There was no one on the roof. She peered over the parapet wall, and then came downstairs again, going through every room, opening every cupboard door until she reached the basement kitchen. Then she opened the door leading to the cellar. At last, she heard voices.

"Come!" she called.

The children were beside her in a minute. Their faces showed no fear, but only a deep, bewildered disappointment.

"Padma!" she exclaimed, addressing the older of the two, "whatever were you doing down there?"

"Looking for the ice," Padma answered on a note of utter defeat, "and we couldn't find it anywhere!"

By nine o'clock, the girls were all asleep, the house wrapped in quiet. Only Subbalakshmi, lying alone in a little room which looked out towards the sea, was wide awake, watching the stars and listening to the still unfamiliar music of the waves. She was happy, happier, it seemed to her, than she had ever even during the best years of her childhood imagined possible, and far too happy to sleep. Now, at last, she would be able to do exactly what she had dreamed of doing.

As she traced the pattern of the constellations, aware of earth's small place in the hazy brightness of the Milky Way, verses from the scriptures sprang, unbidden, to her mind. "Do thine ordained work," Lord Krishna had told the warrior-prince, Arjuna. "With this comfort ye the gods, and let the gods comfort you; comforting one another, ye shall get supreme bliss. For the gods, comforted by the sacrifice, shall give you the pleasure of your desire."

From now onwards it would be possible to give to her girls, and to the girls who would come to the Ice House in the future, a life which would not merely compensate them for much of what they had lost, but which would send them out into the world full of happy eagerness to give to others what they themselves had been given.

It was just possible that some of them might marry again, as Subbakka had done. If they wished to do so, Subbalakshmi would not, whatever orthodox people might say, do anything to try to prevent them. She herself had never, even for an instant, wished to marry again, but she had no doubt that the supreme fulfilment of a woman's life was to be found in marriage and motherhood.

Some of her pupils were grown-up young women who had experienced the joys as well as the pains of marriage and motherhood. There were others, still hardly more than children, who had, as soon as they reached puberty, been roughly deflowered, some by lusty and inexperienced boy-husbands, and some by husbands who were older men, men who were old enough to be their grandfathers and who had been married before, and who had, perhaps, too had a variety of sexual experiences with concubines or devadasis, the temple dancers who formed a caste of professional prostitutes. Girls with such experience were the exceptions here in the Ice House. Most were virgin widows whose husbands had died while they were still strangers and whose deaths had brought neither sorrow nor release.

Suddenly, from one of the inner rooms came a wild, high, terrified scream.

Subbalakshmi sprang up. By the time she was on her feet the scream was being repeated, echoed by other voices, until the whole building seemed to be filled with the uproar.

"Quiet!" she commanded as she opened the door into the big dormitory. "What is it?"

"A snake! A snake!"

"Sister! Sister! It was crawling over me ..."

"It's all right! Chitti called from the far end of the room. She was holding a storm lantern in her left hand and a stick in her right as she leaned over the long body which had now ceased to writhe.

She had killed it. But, since snakes were believed to move in pairs, more lanterns had to be lit and the house searched from top to bottom before anyone was able to settle down to sleep again.

Next morning, as soon as the house was astir again, the leader of the fishermen arrived, accompanied by five or six of his mates. They and their wives and children had been woken by the noises in the night, and the workmen who were clearing up the Ice House compound had just told them what the trouble was believed to have been.

"Lady," the leader of the fishermen told Sister, "this trouble was to be expected. Do you not know that this great house has a curse upon it?"

The place, he went on, not waiting for a reply, was known to be haunted by evil spirits. The fisherfolk wished their new neighbours nothing but good, and were ready to do everything in their power to help them. The evil spirits could be exorcized by sacrifice. All that was necessary was to offer a cock and a goat to the god of the fishermen's temple. If the ladies would provide the money, the men themselves would willingly buy the animals and make sure that the sacrifice was performed with all the correct ceremonies.

Sister thanked them gravely. She knew that a goat and a cock, after being ceremonially offered in the little temple nearby, would make a fine feast for the fishermen and their families. But she was sure that she and Miss Prager and Chitti could help the fisherfolk in much better ways than by pandering to their primitive superstitions. So she refused the offer in the friendliest possible manner, and told the men that as soon as things in the Ice House were a little more settled she hoped to return their visit and to meet their wives and children.

Then she went back to her room. The Ice House, she was perfectly convinced, was going to be as happy as any home anywhere in the wide, wide world.

It was not long before the young widows began to feel that the Ice House was as much their own as if nobody else had ever lived in it. Nobody ever had to tell them how exceedingly fortunate they were.

Of course, the daily walk to school was rather an ordeal. The unpleasantness which Sister Subbalakshmi had anticipated showed no sign of diminishing as the months went by. Every morning, and again each afternoon when school was over for the day, the ladies of Triplicane would come out of their houses and stand on their pials to stare at the girls and call out to their neighbours to come and look too. Often they made cruel and sarcastic comments which the girls, however hard they tried not to listen, never failed to hear.

"Never mind," Sister would tell them when they were safely home again. "You should not disturb yourselves because people who know no better choose to behave in such a vulgar way. Soon it will stop."

She and Miss Lynch and Miss Prager had already decided how the nuisance could be stopped effectively and forever. The right place for the new high school building, when the government agreed to erect it, would be the big stretch of wasteland adjoining the Ice House compound. It was an ideal site, with plenty of room for playgrounds and tennis courts. It would, of course, be useless to attempt to get the project approved until the war was over. In the meantime, the girls would have to learn to be patient, and to make the best of the advantages they already had.

Although the buildings were so shabby and inconvenient and overcrowded, the school was a marvellously happy place. Within its walls, no distinction was ever made between the Ice House girls and the other pupils. Widow was a word which no one was ever allowed to use. Not a single fact about the origins and family circumstances of the girls under Sister Subbalakshmi's care ever appeared in the official records, lest their past misfortunes might create prejudice against them when they went out into the world to earn their livings. The rules required that the caste origins of all the pupils should be officially recorded, but these records were kept locked away and most of the members of the staff did everything within their power to discourage caste consciousness in the school. Rather more than half the girls were brahmins, some from very poor families, and others the daughters of men who were rich and famous. There were also other caste Hindus, Christians, including several sisters from the convent, and Adi Dravidians, children of parents whose occupations traditionally carried the stigma of untouchability.

Many of these last had begun their education in the school which Sister Subbalakshmi had opened, shortly after she had moved into the Ice House, for the children of the fisherfolk. Even among the untouchables there were distinctions which were just as rigid as those which existed amongst caste people, and just as hard to eliminate. One bright and exceedingly pretty little girl, who had learned to read and write at the fisherfolks' school, was the daughter of a scavenger. Scavengers had the lowest place of all in the hierarchy of untouchability, and if the girl's origins had been known when she entered the Triplicane school she would have had no playmates. Sister, who had brought her to the school, was determined that no one should ever discover the child's origins, and nobody did.

Most of the pupils spoke either Tamil or Telugu in their own homes. In the elementary school and in the training section for elementary school teachers most of the classes were in these languages. It was important for girls who might someday wish to enter universities to begin to master English as soon as possible. Besides, English was not only, as Lord Macaulay had called it, the language of modern knowledge. In India, with its fourteen major languages and hundreds of spoken dialects, it was the principal means of communication among educated people. Educated Madrasis, like Subbalakshmi's father and uncles, habitually talked English among themselves as well as when they met people from other parts of the country. Their wives and daughters, like Subbalakshmi's mother and aunt, generally did not, and most of the pupils who entered the Triplicane school knew hardly a word of the language.

Miss Prager and her staff devised novel and stimulating methods of teaching, "We broke all rules." Miss Prager told me in one of her letters. "Every possible attractive method of teaching English was resorted to. The girls understood the outlook. They knew their future depended on it. Slowly the news spread abroad. There were enemies without ... Suddenly questions were asked in the Legislature. The crisis had come."

Mr V S Srinivasa Sastri, who a little later was to become a member of the Imperial War Cabinet, had for some years taught English to the boys of the Hindu High School in Triplicane, and his own mellifluous English had earned him the title which people still use when they speak of him today. He was the Silver Tongued Orator. His style was so pure, his grammar so meticulously obedient to every rule, that later on Gandhi, when he was planning to publish his autobiography in English, sent the manuscript to Mr Sastri for correction.

Mr Sastri thought it was too much of a strain for the little girls at the government school in Triplicane to be learning so many of their lessons in English, and in a speech in the Madras Legislative Council on 3 February, 1916 he said so. The children in the lower classes were, he declared, being subjected to a great mental strain. Perhaps, he suggested, they were being compelled to listen to lessons in English because there were not enough teachers capable of imparting instruction in the children's mother tongues. In any case, and whatever the reason for the present state of affairs, it would be better for the girls to be spared from learning a foreign language until they reached the higher forms.

As a result, it was decided that members of the Legislative Council, together with the Director of Public Instruction, should visit the school and find out for themselves what the situation was. When they arrived, they were received by Miss Prager, several members of her staff, and a group of girls. As soon as the formalities of greeting were over, the teachers excused themselves, leaving the pupils and visitors together. The girls had strong views. They were not in the least shy, and answered questions and expressed their opinions in a fashion which clearly showed that they already had a remarkable command of the English language. The visitors went from classroom to classroom, questioning everyone. "After five hours," Miss Prager wrote, "they departed. Nothing was said. We went our own way – and continued to break the law ... I always felt that those marvellous men had never before taken the trouble to realize and appreciate the intelligence, charm and appeal of their own kind. Anyway, the girls had won – off their own bat – the first round of Success – and they were inspired to go on!"

They loved their teachers. Mrs Elizabeth, an Indian Christian who had been educated by the missionaries, was a bit of a sergeant-major, and the girls as well as some of the other members of the staff would burst into laughter as they watched her go out into the street at the end of afternoon school to police the traffic, directing rickshawalas to one side and bullock carts to the other so as to make room for Mrs Annie Besant's Rolls Royce, which had come to take beautiful little Rukmini home to Adyar. Miss Glynne-Barlow, whose father was the editor of the *Madras Times*, taught English and wrote the funniest and nicest poems about life in Madras. Miss Iles, who had given up a studio in Bristol and come to teach English singing in Madras, was delightful too. "And so were all the others," I was told by the headmistress of a big girls' school who still remembered just how she had felt when she was one of Sister Subbalakshmi's little widows. "There were so many – more than thirty in all – that I can't remember all their names. They were so friendly and kind and took such an interest in us that they were really more like mothers than teachers."

The only male member of the staff was the visiting master

who taught Indian music. He used to arrive with his miniature harmonium – an instrument which is still very popular in India today – tucked under his arm. Miss Prager, like most people of cultivated taste, thought it a most abominable thing, and whenever, from the other end of the corridor, she glimpsed the music master's brilliantly coloured turban she would run away and hide. The music master hid from her, too, for a long time. Then he plucked up his courage, presented her with a lemon, and suggested that he should teach her to play.

She refused.

She and Subbalakshmi, with their different backgrounds, were equally determined that the girls should study and should help to revive the traditional arts of India. Knowledge of English was not to mean that the Triplicane girls were to become, like so many educated Indians, imitation Europeans. The Triplicane school was the first government institution anywhere in the South, and possibly anywhere in India, to relate the teaching of drawing, painting, and music and dancing to Hindu religious tradition. Subbalakshmi devised dances, based on kummi and kolattam, to interpret the movement of the seasons and the festivals of the Hindu year. Sometimes the girls gave public performances. Then the dancers would all be dressed in traditional fashion, with long, brightly coloured silk skirts topped by dark velvet blouses which were fastened at the waist with gold belts. Their beautiful hair would be dressed in thick, four stranded plaits interwoven with palm and fastened at the ends with gold coloured decorations. Visitors from the city and guests from foreign countries could not help comparing these girls with the poor widows who could be seen going along the streets of Triplicane, to and from the temple, their heads tightly covered and their breasts only half-concealed by the single garment in which their bodies were wrapped.

Visitors, lady visitors that is to say, were always welcome at the Ice House. Now that there was plenty of room, it was possible for Sister to invite brahmin ladies from country districts to come and stay for a few days, so that they could satisfy themselves that orthodoxy was being observed and that it was a fit place to which to send young girls. "In this way," Miss Lynch wrote, "I succeeded in getting three young widows from the orthodox zamindari of Punganur, for the parents, who hearkened not to my words or to those of the brahmin teachers of the Punganur High School, waived all objections the moment a favourable report was received from the trusty messenger who was deputed to go to Madras to examine the cooking and other domestic arrangements of the Widows' Home."

A few people still carped. "I trust," a Madrasi lady who was a vaishnavite brahmin remarked one day to Sister Subbalakshmi, "that in the Ice House the preparation of food for vaishnavite and smartha girls takes place in different kitchens?"

"Certainly not," Sister answered sharply. The questioner, so Sister had been told by people on whose word she could rely, had more than once been sitting with her husband behind one of the pillars of a European restaurant in Mount Road, tucking into omelettes, mutton cutlets and goodness knows what other forbidden foods. "It is enough," Sister continued, feeling as she spoke that she had never in all her life come across such disgusting hypocrisy, "that our girls should be brought up as pure vegetarians and that all the laws of hygiene discovered by our ancestors should be strictly observed. It would not be either sensible or right to make distinctions between girls whose families happen to belong to different religious denominations."

Most visitors agreed with her. At last, criticism was beginning to diminish. It was no longer necessary for Miss Lynch to implore parents in country districts to send their daughters to the Brahmin Widows' Home. Many were doing so of their own free will. The big house was slowly being filled.

It had become a beautiful place. In less than a year the compound had been transformed, with the magical speed that is possible only in the tropics, into a picturesque and well-kept garden, with young trees and flowering shrubs surrounding the newly made tennis and badminton courts. Sister was again able to keep silkworms out of doors in palmyra umbrellas, and every morning there was a great profusion of fresh flowers from which to choose decorations for the puja room and specimens to be used in botany classes at school.

When the Ice House girls came home from afternoon school they were free to amuse themselves in any way they liked. No one was allowed to study before suppertime. Those who did not want to play games could sit in the shade and watch, or else go down to the beach with Chitti and tuck up their skirts or saris and plunge into the sea. Chitti would wade in too, standing thigh deep among the breakers as if her swollen, shapeless legs were no handicap at all, and would watch to make sure that no one got into danger.

On newmoon and fullmoon nights, when people from the city would come to bathe, Sister and Miss Prager would often take the girls to the Elphinstone Cinema. The owner of the cinema was eager to do whatever he could to help provide the young widows with some innocent enjoyment, so he willingly agreed to allow Miss Prager to see every picture before it was shown to the girls and to cut out whatever she thought might be unsuitable for their eyes.

The girls did not expect to be given free seats. They liked to feel that they were independent and could afford to pay for themselves. And, miraculously, they could. Out of the fifteen rupees a month which each young widow received as the government stipend, only ten were collected to be put into Chitti's housekeeping account. As the war dragged on, prices of foodstuffs rose to a level which would have seemed inconceivable when the first group of girls went to live at Adi Cottage. Yet somehow Chitti managed to keep everyone well fed and to provide sweets and other little luxuries on festival days. The girls were allowed to keep the balance of their stipends, and if they chose to spend their money foolishly they were free to do so. The mistakes they made now would teach lessons which would probably help to save them from getting into difficulties when they began to earn.

Some parents were able to pay for their daughters' maintenance. Presently, too, as news of the excellent education which the girls were receiving began to spread, the parents of girls who were not eligible for admission to the Ice House would seek Sister Subbalakshmi's advice.

One of these was a stranger whose name Sister already knew. In 1912, an article had appeared in *The Indian Social Reformer*, a weekly paper published in Bombay, describing the opening of the Brahmin Widows' Home at Adi Cottage. The same issue had also reported the celebration of a social reform marriage in South India in which the bride had been a young brahmin widow.

It was the father of the bride who had come now to see Sister. The bridegroom, he said, had been a young university graduate from a poor family. He had demanded, and had been given, a very large dowry. A little later, when his girl-wife went to live with him, he had made it plain to her that he had married her only for her money. As a widow, he had said, she had been very fortunate to find a husband at all, and it was now her duty to repay his generosity by begging more sums from her father. She obeyed. As time went on, the father found it quite impossible to satisfy his son-in-law's rapacity. The girl, made increasingly wretched by her husband's nagging and bullying and his constant reminders that she had once been a widow, at last ran away and returned to her parents. She was now nearly seventeen, ignorant but intelligent and anxious to be educated and to be trained for a profession. Could not Sister, the father asked, find room for her in the Brahmin Widows' Hostel?

There was plenty of room, and Sister would have liked to say yes. But, since the girl was no longer a widow, she was compelled to refuse. Instead, she suggested the name of a boarding school to which the girl could be sent.

When Sister mentioned this incident to Miss Lynch and Miss Prager, both of them agreed that the government ought to be asked to relax the rules governing admission. Some of the young widows had little sisters who were not yet married and whose parents wished to send them to the Ice House as paying boarders. If these girls stayed at home in their villages they would inevitably be married off, and quite conceivably widowed, by the time they were twelve or thirteen. And what, the three ladies asked each other, was the use of making speeches against child marriage at meetings of the Sarada Ladies' Union if they themselves did not do what they could to help discourage such marriages?

By this time Miss Lynch had been promoted. As director in charge of the education of girls and women throughout the Madras Presidency, she had no difficulty in persuading the government that the rules must be changed. Soon a few single girls, though not many, were accepted as paying boarders. More would come later, though they would remain a small minority. As long as there were child widows to be educated the Ice House would continue to be, above all else, their home.

At last, in the summer of 1917, the ambition which had fired Miss Lynch almost twelve years earlier was almost within sight of fulfilment. The three senior girls, Ammukutty, Lakshmi and Parvathi, sat for the secondary school leaving examination. All three passed. Ammukutty and Lakshmi were both very intelligent and Parvathi showed signs of becoming a brilliant mathematician. Ammukutty would spend the summer holiday with her little daughter, and Lakshmi and Parvathi with their parents. They would not return to the Ice House. Instead, when autumn came, all three would enter Queen Mary's College and begin to study for the Bachelor of Arts degree of Madras University. In another three or four years they would be ready to go out into the world and teach others.

Living in the World

THE GREAT WAR was over. At the Ice House, there was another cause for rejoicing. In March 1918, Miss Lynch had become Mrs Drysdale. To the young widows, many of whom could hardly even remember their own weddings, it seemed very strange, and also very romantic, that a lady who was said to be getting on for fifty and who might have been a grandmother years ago, should be marrying for the first time. They clubbed together to buy her a silver box and a silver picture frame and a beautiful garland, and were more delighted than ever when they learned that she was not going to leave them. Mr Drysdale had business in Madras, and the government was not only willing but anxious that his wife should remain in the public service.

She and Subbalakshmi and Miss Prager and Chitti were all

busily occupied. The girls, both at the Triplicane School and the Brahmin Widow's Hostel, were continuing to justify their teachers' highest expectations. Three of the Ice House girls had gone to Delhi to study at the Lady Hardinge Medical College. Twelve had already become teachers.

One of these, Meenakshi, had already been shorn when she first came to the Ice House, and her outlook had been so very orthodox that although she wished to be educated and to earn her living, she had told Sister that she did not want to allow her hair to grow and would prefer to continue to dress in the fashion proper to all shorn widows. Her wishes had been respected. Now Meenakshi had gone to teach at Mayuram, a town in the far South which was noted for its orthodoxy. In such a place her appearance and style of dress were very positive assets. Brahmin parents who had hitherto refused to send their little daughters to school for fear of them learning anything undesirable or improper felt that their children could safely be entrusted to the care of Meenakshi.

In the Ice House itself, there were now more than seventy girls in residence, and never a month passed without several new arrivals. The place, visitors often remarked, was like a little island of happiness in a world of apparently unending and often almost unendurable suffering.

The war had not touched it directly except for a few brief moments, but now famine, disease and death stalked the land from end to end. In many areas poor people, who had been accustomed to hunger all their lives, were dying of starvation. Millions fell victim to the influenza epidemic that was raving the world. In India the disease, usually so mild, caused thirteen million deaths – more than twice the number of fatal casualties suffered by combatants on both sides during more than four years of war.

The Ice House was not immune, but thanks to Chitti's nursing and the wholesome food which she still managed to provide, everyone recovered. They were still in the early stages of convalescence when Mr Gandhi, Mahatma Gandhi as more and more people were beginning to call him, paid a visit to Madras which, though few people realized it at the time, was to be the turning point of modern Indian history.

Two Bills restricting the civil liberties of Indians had been introduced into the Central Legislature in Delhi, and one of them was about to become law. In Madras, Gandhi was discussing with old and new friends the methods by which popular protest against these measures could be most effectively expressed. It was decided to call a national hartal, a day of mourning, of fasting and prayer, in which shops would be closed and everyone would stay away from work. On 18 March, the day before this decision was made, a great meeting was held on the Madras beach, within sight of the Ice House windows. Gandhi's speech was reported in the newspapers next day.

"There are times," he said, "when you have to obey a call which is the highest of all, the voice of conscience, even more, separation from friends, from family, from the state to which you may belong, from all that you have held as dear as life itself."

Then, a few days later, he called upon the people of India to join his movement, and urged that government servants, as well as ordinary citizens, should celebrate the hartal by fasting and by abstaining from work.

The hartal, which took place on 6 April, was the first great nationwide demonstration to be held under Gandhi's leadership. Subbalakshmi did not take part in it, or in the great political agitation of the years that followed. Her first duty was to her girls, and it was perfectly clear to her that she could serve her country in no better way than by helping them to grow into women worthy and capable of filling whatever demands the future might make of them.

Very many little girls all over India had been widowed by the influenza epidemic. A few – so few as to be only drops scooped up from the vast ocean of sorrow – were brought to the Ice House. Yet, compared with the rate at which the Widows' Home had so far been growing, the number of new entrants was exceptionally large. As long as applicants for admission were not suffering from any communicable disease and showed no sign of being mentally retarded, Sister would not allow anyone to be turned away.

Some of the Influenza Widows, as they were ever afterwards to call themselves, were almost unbelievably ignorant.

"Do you really think it is possible to educate that girl?" Mrs Drysdale enquired of Sister when she first saw Rukmini.

This Rukmini – the name was a fairly common one – had come from a village hundreds of miles away, in Tinnevelly District.

"You could almost fill a book," one of the other widows, Mrs V Saraswati, told me, "with the story of all the struggles and difficulties of getting Rukmini as far as the Ice House."

Rukmini, who was sitting beside her, was as bright and plump bosomed as the sparrows who were building their nests, a yard or so above her head, in my window curtains. She looked, too, just as chirpy.

"Well, why shouldn't I tell you what happened?" she asked,

in a quick voice that was full of gaiety as if she had never shed a tear in all her life. "I have never had any secrets. And I promise you that every word is true."

She was ten when she married, and her husband twenty. He was a clever boy with good prospects, and Rukmini, who was a gay, carefree little girl, looked forward with the liveliest pleasure to the day when she would go and live with him and his parents. So when, shortly before her twelfth birthday, her first menstruation started, she was not at all distressed. A telegram was at once sent to her parents-in-law who, with their son, were in Trivandrum on holiday, and it was arranged that the nuptial ceremony would take place in a fortnight's time.

Rukmini's mother then went off to Madras to buy the gifts which would have to be presented to the boy and his parents. Rukmini and her father remained at home, and the father's sister, whose husband was away at the war, kept house for them both. Rukmini's aunt was in the habit of spending many hours each day performing puja, making offerings and praying to the gods that her husband might return home safely. She was not a very cheerful companion for the little girl, but Rukmini was so bubbling with happiness that she did not really mind that her aunt seldom seemed to be listening to what she said. Besides, her mother would not be away for more than a few days.

Her mother was still in Madras when a telegram arrived from Trivandrum, to say that Rukmini's husband had caught influenza and was dangerously ill. Rukmini's father, who was on friendly terms with the boy's parents, at once left for Trivandrum. His train had only just started when another telegram arrived. The young man was dead.

Rukmini's aunt, who opened the telegram, burst into loud lamentations. Neighbours rushed in to condole with the weeping woman whose husband, they at once guessed, must have been killed at the front. She, incoherent with grief for her little niece, was for some time unable even to find words to explain to them that they were mistaken. When the mistake was discovered and the woman gathered around to mourn for Rukmini, the girl began to weep with terror. There was no need for anyone to try to prepare her for what would happen on the tenth day, when the barber would be sent for to shave her head and she would be dressed for the first time in the hideous costume of widowhood. She knew what to expect.

Next day, her mother's brother arrived from Madras. Rukmini was very fond of her uncle, and when he asked her to go upstairs with him, she obeyed at once. He took her into a room, closed the door and spoke to her more seriously than anyone had ever done in all her life. He could, he said, save her from having her hair cut off and from all the other dreadful things which happened to widows who had attained their age. If she agreed, he would take her with him, before the days of mourning were over, back to Madras. There she would be able to go and live in a big house and be taken care of by a beautiful lady who already had many virgin widows in her care. Rukmini would go to school. She would be happy. When she grew up she would be able to go out into the world and earn money. She would be free to live as she liked.

Rukmini had never been to school, and the prospect of sitting in class all day with other girls and trying to learn to read and write and do arithmetic simply terrified her.

"No," she replied, "I can't go. I won't!"

"Listen to me," her uncle said, "for just a little longer." He talked to her, as nobody had ever done before, of what would happen when she became a woman. Supposing, he asked, that something were to happen to her father, and she and her mother were left alone in the world? Of course, he himself would care for them as long as he lived. But after that, to whom would the two poor widows be able to turn for help, for the little that they needed to keep alive? If Rukmini went to school now, she need have no such fears. She would be able to look after her mother whatever happened.

"Now," he finished, "you must sleep. When you wake up, I want you to think about what I have said. You had better not talk to anybody else, so I shall lock the door before I go downstairs. I'll come back soon."

He kept her a prisoner for more than a week. She never knew what her mother and aunt said when her uncle told them what he proposed to do. It was he who brought her meals upstairs, and he spent many hours each day trying to persuade her that he was right.

When, at last, she consented to go to Madras her father was still in Trivandrum, where the period of mourning was not yet over. Rukmini was still not sure that she really wanted to be educated or that she would be happy at the Ice House, so her uncle took her first to stay with some lady missionaries, and it was they who finally convinced her that her uncle was right.

At the Ice House, she was put into the preparatory class. Sister did not agree with Mrs Drysdale that the child, whose high spirits seemed to lead her into every kind of foolishness, was ineducable. She had everything to learn and she must begin, Sister decided, by discovering from her own experience what hard work meant. Rukmini spoke Tamil with immensely fluent inaccuracy. She would have to learn to speak it correctly. The mother tongue of her parents was Telugu. Rukmini, Sister said, must learn that too. This meant that, including English, there were three alphabets to be mastered at once, as well as the mysteries of addition, subtraction and multiplication.

It was the custom for the younger girls to do their homework in the company of one or other of the seniors, who would keep an eye on them and help them with small difficulties. Rukmini was so gay that no one could help liking her. But she was, so she herself told me, a dreadful little chatterbox.

She said, "I suppose that is one way in which I have not changed very much. When I first went to the Ice House, I was always breaking the rule that everybody had to talk English all the time. Of course, I didn't know a word of the language, and all my pocket money used to go in fines because I would babble away, talking any kind of meaningless nonsense, rather than keep silent. It really wasn't a bit surprising that Mrs Drysdale thought I was half-witted."

In fact, she learned quickly and was soon able to enter the high school. For the first three years she did not go home for the summer holidays. If she had done so, she would certainly never have been allowed to return to Madras. As it was, Rukmini's uncle found himself outcasted from the family. "My grandfather," Rukmini went on, "felt the disgrace, as he called it, so keenly that he left home and went to Courtallam to cleanse himself from the family's sin by bathing in the sacred falls. He stayed there for many years. By the time he came home I was growing up and already thinking about my future profession."

Another girl who entered the Ice House at about this time

was Meenambal, who had been named after the fish eyed goddess Meenakshi, to whom the great temple at Madurai is dedicated. Her mother had died when she was still a baby, and she was brought up by her grandmother and her father. She was sensitive and warmhearted, and until she was almost thirteen she had never known a moment's sorrow.

Then her husband died. Meenambal had been married for nearly two years, but she had not yet come of age and the boy was still a stranger. Meenambal's father, a lawyer by profession, was an enlightened man and thought it very wrong that the burden of widowhood should have to be borne by an innocent little girl who had never done the slightest wrong to anybody. He was so brokenhearted at her misfortune that each time he looked at her tears would spring into his eyes. But although he agreed with social reformers that young virgin widows ought to be allowed to remarry, he could not bring himself to defy convention by seeking a second husband for his child.

It was from one of his clients that he learned about the Brahmin Widow's Home. This, he decided, was the place for Meenambal. The girl's grandmother disagreed. She was a very orthodox old lady. Although she was greatly distressed by the child's sufferings, she believed that it was Meenambal's duty to bear them and that only by doing so could she wash away the sins committed in her previous birth.

As the months went on, Meenambal, who had always been so chubby and bright eyed, grew thin and listless.

"It wasn't any physical illness," Meenambal told me. "It was just that the sorrow was too much to be borne. Besides, I knew perfectly well what would happen to me when I attained my age, and the sort of life I would have to lead when I grew up and my father passed away ... Sati," she went on, "would have been preferable. When widows were burned on their husband's funeral pyres, their sufferings were soon over. However terrible their agonies may have been, they could not compare with the long years of hunger and cruelty and misery and pain which the poor creatures had to go on enduring until god in his mercy took them away."

At last, friends of Meenambal's grandmother who had been to Madras and had met Sister Subbalakshmi persuaded the old lady to yield to her son's wishes.

"When my father took me to the Ice House," Meenambal went on, "I was nearly fourteen. I didn't know a word of English. I didn't even know that two and two made four. I knew absolutely nothing. I sat waiting while my father talked to Sister in her office, and when they came out together and I looked at Sister for the first time, I thought I was seeing an angel."

Sister walked beside her up the wide, curving staircase. Meenambal gathered her courage to ask the only question about the future which seemed to be of any importance. This beautiful stranger, she was sure, would never say anything which was untrue.

"If I stay here," Meenambal asked, "will I still weep?"

She did not see the tears which sprang into Sister's eyes. "No, no," the firm voice answered, "you need never weep again. Everybody is happy here."

Subbalakshmi herself was happy, but not contented. She realized how ignorant, how secure in the cage of her private happiness she had been when, still hardly more than a girl, she had resolved to dedicate her life to those who had been less fortunate than herself. She had known something, though by no means all, of what it meant to be a child widow. But in those early days she had scarcely the faintest inkling of what it meant to be a child wife.

Now she knew. Even parents with advanced ideas often found it very difficult to postpone the consummation of their daughter's marriages. If they appeared to hesitate, the husband's parents would, quite probably, threaten to end the marriage and take a second wife for their son. Pre-puberty consummation, though not common, had occurred in a number of cases within Sister's own experience.

One little girl whom Subbalakshmi had tried to help had been married when she was ten, and the marriage had been consummated before her eleventh birthday. The child's mother-in-law was dead, and she found herself the only female in her father-in-law's household. For more than a year she was compelled to toil at housework and cooking from five o'clock every morning until ten each night. She was just twelve when she was taken to hospital suffering from severe pains which the doctors diagnosed as being due to a displacement of the womb brought about by excessive strain and heavy manual labour. Her husband and father-in-law insisted on taking her away from the hospital before her cure was completed, and she was obliged to return for further treatment three times during the next three years. She was at the mercy of her menfolk, and there was very little that Sister or anybody else could do to relieve her sufferings.

Sister's own girls, whatever else they might have suffered, had at least been saved from such miseries as this. It was probable, too, or at any rate possible, that the parents of single girls who were paying boarders at the Ice House would agree to postpone their daughters' marriages, at least for a year or two. But there would be countless thousands of little girls who could not be helped in any direct way. They could be saved only if the general attitude towards marriage was completely transformed.

And how was that to be achieved?

Sister had made it a habit to open all the letters which were delivered at the Ice House. When bad news came, as it sometimes did, she could break it gently, and she could also be sure of knowing when any of her girls needed special help.

One morning the postman brought a letter for Gita, who very seldom received a letter from anybody.

Gita was born in an exceptionally happy and affectionate family, and her marriage had been arranged with more than the usual care. Her husband was said to be a good and intelligent boy. His parents were well-to-do people, and so kind and openhearted that it seemed certain that when Gita went to live with them she would be spared the torments which most young brides suffered at the hands of their mothers-in-law.

She never did go. When the news came that the little girl had been widowed, Gita's mother was so prostrated with grief that she fell seriously ill. Within a few months she too was dead.

Gita's father had been devoted to his wife and could scarcely imagine how he would be able to tolerate existence without her. He had, besides Gita, three other children to bring up, two boys and little Indu, who was the baby of the family. He

---

Gita, as I have called her, is a pseudonym. So is Indu. "It will not lessen the interest of our story," Gita wrote to me, "if you do not use our real names."

Living in the World

took the advice of friends who urged that since he had no woman relative to keep house and look after his boys and girls it was his duty to marry again.

Gita's stepmother was a young girl from a poor family, ignorant and pathetically incapable. She was unable to make friends with the children, and the atmosphere of the home became more and more unhappy. Gita's father, burdened by troubles which he felt that he had brought upon himself, could hardly bear to think of the future which awaited his widowed daughter when his own life came to an end.

He turned for advice to another friend, Subbalakshmi's cousin Krishnaswami, who was the local superintendent of police. It was Krishnaswami who suggested that Gita should be sent to the Brahmin Widow's Home in Madras to be educated.

She was happy there, and made rapid progress. Then her father fell ill. Friends brought him to Madras, and he was admitted to the General Hospital for treatment. Gita, of course, visited him regularly. She was old enough by this time to realize that his condition was serious. His illness could have only one end.

His death was not the last of his children's misfortunes. The two boys and little Indu had been left in the guardianship of an uncle. Six months after their father's death the children's guardian also died. They continued to live in the house of his widow, a harsh, dominating woman with a grown-up son. They were utterly dependent on her, since their father's savings had all been expended on his wife's and his own illnesses. Gita, with her government scholarship, was able to keep herself. There could be no doubt that when she obtained her secondary school leaving certificate she would be able to get another scholarship to enable her to study for a degree and afterwards train to be a secondary school teacher. Her brothers were at school, and in due course would be self-supporting. But poor little Indu, who was a bright child and had already managed to learn to read and write, would be wholly dependent on the charity of her uncle's widow until her sister and brothers were able to maintain her and put something by to provide her with a dowry.

The letter to Gita was, as Subbalakshmi guessed before she opened it, from Indu.

"Dear Akka," she had written, "please come and save me. The people in this house are going to marry me to a man who is fifty years old. I cannot bear it. If they make me do this thing it will kill me. They said next week. So please come quickly."

Someone was at once sent to give the letter to Gita and to tell her to come to Sister as soon as she had read it.

Indu, Sister knew, could not be more than twelve. Some years ago, before the Great War began, Mr Srinivasa Sastri had introduced a Bill into the Madras Legislative Council to prohibit the marriage of girls under the age of fourteen. Later, the Bill had been withdrawn because it was feared that it would not achieve its purpose. Since then, although criticism of the institution of child marriage had begun to grow, there was still no legal way of preventing such marriages from taking place. All the same, Sister told herself as she waited for Gita to come downstairs, little Indu must, even at the cost of some illegality, be saved from becoming the wife of a man old enough to be her grandfather.

She could not think what to do. Her own views were by

this time so well-known that if she tried to dissuade the girls' aunt she would probably only succeed in making the coldhearted woman even more determined to carry out her wicked scheme. Yet who else could possibly intervene?

Then Gita entered the room. A plan had already formed itself in her mind. There was no need, and no time, to waste words. "Sister," she suggested, "I ought to go at once. If Chitti could come with me I think she would be able to manage things."

Sister agreed, and Gita and Chitti left Madras by the next train.

Gita's aunt greeted them with chilly surprise, but, the laws of hospitality being what they were, was obliged to invite them to be her guests for as long as they chose to remain. Indu, who was usually so gay, looked pale, and her eyes, red with weeping, were narrowed, screwed up as if she had not slept for days.

The aunt guessed at once why they had come. Nothing that Chitti could say moved her in the least. She was adamant. A girl without a dowry could consider herself lucky to find anyone willing to marry her. Everybody knew that widowers, old men, were the only possible husbands for penniless girls. The marriage would take place. Although Chitti and Gita could not, as widows, attend the ceremony, they would be welcome to remain in the house until it was over.

It was evident that there was only one thing to be done if Indu was to be saved. Chitti and Gita would have to kidnap her.

The marriage ceremony was due to take place during the next few days. The two girls, Chitti advised, must be patient. It would be worse than useless to try to escape unless there were a fair chance for the three of them to get on the Madras train before their absence was noticed.

At last, the house was empty. The children's aunt and her son had gone out to pay visits and would probably not return for two or three hours.

Chitti and the two girls hurried, as fast as they could go, to the railway station. The Madras train was not due to arrive for another hour. Then there would be another twenty minutes of danger and suspense before it steamed out again.

Chitti bought the tickets, and then joined the two girls in the ladies' waiting room. The three of them knew that when their absence was discovered, the girls' relatives would have no difficulty in guessing where they had gone. Once Indu was safely in Madras it was as certain as anything could be that no one would attempt to fetch her back. Indeed, her bridegroom would probably no longer want her. In an hour or so the danger would be over.

The train arrived. Luckily it was not crowded, and Chitti had no difficulty in finding seats for herself and the girls. The platform was thronged with passengers getting in and out of the train, with visitors coming to meet their friends or to see them off, with water carriers and vendors of coffee and fruit and packages of food, with child beggars and lepers and the arrogant servants of the Europeans. The girls sat perfectly still. Then, as the minutes passed, they fancied that they could hear their own hearts beating so loudly that the sound seemed to drown every other noise.

The first bell rang. In another minute the train would begin to move.

Then, before the second bell could ring, the girls' cousin

pushed his way through the crowd and wrenched open the door of their compartment.

"Come!" he cried, thrusting his head and shoulders in and flinging out both arms to seize Indu's wrists.

"No!" she yelled.

She was small for her age, thin and delicately made. Her cousin tugged with all his might. Meanwhile, Chitti and Gita had grasped her legs, holding firmly and trying to draw her back as she was about to topple, head first, out of the door.

None of them heard the second bell. The door was still wide open and the little girl was still being pulled both ways as the train gave a jerk and began to move. The two widows, the slender young girl and the strong, mature woman, were using more strength than either had ever known she possessed. They were too much for the man. As the train gathered speed he lost his hold. Perhaps he crashed on to the platform. Chitti and Gita did not turn to see. Indu was weeping, bruised and shaken. But at last she was safe, and presently she was able to smile.

Chitti, although she did not say so to the girls, was still worried. How was Indu to be provided for? Only widows were eligible for government scholarships. Unmarried pupils were maintained by their families, who also paid their school fees. Times were so hard and prices so high that even though Subbalakshmi and her parents would help all they could it would be almost impossible to provide for the child.

"Indu," Sister finished when she had told me all this, "was always lucky, and Chitti need not have spent all those hours distressing herself about the child's future. A few days before she arrived, and when I didn't know whether she would be rescued, a gentleman came to see me and said that he would like to give a donation of twenty rupees a month to help one of our unmarried girls. So when Indu reached the Ice House everything was easy. It was a real happy ending."

"And what," I asked, "became of the two sisters?"

She smiled. "I shall tell you that later."

In the summer of 1920, Subbalakshmi was awarded the Kaiser-I-Hind Medal in recognition of her services to the girls and women of the Madras Presidency. She had never dreamed of or imagined such a thing, and when she received the news in a telegram from Lord Willingdon, who had succeeded Lord Pentland as Governor of Madras, she was simply overwhelmed with astonishment and happiness.

There was still criticism of the Widows' Home. There probably always would be. But now its success was undeniable. The Ice House was comfortably full, with just over a hundred girls in residence. The overwhelming majority were child widows. Some came from very poor homes. Others, like the single girls, had parents who could afford to pay for them. Girls whose husbands were living were not usually accepted, though exceptions were made in special circumstances.

"Did I ever tell you," Sister asked me one day, "about the young widow who remarried, and who left her husband because he was so rapacious and cruel?"

"Yes, you did. But didn't you say," I asked, "that when she was brought to you it was impossible for you to accept her?"

"Yes. When she first came, that was so. Then, when the rules were changed, her father again asked me to take her. I did. She was a very nice, intelligent girl, and settled down happily and made a lot of friends."

One of these friends, Sister continued, was a single girl of about the same age, whose parents lived in Madras city.

"The father of this second girl," Sister said, "was anxious to find a husband for his daughter who was not merely in a good position but who would appreciate having an educated wife. He put an advertisement in the newspapers. A week or two later, he came to the Ice House to tell the girl that he had had a reply from a young man in Calcutta who appeared to be in every way what was wanted. The father was a rather modern minded man who would not have made any arrangement without consulting his daughter. He gave her the young man's letter to read, and she was very much taken with the idea of marrying him. So after a short time the father went off, saying that as soon as he had spoken to his wife he would send a telegram to Calcutta, telling the young man to come to Madras at once."

He left the letter with his daughter. She was reading it for the second, or perhaps third, time when her unhappily married friend came into the room, sat down with a book, glanced up, stared, and, after a long minute, said, "I think I know that handwriting."

She was not mistaken. It was that of her husband. The two girls rushed to Sister to tell her of the discovery.

Sister at once sent a message to the father of the bride-to-be. "Luckily," she told me, "the telegram had not yet been sent off. The young man was, of course, told that he was not wanted, and both girls stayed at school for some time longer."

The Triplicane school was phenomenally successful, and

the eagerness of many Madrasi parents to educate their daughters was now proved beyond doubt. At the end of 1913, the year in which the school opened, there had been a total of two hundred and twenty one girls in the elementary and high school sections, and twenty nine students in the teachers' training department. Now, after seven years, there were four hundred and fifty five pupils and seventy nine student teachers. Although numbers had been restricted because of lack of space, the high school section, in which there were one hundred and sixty three girls, was considerably bigger than any other Hindu high school in the Madras Presidency.

It was also, in the opinion of experts from other parts of the country, the best school of its kind in India. Everyone who visited it was struck by the frank and easy manners of the girls and the bright, unselfconscious friendliness with which they talked to strangers. They were struck, too, by the originality of the teaching methods and by the alert, absorbed interest which the girls took in their lessons. Their physical exercises and traditional dances, as well as the plays which they acted after school hours, were delightful to watch. So were their exhibitions of blackboard drawing, in which many of the pupils appeared to be as quick, and almost as skilled, as professional cartoonists. But to most visitors the botany lessons were the most fascinating of all. The windowsills in the dismal rooms were decorated with flowers, potted plants and germinating seeds. Even the smallest children, one visitor noted, would bring their own botanical specimens to school, and would learn to observe with remarkable exactness every stage in the processes of growth and reproduction.

The girls, whatever their circumstances and backgrounds,

seemed to mix with each other on terms of perfect equality. In fact, the only thing that was wrong with the school, so it seemed to most visitors, was the dreary unsuitability of its premises.

Now, at last, a change was to be made. The government had agreed that a new school should be built exactly where Sister and Miss Lynch and Miss Prager had hoped to see it, just around the corner from the Widows' Home. The new building would not be ready for occupation for another two years, but everyone was so overjoyed at the decision to construct it that the long wait did not seem to matter very much. At last, everyone could look forward to the future with real confidence.

Then the storm broke.

There had been a rumble of thunder, close but not very loud, three years earlier, when the Viceroy, Lord Chelmsford, and the Secretary of State for India, Edwin Montagu, had visited Madras. Both had been struck by the intensity of ill feelings between people of different communities. Montagu was told, so he recorded in his diary, that "the English hate the Indians, the Indians hate the English, and this new violent opposition of the brahmins to the non-brahmins had become the guiding principle of the place.

Inter caste rivalry and bitterness were not, in fact, new features of South Indian life. When the British East India Company had set up its trading station at Fort St George in 1639, and had begun to weld a collection of scattered villages into a city, most of the Indian clerks whom they had taken into their employment were brahmins. Although the brahmins formed only three per cent of the population, they were the only educated people who were,

---

An Indian **Diary** **by** Edwin S Montagu, Heinemann, 1930, pp. 113-4.

for the most part, propertyless and eager to accept any work which offered a salary. Since then, some South Indian brahmins had grown rich. Those who rose to positions of responsibility in government service used their power as best as they could to help their relatives and others who belonged to their own community. For some years before Lord Chelmsford and Mr Montagu visited Madras, educated non-brahmins had been complaining, not without justification, that they were not being given a fair chance in the public services.

One charge of unfairness led naturally to others. Lord Chelmsford sent for Miss Lynch. Why, he demanded, was the Widows' Home in the Ice House reserved exclusively for girls from brahmin families? Surely such discrimination was very unjust?

There was, Miss Lynch answered, really no discrimination. Widows young enough to be able to benefit from a secondary education were hardly to be found outside the brahmin community. Her sympathy with the educational ambitions and needs of non-brahmins was, she said, just as keen as with that of the brahmins. She had shown this by obtaining government sanction for the opening of hostels for both Christian and non-brahmin Hindu girls who were attending the Triplicane school. She had, too, though she did not mention this to Lord Chelmsford, helped Sister and the Members of the Sarada Ladies' Union to raise the funds needed to build and maintain the school for the fisherfolks' children.

Lord Chelmsford seemed to have been satisfied and other critics, for the time being, silenced.

By the autumn of 1920, the new constitution for India which Chelmsford and Montagu had begun to devise in 1917 had taken shape. The Indian National Congress, under Gandhi's leadership, was planning to boycott the forthcoming elections. In Madras, wealthy non-brahmins who disliked what they regarded as Gandhi's revolutionary aims had formed a new political party on a regional and caste basis. The Justice Party, as its founders named it, demanded, as the main item in its programme, an allocation of jobs in the public services in proportion to the castes and religious beliefs of the various sections of the population of the Madras Presidency. A member of the new party wrote to the newspapers repeating Lord Chelmsford's criticism. The Ice House Hostel, he declared, should either be open to all widows, irrespective of caste, or should be closed altogether. Certainly no single girls should be allowed to live there.

This was followed by a criticism from an unexpected quarter. A teacher on the staff of the Triplicane school wrote to a leader of the untouchables. Sister Subbalakshmi, she complained, had presided over the teachers' meeting which had been held at the end of the summer term and had succeeded, against all reason and justice, in preventing any girl who was not a brahmin from being promoted to a higher form. Two girls – one of them the daughter of a fisherman whom Sister had come to regard as a personal friend – wrote to the newspapers making a similar complaint.

The Director of Public Instruction was asked to make an official inquiry. Sister and Miss Prager, who had tried hard and on the whole very successfully, to keep caste consciousness out of the school, were terribly distressed. Records of the pupils' caste origins, which had been carefully locked away, had to be brought out and examined. Although the charges against Sister were easily disproved, it was not going to be by any means easy to restore the old happy atmosphere.

In fact, grievances multiplied. Why, critics demanded, should the hostels for Christian girls and non-brahmin Hindus be situated in the crowded, dirty streets of Triplicane while the brahmin girls were housed in a beautiful mansion beside the sea? It was useless for Sister Subbalakshmi to point out that a lucky accident had, so to speak, thrown the Ice House into her lap at a moment when the young widows were literally homeless and that, much as she wished that all the boarders who attended the Triplicane school could live in equally beautiful surroundings, it could hardly be expected that such luck would be repeated.

This issue, too, was taken up by members of the Justice Party. Their influence was growing, and in January 1921 the governor, Lord Willingdon, invited the Justice Party leader to form a government.

Lady Willingdon had, ever since she arrived in Madras, taken the liveliest interest in both the Triplicane school and the brahmin Widows' Hostel. Sister Subbalakshmi was frequently asked to arrange for the Ice House girls to give a short entertainment to distinguished visitors who came to stay at Government House. When the governor's wife happened to be alone, she would often stop at the Ice House on her way home from her evening drives to chat with Sister and the girls and perhaps arrange some special treat for them, such as a trip in the governor's barge to visit the ancient monuments at Mahabalipuram. It seemed to everybody only right that the new high school which was being built, and the teachers' training college which was to be associated with it, should be named after the Triplicane school's most powerful friend.

Nobody could doubt that Lady Willingdon's name was magic. The site for the new training college bordered the Marina. Soon after the contractors had begun to work, Miss Prager, walking past, noticed that the foundations had been laid edge-to-edge with the pavement. She at once went to call on the governor's wife. "A college which is to bear your name," she urged, "ought not be built where every passerby can stare in at the windows. It should be set well back from the road, with a wide lawn and gardens in front of it."

The foundations were moved and a big garden laid out between the front of the building and the boundary wall. But Lady Willingdon did not, and doubtless could not, intervene when, in March 1921, Mr Subbaroyalu Reddy, who was at that time the leader of the Justice Party, paid an official visit to the Ice House.

Sister and Chitti, and Miss Prager too, had for some time been looking forward to this visit with the most anxious foreboding. If they were now to be compelled to admit girls from non-brahmin families to the Widows' Home, the battle for the support of orthodox people, which was not more than half-won, would have to be fought all over again. Pious Hindu parents, non-brahmin as well as brahmin, would certainly disapprove of any institution in which people of different castes sat down to meals together. Even Mr Gandhi had recently expressed disapproval of what the social reformers called inter dining.

Mr Subbaroyalu Reddy turned out to be pleasant, even cordial. He paid Sister Subbalakshmi and her aunt, Mrs Valambal, many compliments on the admirable work which they had already done, and expressed the hope that they would continue to manage the Ice House for many years to come. All the same, he told them, the rules by which it was managed were to be changed. In future, the hostel must accept non-brahmins and girls who had not been widowed must, whatever their caste, be excluded.

The consequences of these decisions turned out to be less undesirable than Sister and Miss Prager had anticipated. A new hostel, financed from private sources, would have to be opened for single girls and young wives. As to the non-brahmin widows who were to be admitted to the Ice House, arrangements could be made for them to take their meals in a group by themselves. Although they would almost certainly be too old to enter the high school, they could, like the older brahmin entrants, be trained as elementary school teachers. If there were not too many of them, they would soon learn to fit into the settled pattern of living.

In fact, one non-brahmin girl was already living at the Ice House. "She," Sister told me, "was the daughter-in-law of a zamindar who had become a Theosophist and who had taken a house at Adyar so as to be near Mrs Besant and the headquarters of the Theosophical Society. He was a religious and kindly man, but his son, the husband of this girl I am telling you about, was the most disgusting, degraded creature imaginable. He had been ill treating his wife, who was then about sixteen or seventeen, in the most vulgar way."

"Vulgar?" I repeated.

"Yes. He did things to her which I cannot possibly tell you – things which are too horrible to speak about, don't you know. Then he went off to Europe. For some time, his wife was left in peace. But the things the poor girl had suffered preyed on her mind to such a point that one morning she slipped out of the house and walked along to Elliot's Beach, intending to drown herself."

The girl had expected to find the beach deserted. As dawn broke and she moved towards the water's edge, she noticed that a fisherman was watching her. She strolled on. The fisherman followed. He did not come close or attempt to speak to her. Nor, on the other hand, did he allow her out of his sight. With a rescuer so close at hand it was, of course, pointless to get into the water. She was obliged to turn round and go home again.

The fisherman followed at a discreet distance. When he reached the house, he asked to see the zamindar and described what he had seen.

"The poor father-in-law," Sister went on, "was advised by his friends to bring the girl to me. I told her that if I took her into the Ice House she would have to study just as hard as all my other girls. "That," she said, "is what I want to do, I cannot stand any more of married life. If I learn to work then I can be free."

She was put into the preparatory class. She seemed intelligent, yet she was quite unable to learn. She seemed to want nothing but to be alone with Sister and to pour out her troubles.

Sister spent many hours listening, hoping that if the girl could unburden herself completely she would be liberated from her memories.

It did not happen.

"If you don't make some progress with your studies," Sister

warned her, "you will never get into the high school or be able to earn and become independent of that man."

"I will study," the girl answered. "I will really. And I'll never go back to that man – never!"

"Suppose," Sister asked, "that your husband should take a second wife?" Even the most respectable men, kindly and devoted husbands, often would not hesitate to take a second wife if their first had failed to bear a son. "If he should do that," Sister went on, "and the new wife became a mother, you would lose all your rights to the zamindari property. Then what will you do?"

"I shall work! I really shall!"

Then her husband returned, and a few days later sent his lawyer to call on Sister Subbalakshmi.

The young wife, said the lawyer, must at once go back to her husband. If she did not go, Sister Subbalakshmi would be charged with having taken the girl away. The word kidnapping was not used, but the meaning was perfectly plain.

"So I told him," Sister recalled, "that he was talking nonsense. It had been at the father-in-law's request that I had taken the poor girl and I had never made any secret of where she was. Then the lawyer tried another line. "Madam," he said to me, "you call yourself Sister. Will you not be a Sister to my client?"

Sister looked at me. "Imagine the impudence! Would it, I asked him, be sisterly for me to force that girl to go back to the life which had almost driven her to her death? I told him that she was free to make her own choice. She refused to go. The husband threatened to petition the courts for the restitution of conjugal rights. He did not do so. If he had, his infamy would have been reported in the newspapers, and I suppose that is what stopped him."

"So," I asked, "the girl stayed with you?"

"Not for long. She heard that her husband had taken a second wife. When she came to me with the news she said, Now I had better go and see if I can make him give me a son. If he does, I can leave him again and he will have to give me the money I need for the rest of my life. So off she went. I don't know whether she had a child. I never heard of her again."

It did not take long to find a house near the Triplicane school which could be turned into a hostel for girls who had not had the misfortune to be widowed. It was situated in a narrow dirty street, but it was commodious and reasonably well built. The rent, one hundred and fifty rupees a month, was high, and the strictest economy would be necessary if the boarding charges were to be kept at a level which middle class parents could afford. The Ladies' Union, with Dr Muthulakshmi Reddy as its president for the year and Sister Subbalakshmi still as secretary, were confident that they would be able to manage.

In many ways, they were glad to be free from government control. They would still have all the help that Mrs Drysdale and Miss Prager could give them unofficially, and they would be free to make experiments without fear of official interference. Later, perhaps, they might find ways of helping girls whose parents could not afford to pay for their maintenance. Even now, they were sure that they would be able to find the money needed to educate girls who were both very poor and especially deserving.

By July 1921, the house was ready for occupation and twenty

one girls moved into it. In addition to those who came from the Ice House there were several new girls, daughters of country families who had heard about the project and thought it an excellent chance both to educate their children and save them from marrying while they were still too young to become wives.

The Ice House filled up again quickly. The widows were not all children. Alamelu, for example, was twenty three. She was a big, strongly built young woman and had, she told Sister at their first interview, walked nearly five hundred miles to seek admission. She was quite illiterate but she was sure that she could learn and was eager to do so for the sake of her three children, whom she had left with their grandparents. She wanted to educate them but, she explained, there would be no possibility of doing so unless she herself was able to earn.

Alamelu did not in the least mind sitting in the preparatory class with little girls, and it was evident that she would soon qualify to join the teachers' training department. Meanwhile, her strong, disciplined body and forceful personality quickly made her a leader at drill and in organized games. She was perfectly at home in the Ice House.

Saraswati Deshpande, though she was only fifteen, at first felt very out of place among the other girls. Her parents had been too poor to be able to give her a dowry and like so many girls who were similarly situated, she had been married to a man who was old enough to be her grandfather. He was a widower. Saraswati was, she learned when she went to live with him, his fourth wife.

Her husband and her father died within a few weeks of each other. The two widows – Saraswati's mother was then only thirty – were invited to leave their native village and to stay with some relatives who lived in Madras, not far from the Triplicane school. Saraswati, when she saw the young widows passing by on the way to and from the Ice House, longed to join them. Her mother would have liked her to do so, but the relative whose guests they were refused even to listen to such a suggestion. They were, they pointed out, respectable, god fearing people. It would not be right that any member of their family, however poor she might be, should be trained to go out into the world and lead an independent life.

Saraswati and her mother refused to abandon their dream. They returned to their native village, where the young girl's grandfather undertook to teach her English and arithmetic. After some months, mother and daughter visited Madras again, and this time went to see Sister Subbalakshmi. The interview was discouraging. The Ice House was full. Moreover, Saraswati was not young enough to stand a good chance of being awarded a government scholarship. She had better, Sister said, apply for admission to the Government Secondary and Training School at Cuddalore, which was not far from her home.

So Saraswati went to Cuddalore and was enrolled as a pupil. If she did well there, she would be able to train to be an elementary school teacher. This was not what she wanted. The stories she had heard about girls who had already left the Ice House had aroused her ambition. She wanted to study for university degree. When she got it, she would be able to travel, to see the world. Exciting things would happen to her.

She never spoke of her dreams. She worked so hard that at the end of six months she had earned the right to skip a class and study with the senior girls. She was very shy. She could not make friends, and her teachers were struck by the contrast between the sturdiness of her body and the nervous timidity of her manner. Yet, when she really wanted something, she could usually pluck up enough courage to ask for it. She applied to be transferred to the Ice House. This time there was room and she was accepted.

She was so tormented by shyness that she hardly knew how she managed to live through her first day at the Triplicane high school. When the girls returned to the Ice House in the evening and she found that she was not allowed to study, she simply did not know what to do with herself. Some of the girls had gone to the beach with Chitti. Others were playing tennis or badminton or feeding the silkworms or working at their hobbies. The girls whose turn it was to help in the kitchen had disappeared. Saraswati, strolling though the garden alone, felt terribly inferior. She didn't belong to the gay, pretty, laughing creatures she saw around her. Her eyes were hot with unshed tears. She wished she had not come.

Then one of the bigger girls came up. "Won't you," she asked "come and listen to the veena players practising for a concert? I've been looking for you everywhere, and nobody seemed to know where you had got to."

They went indoors together. Nobody fussed over Saraswati. They treated her as one of themselves. An older girl, whose name was also Saraswati and who had come over from Queen Mary's College to spend the evening, told her how shy she had been when she herself had first joined the Widows' Hostel, and how sorry she had been to leave it and, at the same time, how happy she was to be studying for a degree. Other girls chatted with her too. By the time the supper bell rang she was already one of the crowd.

Sister wanted every girl who came to the hostel to feel that whatever she had suffered in the past could be forgotten in the busy life of this huge, new family. Most newcomers had no difficulty in fitting in, but there were some girls whom Sister would not agree to take.

"Dr Muthulakshmi Reddy," she told me, "thought that we ought to accept the daughters of D G's …"

"What," I interrupted, "is a D G?"

"Surely I have told you that before? It means a dancing girl – a member of the caste of devadasis." Sister's face was stilled for an instant, rigid with disapproval. "At the time I am speaking of," she continued, "it was a common thing for respectable men – so-called respectable men – to keep such women. The origin of the devadasis was harmless enough. In ancient times it was customary for respectable families, and even great people like maharajas, to dedicate a daughter to the gods. The girls would live in the temples and take part in the worship. In fact, it was very like the life of nuns in Roman Catholic countries. Unfortunately, after a time the priests began to get hold of these girls and spoiled them. The men who came for worship began to do the same, until the system became nothing more than legalized prostitution. Dr Muthulakshmi Reddy tried to get a bill passed to stop it all. In the end, as you know, she succeeded. Of course, the poor little children of such women were not to be blamed, but some of them knew too much and I thought it better that they should not mix with our girls." She paused again, this time for long enough to allow a whole procession of thoughts to pass through her head.

I waited.

"Well," she asked at last, not addressing me but speaking, it seemed to the air around us, "what is the consequence of doing away with the devadasis? Nowadays so-called respectable young women from good families do all sorts of things which are not at all nice even to think of." Then she looked at me and smiled. "But I suppose it is all part of the times we live in."

In 1921, exciting events were happening in the political world. The Indian National Congress had launched a movement which, Mahatma Gandhi had declared, would bring freedom within a year. All over India, people were being urged to stop wearing foreign cloth, to boycott the law courts, and to take their children away from government schools and colleges. A few parents, not many, took their children away from the Triplicane school. In Madras, as elsewhere, the movement was gathering speed. Many of the outstanding leaders of the Congress had been arrested and were already in jail when the Prince of Wales arrived in Bombay in November 1921.

Some people said that the prince had come to show the goodwill of the British towards the people of India. Others declared that he was being used as a tool by powerful men who wanted to deny to Indians the political and economic freedom that the people of Britain enjoyed. The congress had decided that his arrival in each city should be greeted by a hartal, a demonstration of silent mourning. In Bombay, angry crowds ignored Mahatma Gandhi's injunction that all demonstrations must be non-violent. About fifty people were killed, and more than four hundred injured.

When the royal visitor arrived in Madras, on 13 January, 1922, many people were torn between the desire to express their nationalist feelings and their curiosity to see for themselves the most famous young man in the world. The hartal, which was observed in most parts of the city, produced some rowdy scenes and one violent demonstration in which a man was killed. The route from the Central Station to Government House was lined with police. Behind them, watchers stood, patient, a little tense. Union Jacks fluttered above official buildings, and from the windows of some Indian shops and dwelling houses. There were black flags too, which had been hung defiantly by householders who were bold enough to dare to allow all the world to see that they were observing the hartal.

The Ice House girls and a large party from the Triplicane school were specially privileged. Next day they were going to dance kummi and kolattam before the Prince. Today they stood, shepherded by Miss Prager, Sister Subbalakshmi and other members of the staff in a gallery overlooking the statue of Sir Thomas Munro, the most benevolent governor in the history of the Madras Presidency. Chellam and Gita and Indu and Saraswati and the rest stared down with wonder at the Prince's pale hair, and at the pale, handsome, strained face. Someday, they had learned at school, he would be their King-Emperor, the greatest royal personage on earth and the successor to Emperor Ashoka, who had ruled India more than two thousand years ago and was still remembered as the noblest rulers who ever lived.

That evening, Lord and Lady Willingdon held a reception at Government House. Sister Subbalakshmi, who was among the guests, had been told a few days earlier that her name was on the list of those who were to be presented to the prince.

The Banqueting Hall in which the reception was held, was, as it still is, perhaps the most beautiful room in India. Since Independence, its name has been changed. Now, it is called Rajaji Hall in honour of Chakravarti Rajagopalachari, who was a prisoner in Vellore Jail at the time of the Prince of Wales's visit and was later to become Governor General of free India. Today, when one reaches the top of the great flight of steps which lead up from the gardens, one sees, in the instant of stepping over the threshold, the three lifesized portraits which hang side by side at the far end of the hall, just above the dais. On the left, painted against a background of threatening monsoon clouds, is Jawaharlal Nehru, his head rising with a kind of melancholy pride from the high neckband of his achkan, the coat which northerners call the national costume of India. On the right is Rajaji, wearing a white dhoti and gibba and a subtle, mischievous and quite un-elder-statesman-like grin. Between these two, a sloppily painted portrait of Gandhiji, dressed in a loincloth and with his hand resting on the gate outside his mud and thatch cottage at the Sevagram ashram.

Nothing else in the hall has changed. Portraits of British governors, in handsome uniforms and with pink, grey, red and purple faces, hang between the doors, which flank the two long sides. These doors open on to terraces which are screened and cooled by the spreading branches of pink mimosa and mango and asoka trees. The walls are cream and ivory, and so are the tall Corinthian columns which support the gallery and which rise from it to the immensely high, curving roof.

On that night of January 1922, while nationalists shouted and waved their black flags in streets just beyond earshot, the crowded hall seemed to epitomize all that was meant by imperial magnificence. An orchestra, concealed behind a screen of potted palms and English garden flowers, played English and German music. The formal evening dress of British civilian officials mingled with the full dress uniforms of soldiers and sailors and threw into brilliant relief the gold-and-white or brilliantly toned turbans of Indian princes and politicians. The gowns of the European ladies were of pale, shimmering silks and satins, which made their white skins look whiter still, almost etiolated in the brilliant light. The Indian ladies who were present wore saris of the finest Conjeevaram or Benares silk, red, green, orange, gold, and the jewels in their ears and noses glistened like sunlight on water as they were touched by rays from the crystal chandeliers overhead.

Subbalakshmi's sari was the colour of winter violets, laced with a border of gold embroidery. She was not in the least nervous. She stood beside Mrs Prager, quietly self-possessed and evidently enjoying every detail of the scene. She watched closely as the gentlemen, and the few ladies, who were to be presented to the prince stepped forward and, as their names were read, took the hand he offered. Then each of them, sometimes after a word or two, stepped back to make way for whoever was coming next.

At last Subbalakshmi's name was announced.

The prince came forward, his right hand extended.

She did not take it. Instead, she made a deep bow and, pressing her own hands together, lifted them until her palms were at right angles to her forehead.

The prince, who since his arrival in India had never once been offered an Indian greeting, stepped back a few paces. A hush fell on the hall. Everyone was staring, frozen with astonishment.

Subbalakshmi rose, and was about to move back to her place when the prince, perhaps thinking that she had not understood what was expected of her, stepped forward again, smiling with great charm as he again proffered his hand.

Subbalakshmi bowed again. She pressed her palms together once more, this time murmuring an almost inaudible namaskaram.

The Prince again moved back. Then, as Subbalakshmi stood up he came forward for the third time. He was about to offer her his hand once more when, it seemed to the watchers, understanding dawned. As Subbalakshmi bowed the Prince of Wales, too, pressed his palms together, bowing as he did so, and returned, in perfect Indian fashion, the greeting he had been offered.

Everyone was enchanted. By next morning, when the story had already got around, the whole city was talking about Sister Subbalakshmi. Everybody knew that, although some of her friends and relatives were supporters of the Indian National Congress, she herself had never had anything whatever to do with political affairs. Yet she had made a supremely nationalist gesture, and the Prince's response, so Miss Prager said when she described this incident in one of her letters to me, had changed some of his critics into sympathetic admirers.

"However did you think of doing such a thing?" Sister was asked.

She seemed to find the question strange. "It is the proper way of expressing respect," she answered in a matter of fact, almost casual tone, "to a prince of the royal house and recognizing the divinity of kings." Then the warmth came back into her voice, and she added on a more emphatic note, "Besides, I would *never* touch the hand of a gentleman!"

"Pray, Sister Subbalakshmi, what is the meaning of this?" Mrs Drysdale demanded one day in the hard, cold voice of authority.

She was seated behind her desk, looking distant and formidable. A newspaper was spread out in front of her. She pushed it across. "You had better read it before you answer."

Sister took the paper. One of the columns had been outlined in red pencil. It contained a report of a political meeting held under the auspices of the Indian National Congress. The last sentence stated "Mrs Subbalakshmi also spoke."

She looked up, feeling a spurt of anger rise within her as she met Mrs Drysdale's icy glance. "Do you think," she asked, "that I am the only Mrs Subbalakshmi in this city?"

"It was not you."

"Most certainly not."

Mrs Drysdale apologized. Her sympathies were still, as they had been ever since she came to India, with the nationalist cause. As a government servant she had always been careful to avoid expressing any of her opinions on public affairs to people outside her own circle of intimate friends ... Now, when the government was doing everything possible to suppress the nationalist movement, silence was more essential than ever. She, like Subbalakshmi, was not concerned about her own future. But it would, as they had often said to each other, be very foolish to jeopardize the work they were doing. They, like Mahatma Gandhi and the other Congress leaders, were devoting all their energies to the struggle for freedom. Both were perfectly clear in their own minds that the political liberty which the politicians were demanding would be of little value unless the people of India, and especially its women, were free to develop their individual capacities, to profit by education, and to choose for themselves how they would use their lives.

The girls at the Ice House were making their own choice.

Gita, who at one time had seemed doomed to endless misfortunes, had made hers, and in a way which surprised everybody, and Sister most of all.

"My dear," Sister had said to her when the results of the secondary school leaving examination were announced, "we are all very happy that you have done so well."

Gita listened, gravely attentive, while Sister explained that she would be eligible for a scholarship and a maintenance stipend at Queen Mary's College. When she had taken her degree she would have to spend a year qualifying herself to be a teacher. After that she would be able to earn enough to help her sister when she too went to the university.

When Sister had finished there was a short silence.

"Sister," Gita said to her at last, "you know that I can never be sufficiently grateful to you for all that you have done for us …"

"My dear, don't speak of it!"

"I must speak of it." Gita's manner seemed a little anxious, as if she were afraid of saying something which might hurt. "I don't want," she continued, "to become a teacher."

It was almost unbelievable, so unbelievable that Sister did not know what to say.

"I made up my mind a long time ago," Gita said into the silence, her voice gathering firmness as she went on. "I intend to be a doctor."

"A doctor?"

"Yes. It was my father's wish, also. We used to discuss my future when I visited him in the hospital. Before he died I promised him that as soon as I was old enough I would begin to study medicine."

Sister was still looking at the girl, no longer with disbelief, but with growing amazement. She did not feel angry or disappointed that Gita had never once spoken of her ambition. On the contrary, she was filled with admiration both for the girl's restraint and the enduring strength of her resolution.

She said, "I wish I could help you, but I am afraid that what you want is utterly out of the question." At this time there were, Sister was quite certain, no scholarships to medical colleges generous enough to cover living expenses as well as fees. She told Gita this. "Who do you think is going to be able to help you to undergo such a long and costly training?"

"That," Gita answered quietly but firmly, "has already been arranged."

"What do you mean?"

"My father, when he was on his deathbed, told me that my husband's family had been good enough to promise to provide for my future. He said that when the time came and I needed the money I had only to ask for it and that they would certainly keep their word."

Sister had never yet heard of the parents-in-law of a child widow behaving with such generosity. The story was almost too much for her to believe. Yet Gita was a truthful girl, and not in the least given to fantasy.

So she questioned patiently, hoping that Gita might not be mistaken.

The girl seemed quite certain of her facts. Her father had told her that her husband's parents had been given a substantial sum as dowry. Later, when Gita's husband died and her father went to offer his condolences to the bereaved family he also asked them to make some provision for the young widow. They were generous, at any rate in intention. They gave an undertaking that Gita should be given, during the lifetime of her father-in-law, the sum of eight thousand rupees. When she needed the money, she had only to ask for it.

"What," Sister asked, "is the name of your father-in-law?"

"I don't know."

Gita had been so young when she married that it was quite possible that she had never known it. Her dying father had not thought to tell her, and it had not occurred to her to ask.

"Your husband's name?"

"I can't remember."

"So how do you think we are to find these people and claim the money?' Sister's tone as she asked the question was not impatient. Now that the poor girl was, almost certainly, about to suffer a disappointment which would determine the whole course of her life it would be cruel to speak to her unkindly.

"We must find them," Gita said. It was as if her dream had seized her so completely that she was living it, far removed from reality.

"Can you remember the name of anyone who might have been connected with your husband's family?"

"I..."

"Just try to think."

The girl was silent for a long time. Then, at last, a name came back to her. It was a fairly common one, so common that unless Gita could remember the initials which preceded it – and of course she could not – there seemed almost no chance of identifying the right person. However, Subbalakshmi's cousin Krishnaswami was still the superintendent of police in the town in which he and Gita's father had become friends. If anyone could help, he was the man to do it.

Living in the World

Sister wrote to him.

Krishnaswami replied that he was fairly sure of the man's identity, though he had never known him well. He had made enquiries and had learned that he was now living at Coimbatore. Unfortunately, it had not been possible to find anyone who knew his address.

Sister was doing her best to prepare Gita for an almost inevitable disappointment. Yet she found that she herself was being infected by the girl's calm certainty. Since little Indu had turned out to be so lucky, why, she asked herself, should not Gita be equally fortunate?

She wrote to the stranger, setting out all that the girl had told her. Then, as she addressed the envelope, she was again seized by misgivings. Coimbatore was a growing industrial town, and many strangers had settled in it during the last few years. How could a letter addressed to one of them, and bearing no street name or house number, conceivably be expected to reach its destination?

Miraculously, it did.

Just twenty four hours after it was posted Sister Subbalakshmi received a telegram from Gita's father-in-law. He and his wife were leaving for Madras that night.

They reached Ice House next morning. Sister could see at a glance that all that Gita had been told about them by her father was true. When Gita entered the room, her mother-in-law was moved to tears at the sight of the beautiful girl who, if things had been different, would have been the mother of her grandchildren.

Her husband agreed that the promise to Gita's father had certainly been made. It would be kept. If the money was needed now, the whole sum would be realized in cash and paid within a week.

It was, and that autumn Gita was able to enrol as a student at the Lady Hardinge Medical College in Delhi.

It was wonderful to have been able to help Gita. It was better still to be able to feel sure, as Subbalakshmi did, that almost every girl who left the Ice House would, when she went out into the world, devote her energies towards making India a finer country for women and children to live in.

There had been many changes in these past few years, but the pace, Subbalakshmi felt, was far too slow. For a long time now she had been asking herself what more she could do. At first, there had seemed to be no answer. Yet now, she slowly began to realize, she was doing more. The question was answering itself.

In May 1918, before the war ended, Subbalakshmi and her mother had been invited to attend a conference on social problems at the ancient temple city of Conjeevaram, about forty miles west of Madras. Most of those present were Congressmen who were also social reformers and the sessions were presided over by Mrs Sarojini Naidu. Subbalakshmi found the conference a stimulating, but in some ways disagreeable experience. The delegates argued so violently on some of the resolutions which were put to them that pandemonium broke out and it almost seemed that they would come to blows. Mrs Naidu had needed all her famous charm and oratorical gifts to persuade gentlemen who should have known better to behave like civilized beings.

Only a few ladies had attended the conference. To many people it seemed remarkable that any should have done so. In fact, at that time educated women had already begun to demand a voice in the conduct of public affairs. Mrs Annie Besant, whom many people regarded as a foster mother of the nationalist movement, had already served a term as president of the Congress. One of her followers, Mrs Margaret Cousins, who was Irish, a suffragette and a Theosophist, had taken a leading part in founding the Women's Indian Association in 1917. A deputation from the Association led by Mrs Naidu, had called on Mr Montagu during his stay in Madras, and had presented him with an address in which they asked that Indian women should be granted the same political rights as men.

If, the address continued, these rights were to be exercised wisely, the educational system would have to be reformed. Only one Indian village out of every six possessed any kind of school. Of every hundred boys in the country only thirteen received any education, and out of every hundred girls only one. Compulsory and free primary education for both boys and girls should be introduced as soon as possible. To achieve this, there must be a big increase in the number of training colleges for women teachers. Widows' homes should be established in every part of the country, and scholarships granted to widows and others who were willing to be trained for the teaching profession.

Montagu's diary gives the impression that he regarded the members of the deputation as processional agitators, too unrepresentative to be taken seriously.

He was mistaken. Some, it was true, were active in politics, but the views they expressed had been endorsed by the rank-and-file members of many women's organizations, including the Sarada Ladies' Union. The leaders of the deputation, Mrs Naidu, Mrs Besant and Mrs Cousins, knew, from firsthand experience, what they were talking about. Their hopes for the future were based on achievements which they had witnessed for themselves. All of them had watched the fantastic progress of the illiterate and semi-literate children who had entered the Ice House and who, after only a few months, had been able to compete in the Triplicane high school, with some of the most fortunate girls of their own age.

During the next few years the members of the Women's Indian Association struggled hard, and with more success than most of them had dared to hope, to obtain full political rights for women. Under the new constitution, which came into effect in 1920, women were not given the vote directly. Instead, members of the provincial legislatures were given the power to confer votes on women if they thought fit. The Madras Legislative Council was the first to do so.

That was in March 1921.

The new power which had been conferred on the women of the Madras Presidency, Mrs Annie Besant pointed out, was not, in fact, an innovation, but a return to an ancient tradition. Her study of old records had, she declared, proved that in the past women had not merely voted in the elections to the panchayats, the village councils, but had served on village committees, including, in at least one instance, the committee which administered justice.

Although Sister Subbalakshmi was, as a government servant, debarred from taking part in the political agitations conducted by the Women's Indian Association, it seemed to her that it should nevertheless be possible to help forward many of the reforms which were of special concern to women voters. Leaders of the Association were, from time to time, invited to address members of the Sarada Ladies' Union. The weekly meetings were usually crowded. Many of the members, Miss Prager told me in one of her letters, were so avid for knowledge that they would ask to be allowed to come to the school and sit in classes with the girls and join them in their studies. They learned to formulate their ideas clearly, and to address small audiences without getting into a flutter. As they gained confidence they began to lose the fear of expressing unpopular opinions.

Sister was sometimes asked to speak at meetings of other organizations. Whenever she could find the time she did so. During the early twenties that was not very often. Looking after her girls seemed to take most of her time.

In July 1922, Miss Prager had been promoted, and went away to be assistant inspector in the Southern Circle, the region in which Miss Lynch had first begun her activities. In future, she would no doubt visit Madras fairly often, but neither Sister nor the girls could bear to think that she would not be with them every day. Miss Ryan, who was to succeed her as superintendent of what was soon to be the Lady Willingdon School, was pleasant and competent. Everybody liked her, but nobody could believe that she would ever become as completely one of themselves as Miss Prager had been.

The Lady Willingdon High School was opened in December 1922. It was, though nobody guessed it at the time, Mrs Drysdale's last achievement in Madras. Six months later, in May 1923, she went to England, intending to take two years' leave. By now, everybody knew that although Mrs Drysdale had sometimes seemed to be made of granite, her heart was as warm as summer in Madras, and her stony seeming exterior really had a precious, diamond like hardness which could cut through every kind of obstruction when she had a worthwhile end to achieve. Chitti and Sister and the rest talked about how much she would be missed, how quickly the next two years would pass and how very much everyone would look forward to the day of her return.

She did not come back. She was greatly missed. The nationwide chain of homes for young widows which the members of the Women's Indian Association had envisaged in 1917 might very possibly have come into existence if Mrs Drysdale had remained in the Indian Public Service. As it was, the few hostels which already existed continued to do good work, but their number did not increase.

During the mid 'twenties opposition to the institution of child marriage was growing steadily.

Gandhi had given the movement his support. The marriage of children, he declared had not the sanction of holy writ. Orthodox priests and pundits disagreed. "According to the Hindu sastras," a South Indian purohit wrote, "a girl should be married before she attains puberty. If the husband of a girl fails to have sexual intercourse with her just after puberty, he will be considered to have been guilty of killing the child in its embryonic stage …"

The British had always been reluctant to interfere with the religious beliefs and customs of their subjects. In 1828, the governor general, Lord William Cavendish Bentinck, had prohibited Sati in the face of most determined opposition from his official advisers. Indian opponents challenged the decision in the courts, but their claim that widow burning should be permitted as a religious ritual was rejected. Inspectors were appointed to see that the law was obeyed. In most parts of British India widow burning rapidly died out.

Legislation designed to curb the far more widespread practice of child marriage was both limited in scope and half-heartedly administered. An Act of 1891 had prohibited the consummation of marriages before the bride was twelve years old. The law was seldom enforced. Thirty years later very few people other than lawyers even knew that it existed. Even if they had, enforcement, it was generally acknowledged, would have been difficult to secure.

In most parts of India, child marriages were common among Hindus of all castes and also, except in North West Frontier Province, among Muslims. In Bhopal, sixty three per cent of Hindu girls and almost fifty two per cent of Muslims were married before their fifteenth birthday, very many of them while they were still tiny tots. The situation in most other parts of British India was not much better. It was only on the North West Frontier and in the Madras Presidency – where seventy five per cent of marriages took place after the bride's fifteenth birthday – that child marriages were the exception rather than the rule.

For years, reformers had been demanding new and more effective legislation for the protection of girls. At last, in 1925, the Government of India raised the age of consent – the age at which a girl might be considered capable of rational consent to sexual intercourse – to fourteen for single girls and to thirteen for those who were married. It was seen evident that the new law was just as ineffective as the Act of 1891 had been. It was doubtful, disappointed reformers declared, whether even one person in every hundred thousand was aware that this Act existed while the few who did felt that they could afford to ignore it.

The government, critics argued, had been timidly concerned to avoid giving offence to the most rigid and reactionary upholders of orthodoxy. It was for Indians themselves to demonstrate that more sweeping reforms were not merely needed but wanted.

"Where," Gandhi asked, on 7 October, 1926, "are the brave women who will work among the girl-wives and girl-widows, and who will take no rest and leave none for men until girl-marriage becomes an impossibility?"

The answer, of course, was that they were already hard at work.

The few women of Subbalakshmi's generation who had been educated and trained for entry into the professions were now mature, experienced, and still in the prime of life. They were winning, with the help and support of progressive minded men, their full rights as citizens. Sometimes they found that men were challenging them to advance more boldly and in new directions.

One such challenge was offered in 1926 by a British official, Bengal's Director of Public Instruction. "You have asserted yourselves," he began, "in the field of politics. How long is it to be before you assert yourselves in the field of secondary and higher education? How long are you going to tolerate a manmade syllabus, a manmade examination, and a controlling power in which women have no authority as the dominating arbiter of your educational destinies? ... I would urge that women, who alone can help us adequately, should tell us what they want, and keep on telling us until they get it."

This met with a prompt response from the leaders of the Women's Indian Association. They would, they announced, organize a conference, small but widely representative, to work out a detailed programme for the education of the girls and women. The delegates – fifty at most – should all be experts in the fields of education, medicine or social work, and each of them should be elected by regional conferences at which, it was hoped, housewives and mothers would express their views and help them to frame resolutions for the consideration of the experts. The project had the support of Viscountess Goschen and other British women who could not conceivably be suspected of doing or saying anything which the Government of India might regard as politically undesirable. The conference, it was decided, should be held in Poona where Dr D D Karve was developing a women's university, and it was to be presided over by the Maharani Gaekwar of Baroda, whose husband's State had made remarkable advances in the education of women and girls.

So when Sister Subbalakshmi was asked to help with the organization of preparatory meetings in the Madras Presidency, she agreed at once.

During the summer holidays of 1926, she addressed gatherings of women both in Madras city and in rural areas, and presided over a big conference in Coimbatore. Most of the women in her audiences had never before attended a public meeting of any kind. They came chiefly because they wanted to see and hear Sister Subbalakshmi, whose name they all knew. Some had young relatives to whom the Ice House was at least as dear as the homes in which they had spent their infancy. Other had daughters who were attending school in their native towns and villages and whose teachers had been Sister Subbalakshmi's pupils. There were some, too, who were acquainted with young girls who had run away from their families and had reached Madras, heaven knows how, to seek Sister's help and protection.

They were surprised to discover that Sister was in many ways so much like themselves, simple, modest and homely. Although she was said to speak English perfectly she did not, unlike most educated men, allow a single word of the language to pass her lips when she was talking to people who only understood Tamil. It was evident that she was deeply religious, and her manner showed her to be everything that a brahmin lady should be. If it seemed to her right, as it evidently did, that widows should not be disfigured and should dress like other people, then her opinion was to be respected and, if courage could be found to do so, her action copied.

She was echoing the thoughts and experiences of most of them when she declared that girlhood was simply not allowed to exist among the brahmins. Nearly every woman who listened to her had been flung from childhood into motherhood before her body had reached maturity and before she had learned that she had a soul of her own. Some, when they married, had become the playthings of boys as ignorant as themselves, and others the victims of elderly men for whom they could feel nothing but cowering dread. How, Sister asked them, could it be expected that children born of such unfortunate parents could grow up into healthy, energetic men and women? How different, she exclaimed, India would be if all children went to school and were educated to become good citizens and wise parents! It could happen if people would revive the traditions of ancient times, when child marriages were unknown. To plead for the education of girls would be meaningless if children were not allowed to remain single until they reached maturity. No girl, Sister was convinced, should marry before the age of eighteen.

Everyone recognized that a conference on educational reform would defeat its purpose if it did not tackle the question of child marriage, and the issue was discussed at every one of the twenty two regional conferences which were held in different parts of the country. At the Madras conference, held in mid October, Sister Subbalakshmi, who took the chair, was elected as one of the delegates to be sent to Poona in January.

About two thousand women attended the public sessions of the conference as visitors. They felt, since this was the first national conference of Indian women which had ever been held, that they were making history.

Subbalakshmi, rather to her consternation, discovered that she was famous. She had never thought of herself as a leader. But now, as the delegates settled down to sort out and consolidate the great variety of resolutions which had been submitted by regional conferences, she could not keep silent. She was surprised to find that her resolution on the necessity of moral training in schools aroused fierce opposition.

"Religious and moral instruction," she told her fellow delegates, "are really one and the same thing. There is an eternal struggle going on in everyone to attain the unknown by noble thoughts and good deeds. It is the attainment of this higher self, or god, which is the true aim of education. One side of man's nature is always dragging him down and chaining him to lower things. It is the aim of every being to free himself from these chains." Older children, she continued, perhaps remembering what her father and Uncle Euclid had said to her long ago, should make a study of the different religions of the world so as to develop, as they grew up, a broad outlook. Nothing should be forced on them. The teaching of religion and morals should be planned to help girls, and boys too, to develop themselves.

As Subbalakshmi sat down, another delegate rose to her feet. The resolution, was, she declared heatedly, an insult to teachers. Good teachers could not fail to produce a moral atmosphere, but to attempt to teach morality as a subject was farcical. The home was the proper place for religious teaching. Besides, Sister Subbalakshmi's proposal would, if accepted by the conference, embarrass the government. It must be rejected.

Five other delegates spoke in a similar vein, but when the resolution was put to the conference only four voted against it, and it was carried by an overwhelming majority.

The only other resolution on which the delegates were unable to achieve unanimity was that which recommended that English should be taught compulsorily as a second language in all higher elementary and secondary schools. The opponents were mainly Congress supporters, who repeated views which Gandhi had been expressing for at least twenty years. English, they insisted, was foreign to the Indian temperament and quite unfitted to become the common language of the Indian people. The national language of the people of India was, they continued, Hindi and Hindi, not English, should be taught compulsorily to all children who had not learned it at home as their mother tongue.

Tempers rose.

"But for English," one speaker pointed out, "we should

not be here today understanding one another."

That was undeniable. The women who had attended the regional conference had employed, beside English, at least ten Indian languages. English was the cement, and when the resolution was put to the vote the advocates of Hindi were defeated by twenty one votes to fifteen.

Morals and languages were minor, or at any rate subsidiary, questions. On the big issues that were dividing Indian public opinion, the delegates were united. A member of the Legislative Assembly in Delhi, Sir Hari Singh Gour, was planning to introduce a Bill to raise the age of consent to sixteen. The delegates agreed unanimously that the Women's Indian Association should sponsor a nationwide propaganda campaign in support of the measure and also to demand that the government should introduce legislation to prohibit the marriage of any girl before her eighteenth birthday.

They then settled down to work out details of all the educational reforms, at every level from primary school to university which they wished to see. Their recommendations, based both on the wishes of parents and experiences which many of the delegates had had as teachers, were comprehensive, imaginative and sometimes daring. It would, these women realized, take many years, perhaps longer than the remaining lifetime of any of them, to gain what they wanted. But they had chalked out a programme, and each one would do whatever was in her power to ensure its fulfilment.

When Subbalakshmi got back to Madras she received an official warning. If she continued to take part in the activities of the Women's Indian Association, she would be required to resign her posts as superintendent of the Ice House Hostel and as headmistress of the Lady Willingdon Training College.

Sister could not possibly leave her pupils. Nor could she even dream of leaving the Ice House. But to stop campaigning for the abolition of child marriage was even more unthinkable. If she could not speak on the platforms of the Women's Indian Association, she would continue to do so under other auspices. She would not always be a government servant, and when she was free she would do as she liked.

Dr Muthulakshmi Reddy had been nominated to the Madras Legislative Council, and her fellow legislators had elected her as their vice president. Many of them, though not all, accepted her views. Madras, like the rest of India, was sharply divided.

Sir Hari Singh Gour's Age of Consent Bill was still being considered when another member of the Central Legislature, Rai Sahab Harbilas Sarda, introduced a Bill to prohibit the marriages of Hindu girls who were under the age of fourteen, and of boys under eighteen, and to invalidate such marriages if they were celebrated in defiance of law. The Bill was referred to a Select Committee, whose members refused to endorse the proposal to invalidate premature marriages and recommended, instead, the imposition of fines to be paid by parents, guardians and priests.

While reformers and upholders of orthodoxy were arguing over these proposals, foreigners were stirring world public opinion. The most widely known was an American woman, Katherine Mayo, whose book *Mother India* drew a lurid picture of the horrors of child marriage, premature motherhood, the exuberant sexual vitality of Indian men and boys and the general physical feebleness of the Indian people. Gandhi, who described the book as "a drain inspector's report'" warned British and American readers against believing that Miss Mayo had presented a true and complete picture of the state of affairs. But, he wrote, it was a book which every Indian could read with some degree of profit. "We may," he continued, "repudiate the substance underlying many of the allegations she has made."

At the time when this article appeared, Subbalakshmi and the members of Sarada Ladies' Union had already launched what was eventually to become the biggest and most successful of all their enterprises. This was the Sarada Vidyalaya, which was opened on 1 July, 1927.

During recent years there had been more applicants for admission to the Widows' Home than it was possible to accept. The Madras Government, far from being willing to open a second home, had reduced the number of widows' scholarships. Clever girls were often rejected because their parents could not contribute towards their maintenance, and backward young women now had little chance of being educated and trained to earn their own livelihoods.

The girls who had been brought to Sister when the Widows' Home was first beginning to grow were happily and usefully employed. Now, when people all over India were awakening to the need for more schools and more teachers, it was intolerable that girls who were just as promising should be denied similar opportunities.

They were not all widows. Some had been deserted by their husbands and a few were single. Those whose parents could afford to pay for them were able to become boarders at the Sarada Home. The Home was of course, self-supporting, but Subbalakshmi had always felt unhappy when she had found herself obliged to turn away girls who were eager to study but who had no relatives who were able to or willing to pay the little that was needed to maintain them. Nothing, it was clear, could be expected from the government.

Sister proposed to the members of the Sarada Ladies' Union that they should open an educational institution – a vidyalaya – of their own to train backward but intelligent and promising girls and young women for the teaching profession. Four years, Sister had learned from experience, was long enough to transform an illiterate, or almost illiterate, girl into a well informed, disciplined young woman, capable of teaching children up to the higher class in the elementary schools. When, at the end of their training, these young teachers went home they would, with the assistance of their parents and friends, be able to open their own schools.

The plan was enthusiastically accepted. The members of the Ladies' Union agreed to form an education committee, in which any lady who was prepared to contribute rupees three a month towards the cost of maintaining the vidyalaya would be welcome as a member.

The wealthier members gave generously. A house was rented in Triplicane, near the Sarada Home. Twelve girls were accepted as residents – five brahmins, six non-brahmins and one from an untouchable community. The parents of six of them were able to contribute a little towards the cost of the daughters' board and lodging, while the remainder were too poor to pay anything.

At first, all the teaching was done by volunteers. Subbalakshmi and her sisters gave every hour they could spare to the vidyalaya, and a number of other trained and gifted women sacrificed most of their leisure to help with the work.

Donations continued to arrive, some of them from old students of the Widows' Home who wanted to help others towards the successes which they themselves were now enjoying. When autumn came, it was decided to allow girls whose homes were in the city to attend as day scholars. Parents who could afford it were asked to pay a tuition fee of rupees three per month. The poor paid nothing, and no girl was turned away as long as she seemed capable of benefiting from the opportunities which the vidyalaya had to offer.

The institution grew fast. At the end of its first year the girls from the Sarada Home came to live under the same roof, bringing the total number of pupils to rather more than one hundred. They were of all ages and classes. The oldest, who was about thirty, was the daughter of a rich and noble family and had come to be trained to do social service. A dozen or so were aged between twenty and thirty. Most were still children. Nearly all of them, Sister felt confident, would be allowed to remain single until they had completed their secondary education, and many would not marry until they had spent three or four years at a university.

Meanwhile, the fate of the two bills which had been introduced into the legislature in Delhi was still undecided. Reformers were impatient while opponents of the measures were vociferous, fearful and angry. The government, pressed hard by both sides, had to do something.

In June 1928 it appointed a committee.

The Age of Consent Committee, as it was officially termed, was presided over by Sir Moropant Vishwanath Joshi, who had served as home minister of the government of United Provinces. All his colleagues, except for a British woman doctor, were Indians. Two were judges. Four were eminent lawyers. One was Mrs Rameswari Nehru, whose nephew was to be the first prime minister of free India.

They did their work with great thoroughness. They spent months travelling, visiting every part of India, and interviewing some four hundred witnesses. They reached Madras City in November 1928, and the evidence which they collected during their visit filled more than five hundred pages of small print.

Sister Subbalakshmi's evidence was crucially important. Her belief that education was one of the surest means of preventing early marriages was constantly being fortified by experience. On the very day before she was called before the committee, she was visited by a gentlemen who brought his two little girls, aged twelve and thirteen, with him. If, he said, Sister would take them into the vidyalaya, he would willingly promise to postpone their marriages for five or six years. At the end of that time there should be no difficulty in finding them suitable husbands. Parents of boys were beginning to realize that an educated wife, far from being a liability, was a precious asset.

Generally speaking, Sister wrote in the memorandum which she prepared for the committee, the age at which marriages took place was at last beginning to rise. This was partly because people in the South were developing a new outlook, partly because it was impossible for the parents of girls to satisfy demands for big dowries and expensive wedding gifts. The next step forward, she urged should be prohibition by law of all marriages where the bride was below the age of sixteen. "Personally," she added, "I have more faith in the progress of social propaganda. But for the welfare of the people laws are absolutely essential. Even though the mass of the people may feel that these laws are unjust at present, in the course of time and with the spread of education, *especially among women,* they will begin *to appreciate and abide* by these laws willingly."

Sister had, she told the members of the Committee when she met them, come across at least half a dozen cases during the past two or three years of girls whose marriages had been consummated in their eleventh year. Other witness had similar experiences. "I know of a case," wrote one of Sister's colleagues, the headmistress of the Government Secondary and Training School at Cuddalore, "where the girl attained maturity in her tenth year, and gave birth to her first baby in her eleventh year. It was stillborn. She gave birth to a second and a third and a fourth in her twelfth, thirteenth and fourteenth years respectively, all stillborn likewise. The husband was healthy. The mother was healthy too, except that she was very puny."

Medical witnesses working in different parts of the country agreed in contradicting the common belief that Indian girls reached puberty at a much earlier age than girls in the West. The average difference was about a year, certainly not more. Several women doctors had reported cases in which little girls had become insane as a result of the shock and agony of childbearing. All over the Madras Presidency, Sister told the members of the committee, were tens of thousands of young mothers of fourteen or fifteen, who besides looking after babies, were expected to do all the domestic work of the households in which they lived and who were constantly chided and scolded if they did not satisfy every whim of their husbands and parents-in-law. In the old days it had been customary for girls to go to the homes of their parents to be confined and they would often remain there for as long as a year after each of their children was born. Nowadays, so Sister Subbalakshmi told, young wives were often forced to return to the homes of their parents-in-law as soon as their babies were a month old. Before many weeks passed they would find that they were pregnant again.

They often miscarried. Sister knew, she said, a number of girls of fourteen and fifteen who, forced into premature motherhood, had as many as three or four abortions in a single year. Many babies who were born alive did not live for more than a few days. According to the official records, more than seven per cent of the babies who had been born in Madras city during the year 1926 died before they were ten days old. Altogether, more than a quarter – 279.3 out of every 1000 – did not survive until their first birthday.

People often said that the custom of child marriage had grown as a result of the Muslim conquest of India, though in the south the conquest had never been complete. Whatever its historical origin, the survival of the custom, Sister believed, was due to the desire to protect young girls in the big mixed households of the typical joint family. The danger that an unmarried girl might be seduced by one of her male relatives arose, she insisted, only when girls had no interests of their own. "If they are given education and made to move in a better atmosphere," she continued, "they will not go wrong at all." For no reason whatsoever could early marriages be condoned or justified.

"Do you," the chairman of the Committee asked her, "belong to the Theosophical Society?"

"No." It was important that the question should be asked and the answer should be recorded in the official transcript of evidence. People who were as forthright in their demand for the abolition of child marriage as Sister Subbalakshmi had shown herself to be were constantly being accused by their opponents of being cranks, Theosophists and social reformers.

"Have you," Sir Moropant persisted, "ever declared yourself to be a social reformer?"

"No."

This was the answer which most of the members of the Committee, and perhaps all of them, wanted to hear. When the time came for them to present their report it would be important to be able to demonstrate that Hindus who accepted and followed most of the traditional customs of their faith were as much in favour of this particular reform as those who called themselves social reformers and who, it was often alleged, wanted to destroy Hinduism itself.

"May I take it," asked Mr A Ramaswami Mudaliar, "that in the Widows' Home orthodoxy is observed to some extent?"

He was a Madrasi and a leader of the non-brahmins. Subbalakshmi suspected, mistakenly, that the question was a trick, designed to elicit some statement which might damage her activities in the future. "Orthodoxy," she replied cagily, " is observed to satisfy all parties, and to that extent only."

"May I take it," Mr Ramaswami Mudaliar went on, "that you will not wilfully violate anything that orthodoxy sets much store by?"

Sister, obstinately truthful, was still trying to evade the trap which she fancied to be there. "These," she replied coldly, "are minor points. We are trying to get a wider and more liberal outlook on things."

The questioner became more explicit. "We have been told," he reminded Sister, "that only interested social reformers are interested in this reform. May I take it that you are neither a social reformer nor a Theosophist, but you represent orthodox opinion?"

She ignored the first part of the question, perhaps because she had answered it already. "I myself have tried," she told Mr Ramaswami Mudaliar, "to define orthodoxy, but I have not been able to do it."

"I mean," he explained, "orthodoxy as generally understood. Do people, for example, look on you as a heterodox person, out to ruin existing institutions? Do you inter dine with people of your community?"

This was a key question. A strictly orthodox Hindu would not only refuse to eat in the company of anyone of a different caste, but a brahmin would refuse to sit down to a meal with a fellow brahmin who was not a member of the same sub sect as himself.

"I have been keeping orthodox customs," Sister at last conceded. But her conception of orthodoxy had begun to change. She added, "We not only interdine. We intermarry also."

She had already made it plain, in her memorandum, that her views were based not only on her own experiences but on what she believed to be the correct interpretation of the original teachings of her faith. "According to the Hindu religion," she had written, "marriage and consummation of marriage would come very late in life. According to the ashrama dharma, every boy and girl should lead a brahmachari life" – life of chastity and concentrated attention on learning – "during their studentship. If the Hindu religion be followed to the letter, marriages will be ideal and perfectly satisfactory. All the present troubles have come because we are not following what has been laid down in the ancient books."

She was, she pointed out, not alone in this opinion. Scholars who considered themselves to be orthodox differed widely in their views as to the nature of the marriage customs sanctified by holy writ. Sister, replying to the question of the members of the Committee, quoted several eminent authorities in support of her own interpretation. The Right Honourable Srinivasa Sastri, who had not only been a member of the Imperial War Cabinet, but was acknowledged by everybody to be a man of great learning, had collected a number of authorities to support the view that young women as well as young men should undergo a prolonged period of study before they entered married life.

"Do you mean," asked a Muslim member of the Committee "that according to Hindu religion girls should remain unmarried up to twenty five?"

"That," Sister Subbalakshmi answered firmly, "is the ideal thing."

It was also, of course, much further than the members of the Committee were prepared to go. In fact, Sister would have been fairly satisfied if they had recommended as a first step that the marriage of any girl under sixteen should be forbidden.

When the Report appeared, in June 1929, she was disappointed. The committee recommended that the minimum age of marriage for girls should be fixed at fourteen. At the same time, they proposed, it should be made an offence – to be called "marital misbehaviour" – for a husband to have sexual relations with his wife before her fifteenth birthday. It was also recommended that for unmarried girls the age of consent should be raised to eighteen.

Although the report failed to satisfy many reformers, it was greeted by howls of anger from the orthodox, who condemned the Committee's recommendations as wicked and dangerous. "By legislation against the wishes of the Madras orthodox brahmins," a Madrasi brahmin threatened, "you do the greatest injury to yourselves. India would become a constant prey to earthquakes, hurricanes and many other disasters, like the countries of the West ... Some say that child marriages cause only widowhood. I say that widowhood is not caused by child marriages, but by those child widows having acted against their husbands in previous births. Adultery, teasing, et cetera might have been the cause. If anybody says that widowhood is only a chance happening, I am sure he is a rank atheist and will have the wrath of god upon his head. Child widowhood is horrible, no doubt, but it is the effect of the wrath of god upon man. If the brahmins were given a separate world to live in, free from the interference of others whose religion is no religion, it would be better ..."

"I am still," Sister remarked to me one day, "an excellent sleeper. Perhaps that is part of my good fortune."

"Or your good conscience?"

She laughed. She had never, it seemed, had any trouble with her conscience. "When I lived at the Ice House," she went on, "I used to go to bed at nine, fall asleep at once, and wake at five." Her eyes lit with a sudden flash of recollection. "One evening I took a group of girls up to the third floor veranda just before dark. We watched the sun go down and the stars come out and presently started naming the constellations and the planets. We were all enjoying ourselves so much that the time went by without our noticing it. Then, when we decided that it was time to go indoors, we found that the girls who had been studying in the room inside had locked the door and turned off the lights. They had evidently forgotten all about us when they went downstairs to have their supper. We weren't worried, because we knew the girls would come upstairs again as soon as they had finished. After about half an hour the lights in the room behind us went on again. So I tapped at the window. The girls inside drew back the curtains, but it was so dark outside that they couldn't see anything. They didn't recognize our voices and they were perfectly terrified."

She was laughing again, reliving the experience. "They ran out of the room and rushed down the stairs to call the watchman. He came up with the gardeners. These big strong men thought we were robbers. The more we shouted the more frightened they got, until at last we began to think that that we should have to stay outside until morning."

"But you didn't?'

"No. It was that brave, bold woman, Chitti, who came and rescued us."

Chitti was her help and support in everything she did. When, one morning at daybreak, a thief was spied sitting at the top of a palm tree helping himself to coconuts, it was Chitti who ran to get a length of rope and coiled it around the bottom of the trunk so that the fellow was trapped when he reached the ground. He begged for mercy, pleading that his wife and children were starving, and that if he were sent to prison they would die of hunger. Chitti and Sister agreed to forgive him, and his children were taken into the fisherfolks' school. The girl whom Chitti caught keeping a midnight assignation with a boyfriend in one of the outhouses was not forgiven. She was sent home and nobody ever spoke of her again.

Chitti slept in the entrance hall, at the top of the portico stairs. The slightest sound would wake her. Yet when the sun rose she was always as fresh as the morning, and though there was now the vidyalaya as well as the Ice House to mange, nothing ever seemed to tire her.

The vidyalaya continued to grow fast. In 1929, Sister, with the help of the members of the Ladies' Union, opened a model elementary school, which was attached to the vidyalaya and at which trainee students could practise. The hostel was moved to a much bigger house. It was, it soon appeared, not big enough. Before the year 1929 was over, applicants for admission were being turned away because it was impossible to find room for them.

Sister accepted everyone whom she possibly could. One was the daughter of an unemployed cook. Her father had borrowed rupees three hundred – about twenty five pounds sterling – to provide a dowry. Soon after her marriage, the girl had gone to live in her parent-in-law's household. There, she had found out that her husband already had three other wives, two of whom were living with him. He and his parents and the two senior wives treated the newcomer with extreme cruelty. For some months she suffered in silence. Then her husband told her that he had no more use for her, and that she must go away. Now, in the vidyalaya, she was learning fast and looking forward to the day when she would become a teacher.

From all over the Madras Presidency people wrote to Sister Subbalakshmi, pleading with her to help their women relatives. "I have a sister with seven children," one such letter began. "Her husband, a petty schoolmaster getting rupees thirty per mensem, passed away without leaving a single pie, and I don't know what to do with this widowed sister and her seven children who are intelligent…"

"For the sake of a dowry," another wrote, "a young man came and married our daughter. Being a graduate we felt confident our daughter will be happy with him, so we did not mind giving a big dowry, an amount which was all our savings. After the marriage, the man coolly says that he wanted only our money and not our daughter, as he is living with another woman."

Scarcely a week passed, often not even a day, without some desperate plea for help. To Sister, the young widows were, as they had always been, the most tragically pitiable of all. "In the family," she wrote at this time, "they are surrounded by people enjoying worldly pleasures which are denied to them. Often they are led astray by some male relative … When her shame cannot be hidden, she may go and drown herself. No one pities her. No one defends her. She is pointed at by both men and women, her own kith and kin maybe, and ostracized. The man who spoils her goes scot free, and the woman is told, "Oh! He is a man and he can do anything he likes. There is no punishment for him. But, you, you witch, how can you tempt him? Men never tempt women! It is always the women who tempt men! This is the law of man. This must go, and that too very soon."

Was it possible for her and her friends to do more than they were already doing to bring about the changes they wanted to see?

Sister believed that it was. So did her mother and her aunt and the members of the Sarada Ladies' Union. The next step, they decided, was to raise enough money to enable them to buy a really big bungalow with a large compound in which it would be possible to erect some new buildings. They would then be able to house a much larger number of resident pupils and to develop schools for girls of all ages.

To do all this they would, they estimated, need about a lakh of rupees – at the current rate of exchange something less than seven thousand pounds. By 1930, they had already collected one fifth of this amount. As soon as half the total sum was raised the government would, under the existing regulations, give a matching grant towards the capital expenditure involved.

Meanwhile, the campaign for the prohibition of child marriage continued. Sarda's Bill which was passed on 1 October, 1929 and came into operation six months later, seemed to be achieving very little. Indeed, during the six months' interval before enforcement was expected to begin, its effect was exactly the opposite of what its promoters had hoped and intended.

Although the Sarda Act prohibited the marriage of girls under fourteen and of boys under eighteen, it did not contain any provision for invalidating marriage ceremonies once they had taken place. Moreover, the courts of law were prohibited from taking any action against parents, priests or other responsible persons unless a specific complaint was made. Anyone wishing to lay information that the Act had been infringed was required to do so before a court of law and, unless specially exempt, to give security for his ability to pay, if required, a fine of hundred rupees should the prosecution fail. If a prosecution succeeded, the male parent or guardian of the child concerned, the person who conducted the ceremony, and also the husband if he was over the age of twenty one, were to be penalized either by a fine of not more than rupees one thousand or a term of imprisonment not exceeding one month.

It was right, most supporters of the measure agreed, that there should be some safeguard against the possibility of malicious prosecutions. The government's chief concern, its official spokesmen had made clear, was with its own reputation. "I would rather," said Sir Alexander Muddiman when Sarda's Bill was first debated in the Legislature Assembly, "be charged with going too slowly in this matter than take risks which necessarily follow legislation in advance of general social opinion in the country. About the evil which the Honourable Member who has introduced this Bill has attacked, there can be no possible doubt … Let me warn him, however, that he will not take the people with him, if he goes too far or too fast. If he does not take the people with him, moreover, I know well that the odium of the enactment will fall not on him but on the executive government, and that must be a reason why we should observe a considerable amount of caution in the matter."

The Bill in its final form was carried by sixty seven votes to fourteen. The Home Member of the Viceroy's Executive Council assured legislators that the measures had "the most cordial sympathy and strongest support of the government." Public opinion, he said, had ample opportunity for expressing itself. The evil was "clamouring for a remedy."

This declaration, naturally enough, led both Sarda's supporters and his critics to conclude that as soon as the Act became operative it would be rigidly enforced. Consequently, during the winter and spring of 1929-30, everyone who was opposed to the Act hurried to defy its provisions before legal sanctions could be applied against them. Men who believed that pre puberty marriages were enjoined by the teachings of their religion rushed to find dowries and husbands for little girls, toddlers and even babies, whose marriages might otherwise have been delayed until the approach of adolescence. Ignorant people were given distorted accounts of the provisions of the Act. Many were led to believe that the government had decided to prohibit *any* marriage from taking place for fourteen years after the date on which the Act was to come into force. Later, when the Census of 1931 had been taken and the results collated, it was officially estimated that at least three million little girls and two million boys were hustled into premature matrimony during the six months before the Act became operative.

When it did come into force, the government appeared timidly anxious to avoid affronting those who defied it. On 4 April, 1930, an assembly of twelve thousand Muslims gathered in the great mosque at Delhi, the Jama Masjid, to witness the marriage of a girl of nine to a boy of thirteen. The district magistrate was petitioned to prosecute all those responsible for arranging the ceremony, but the petition was apparently ignored. The headman of a village in the Madras Presidency was found guilty of contravening the Act and dismissed from his post by the collector of the district, only to be promptly reinstated on the orders of higher authority. In Madras city, a vaishnavite judge, who had succeeded in persuading his eighteen year old nephew to marry a girl of eleven, arranged for priests, musicians and cooks, as well as the families of both bride and bridegroom, to travel to Bangalore, in the princely state of Mysore, so as to avoid any risk of prosecution in British India.

A stranger brought a little girl to the Ice House. The child, he told Sister Subbalakshmi, was his daughter. She had been married, the father confessed, in violation of the Act, and her husband had died only a week or so after the ceremony. Would Sister, the man begged, accept the little widow and educate her?

Sister consulted Miss Gerrard, who was now the superintendent of the Lady Willingdon High School and Training College. Miss Gerrard agreed that the girl should be accepted. "But," she added, "we shall have to lay evidence against the girl's parents."

"Certainly the father should suffer," Sister agreed. "But he has already suffered far more by the death of his poor little daughter's husband than he would ever do by going to prison. Besides, people would certainly find out that it was we who started the prosecution, and then those who have misbehaved in a similar way will be afraid of bringing their daughters to us. It is better to allow a guilty man to go free than to run the risk of robbing any girl of the chance that we might be able to give her."

Some hundreds of girls had now gone out to work, most of them in towns and villages in the Madras Presidency, but others further afield. The oldest of them had been, even in their school days and often without being aware of it themselves, the most effective propagandists for the work of the Widows' Home.

Now, in their various jobs, the adult widows who had been Ice House girls were also effective propagandists against child marriage and for the observance of the Sarda Act. They did not, with rare exceptions, make speeches on public platforms. Instead, they were making the education of girls not merely possible but attractive, and were quietly influencing parents as well as pupils.

This, Sister was sure, was the best way of getting the Act enforced. People would have to be taught that child marriage was not really among the doctrines of the Hindu religion. Then, once they were convinced, they would have to be helped to gather enough courage to act in accordance with their beliefs.

Sister was not, of course, alone in this conviction. After the Act came into force, a number of progressive women in Madras decided to organize women's meetings all over the Presidency, mainly for those who in the ordinary way would never attend public gatherings. The Hindu Ladies' Enlightenment Lectures, as they were called, were a great success. Subbalakshmi, who delivered ten of them, found crowded, attentive audiences wherever she went. Then, in December 1930, she accepted an invitation to preside over the women's conference which was being held in Tinnevelly, in the far South. The year had been, for those concerned with big political issues, one of intense agitation, sparked off by Gandhi's march to the shores of the Arabian Sea to offer civil disobedience to the British by making salt and defying the government monopoly. Many thousands had been arrested and were still in prison. In these circumstances it was, to say the least, risky for a government servant to take part in a conference along with hundreds of women who were supporters and members of the National Congress.

Subbalakshmi felt that it was a risk which had to be taken. But when she was asked to attend the annual conference of the Women's Indian Association, over which Mrs Sarojini Naidu, the most famous of all Congresswomen, was to preside, she felt obliged to refuse.

"Do you know," Sister asked me when she was, so she said, getting towards the end of her story, "what it means to come under the influence of Saturn?"

"No."

"Then you had better get someone to explain to you exactly how the influence operates. All I need tell you is that when that particular planet is ruling your life the most unfortunate things are likely to happen. I have twice come under the influence of Saturn. There is no need to speak of what happened the first time. The second period, during which I suffered every possible kind of trial, don't you know, was during the year 1931, I shall tell you what happened then."

To begin with, there was for the first time a serious difference of opinion among the members of the Sarada Ladies' Union. One of the British members suggested that the girls in the Sarada Vidyalaya should be taught some European dances. Sister and most of her compatriots disapproved. Some, indeed, were deeply shocked that the proposal should ever have been made. If the girls learned to waltz and foxtrot, there was no doubt at all that when they went out into the world some of them would start dancing with men.

"Of course," Sister went on, "when the girls got to hear of the suggestion they were all in favour of it. They were typical modern girls, and nothing else was to be expected. The lady responsible – never mind her name – canvassed for support and managed to persuade a number of people who should have known better to vote for her proposal. The upshot of it was that we had to make a break with these people. We decided to move out of Triplicane and set up our headquarters in Mylapore. Then I made a very foolish mistake."

She had already started searching for new premises in which to house the vidyalaya. She had found nothing which appeared suitable when a friend told her that he had bought a big area of undeveloped land in Mambalam, a district where people were just beginning to build. He offered Sister and the members of the Sarada Ladies' Union, as a gift, a site which would be large enough for a hostel, the model school and whatever other educational institution might be needed.

The site was flat, the land waterlogged. The district seemed remote. There were few roads and, it seemed no form of public transport anywhere in the vicinity. Sister, failing to foresee developments which were to take place in the near future, rejected the offer.

Instead, she found a house in Mylapore. The parents of many of the vidyalaya's day pupils lived in the district, and if the school was there it was probable that many more families would send their daughters to be educated. Nevertheless, Sister hesitated. By the time she had made up her mind to recommend to the members of the Ladies' Union that they should buy the house, another purchaser had stepped in and she was too late.

This misfortune, which it seemed natural to attribute to the malign influence of Saturn, turned out to be a blessing in disguise. Sister found a house, very large and situated in a big compound, which was said to be extremely unlucky. Its first occupant had suffered a terrible misfortune soon after he moved in and had hastily vacated it and sold it to the first comer. The second owner had also been unlucky. So had his successor. The place had now been empty for a long time. Everybody believed that there was a curse on it, and Sister found that she could buy it for a quarter of what it had cost to build.

"I told everybody," Sister said, "that no evil spirits were going to stay in the place to harm our girls. I had no patience with such superstitious nonsense, and I was quite sure that after living all that time in the dirt and noise of Triplicane everybody would find the new house a perfect paradise."

They did. But Saturn had not yet finished with Subbalakshmi.

"Now," she went on, "I am going to tell you a most terrible thing. There was a lady on my staff, a very good, clever creature who was doing excellent work. She was unmarried, and a man who should have known much better than to do such a thing – he was a senior government official – was pestering her and making her life a perfect misery. She asked me to take her into the Ice House so that she would have some protection. Of course I did. But that man still would not leave her alone."

I had never seen Sister so agitated, Her hair had worked itself loose and stood out around her head like a silver halo. Her right hand was gripping the battery case of her deaf-aid so tightly that her knuckles shone as if a light were playing on them.

"I may tell you," she lowered her voice, "that this man used to come at nights and write rude things – *very* rude things – on the compound wall. Every morning, I used to send the servants out with buckets of water and brushes to scrub off all the filth before people started out to walk along the Marina. It was so extremely disgusting!"

I asked, "Was the man mad?"

"I suppose he was, in a way. Only in that one way. And it went on for months – many months. Then in April – this was 1931 – Nitya and I and several others decided to go to Burma for a holiday. We had a friend in Rangoon who had invited us to stay with her. On the morning of the day on which we were to arrive she was chatting over the garden wall with her neighbour, an official in the Criminal Investigation Department. She mentioned that she would be going down to the docks later in the day to meet us. He said that he would probably see her there, because he had been instructed to go on board the Madras boat to search the luggage of a political suspect who was believed to be travelling on it. Our friend came onto the boat and we had hardly greeted her when this gentleman from the C I D appeared. Oh! he exclaimed, is Sister Subbalakshmi the lady you have come to meet? She is also the lady whose boxes I have to examine!"

Sister was looking into my face, her expression almost as bewildered as it must have been when the incident happened. Then she tossed her head, screwing up her eyes with disgust. "I don't need to tell you that I had never had anything to do with politics. This poor man from the C I D must have guessed as much. It was very embarrassing for him to look through my things. All the time I was in Burma I was followed about by the C I D – and afterwards I found out that it was this man who had been making trouble in Madras who had arranged for me to be pestered in this way. He had reported that I was engaged in subversive activities!" Suddenly she laughed, long and merrily. "Subversive! Just imagine!"

When she returned to Madras she looked tired. Small worries, of the kind which she was accustomed to taking in her stride, seemed to cause her quite disproportionate anxiety. She was forty six and, by Indian standards, not just middle aged, but elderly. Although she was unwilling to admit it, she needed a rest. Swarnum had recently become an inspector in the Madras government's education department and had been posted to Bellary, near the northern border of Mysore state. She suggested that Sister should apply for a six months' leave and come and stay with her. Swarnum's work took her around a vast, unfamiliar countryside, and when Subbalakshmi was rested the two of them could travel about together.

Sister enjoyed almost every minute of the next five months. Then, in the first week of December, as she was beginning to look forward to her return to Madras, came news of the death of Lady Sadasiva Iyer. This was much more than a personal misfortune. Ever since the foundation of the Sarada Ladies' Union, twenty years earlier, Lady Sadasiva Iyer had been its president – not just a figurehead, but a real leader, full of energy and ideas and skill and courage in the advocacy of new ideas. Sister could hardly imagine how it would be possible to get on without her.

Almost immediately afterwards another blow fell. This was an official notification from the education department, stating that in January 1932 she was to take up the duties of superintendent of the Hobart School.

The school had been founded for girls from Muslim families.

Sister's appointment meant, of course, that she was being moved a step upwards in the official hierarchy. But though she would have more responsibilities and be earning a bigger salary, she could not really regard the change as a promotion. Sister feared that those who suspected her of caste consciousness had contrived to have her, so to speak, kicked upstairs.

Her students wept bitterly when the time came to say goodbye. So did the little girls in the model elementary school which was attached to the training college. Subbalakshmi herself had always found learning delightful, and experience had confirmed her belief that if children were bored in school it was the fault of their teachers. "In thousands of elementary schools," she had recently written, "there is an appalling waste of time and suppression of energy in the children, amounting almost to a crime, due to bored, ill paid teachers who, after finishing the year's work in three or four months, spend the remaining time keeping the children in order." She had proved at the Ice House, and was demonstrative again at the vidyalaya, that the average child's natural pace of learning, as long as the teacher was interested and knew how to be interesting, was much faster than was generally believed. "Both parents and teachers," she had declared, "suffer from the *don't* approach, forgetting all the time that children crave for work and pleasant occupations under the urge of nature of rapid learning ... Don't do this! Don't touch that! Instead of this, if they would take a real interest in their darling children, answering all their interesting and intelligent questions, they would find out how very interesting children are, not a bore as they imagine, how much their children are capable of learning and doing."

At the Hobart School, government regulations made it

impossible to experiment with new educational methods. At the vidyalaya, on the other hand, it was possible to make many innovations. Luckily, the two institutions were near each other, so that Subbalakshmi had no difficulty in managing both.

The vidyalaya was still growing. It was also facing some serious difficulties. The economic crisis which had driven Britain to abandon the gold standard in the autumn of 1931 had severe repercussions in India. Government expenditure was being cut down in every possible direction. The stipend for trainee teachers had been fixed at rupees ten per month for as long as Sister could remember. That had been little enough, but with care it was possible for a girl to manage on it. Now the stipend was cut to rupees four, a sum so small that nobody could possibly live on it. At the same time, charitable people who had been in the habit of giving regularly and generously to the vidyalaya were finding it increasingly difficult to maintain their contributions.

Economies had to be made. Two separate kitchens were organized, one for fee paying pupils whose cooking, except when they were taking cookery lessons, was always done for them, and who were still provided with coffee and other small luxuries. In the other kitchen, which was for scholarship holders, the girls did all the work themselves and the food they ate was the cheapest and plainest obtainable.

The system saved money, but at the cost of threatening to spoil the spirit of equality which had been created among the girls. After a few weeks the experiment was given up. Girls from well-to-do homes agreed that they would rather sacrifice a few comforts than enjoy things which were denied to their friends. The vidyalaya, in its beautiful new surroundings, was a place in which hardships, as long as they were shared by everybody, could easily by borne. Lessons were enjoyable, and there was plenty of room in the big garden for every kind of outdoor game. Sometimes in the evening there were concerts and plays and other entertainment, and now and then, because Mylapore was the intellectual centre of Madras, public lectures or religious discourses which the older students were able to attend.

In the autumn, the members of the Ladies' Union opened a club of their own, with a library, reading room and games room. Sister gave the members a course of lectures on the Gita, and from time to time well-known speakers came to address them. The chief value of the club, most people agreed, was that it encouraged ladies to come out into the world a little, to meet people outside the narrow circle of their own relatives, and to talk about subjects other than child rearing, servant problems, the cost of living and the difficulty of finding suitable husbands for their daughters and the right kind of wives for their sons.

The campaign against child marriage was still being carried on vigorously. The Sarda Act, it had become all too evident, was enforced half-heartedly or not at all. Up to the end of August 1932, only four hundred and seventy three prosecutions had taken placed in the whole of British administered India. Of the one hundred and sixty seven successful prosecutions, only seventeen of the guilty had been sentenced, and none to more than a moderate fine or a few weeks' imprisonment. Among those who escaped with a fine were two Musilms, aged fifty and forty five. Both were convicted of marrying their wards, aged four and two respectively, in order to obtain final control of their property. Although the courts were empowered to levy fines of rupees one thousand, these two husbands, now securely in possession of the property for which they had married, were required to pay only rupees one hundred and fifty each.

Before Sarda's Bill became law, the number of child widows in the country as a whole had begun to decline. Now, as a result of the six months' interval between the passing of the Act and its coming into force, the number of virgin widows was again increasing. "The year that elapsed between the rush of anticipatory marriages and the taking of the census," the Report on the 1931 Census stated, "left time for many infants married in haste to become widows for life, and this is probably significant of sorrows to come." According to the 1921 Census, there had been in that year seven hundred and fifty nine widows under one year of age, ten years later the number had almost exactly doubled, and was one thousand, five hundred and fifteen. During the same period the number of child wives under the age of fifteen had grown from 8,565,357 to 12,271,595.

Soon after Subbalakshmi had taken over her duties at the Hobart School, a British woman member of Parliament, Miss Eleanor Rathbone, visited Madras, and the two of them were invited to address a public meeting on the subject of child marriage.

"What did you speak about?" one of the ladies of Mylapore enquired of Sister on the following day.

"What do you think I spoke about?" Sister retorted sharply. "You know that the meeting was called to demand the raising of the marriage age, don't you?"

Sister, after telling me this, added, "There was a gentleman who also spoke at the meeting. He called himself a social reformer, and he spoke very vigorously about the evils of child marriage. I knew that he had married off his own daughter when she was only eight years old, so after the meeting I spoke to him about it. How is it possible, I asked him, for you to preach one thing and to practise something which is quite different? He answered, We must go along with the times. Of course it is wrong that girls should be married before they attain their ages. I am entirely of the opinion that we should wait until they are fully adult and capable of taking responsibility for their actions. But if I had waited until that time came before I married my daughter, I should have had not a moment's peace in my house. My grandmother would have been after me. My mother would have been after me. My wife would not have let me alone for a minute. I simply could not do it. But is that a reason why I should refrain from telling other people that they ought to do what is right?"

Sister had always known that it was the women, ordinary women who took no part in public affairs, whose views had to be changed. The Sarda Act, she had always known, did not go far enough. The Census Commissioner for Madras had reported that more than one brahmin correspondent had urged that the Act should be taken over, strengthened and enforced by the government. "There seems," he added, "to be a fairly general agreement that as a rather half-and-half effort it is not entitled to much respect." Nevertheless, he continued, it did seem that, at least indirectly, the Act was having some effect. It was being used as an "excuse for later marriage, a reason for beating down dowry claims." It was also, most important of all, "directing a great amount of attention to marriage questions among communities and persons who had previously given them very little thought."

This last, though it did not seem so to many people at the time, was the biggest step forward of all. Miss Rathbone, appalled by all that she had seen and learned of Indian conditions and the complacent indifference of British officialdom, was pessimistic. Deploring drama, she pleaded for dramatic action.

Subbalakshmi and many other women of whom the great British public had never heard were hopeful. Europeans often said that India was a country without a sense of time. This was untrue, but the time scale was different. The seeds of change had already been sown. Untended, they might die. With patience, they could be made to grow.

Subbalakshmi did not stay long at the Hobart School. In January 1933, when she had been there for exactly a year, she was informed by the education department of the Madras government that she had been appointed as superintendent of the Government Secondary and Training School at Cuddalore and was to take up her duties immediately.

Cuddalore, situated on the coast a little to the south of the French Colony of Pondicherry, was not much more than a hundred miles away. To Subbalakshmi, who had never been separated from her family by more than the three miles' breadth of Madras city, the distance seemed enormous. She felt that she was being banished. But she had never tried to evade any duty that had been imposed on her, and she did not try to do so now.

Cuddalore was fair sized town and the school, which had been in existence for some years, was a large one. The pupils were, almost without exception, girls from educated families.

Some were Christians, the rest caste Hindus. They formed a privileged minority. Most of the children in the district had no chance whatever of going to school even for a year or two.

Subbalakshmi had scarcely settled down to her duties when she decided that she and the girls who were under her care ought to make themselves responsible for the education of the poor children of the neighbourhood. Near the school was a slum district, inhabited mainly by fisherman, toddy tappers, potters – all of them untouchables. They were so accustomed to the hostile contempt of caste people that it would not, Subbalakshmi realized, be easy to establish friendly relations with them. They were dirty, often indeed extremely filthy, in their habits. They were also desperately poor, and when they had a little money most of it was spent in trying to drown their sorrows in toddy and arrack. No doubt they were, as far as it was possible, kind to each other within the defensive wall which they had built against the respectable world outside. But they could often be heard fighting, quarrelling, behaving in ways which seemed to justify the worst that could ever be said about them.

If it was going to be hard to penetrate their defences, it was not going to be easy either, to persuade respectable caste Hindus to allow their daughters to mix with the children of untouchables. Yet, there had never, Sister realized, been a better time for making the attempt.

In September 1932, Gandhi, who at that time was incarcerated at Yervada Jail in Poona, had undertaken a fast unto death for the sake of the untouchables. Immediately after the ending of the fast, an Anti-Untouchability Week was celebrated throughout India. During the succeeding months Gandhi, still in prison, devoted himself to the cause of the untouchables, whom he had renamed Harijans, Children of God.

He was released in August 1933. Towards the end of the year he made a tour of the South, and arrived in Madras on 20 December.

"I have come here," he said, addressing a meeting of women, "to ask you to do one thing. Forget altogether that some are high and some are low. Forget altogether that some are touchable and some untouchables." Then, in a second speech delivered on the same day, he told his audience, "If you want to convince Hindu society that untouchability cannot be a part of religion, and that it is a hideous error, you have to develop character. You have to move among the masses ... You will have to bend your backs and work in their midst and assure them that you have gone to them not with any mental reservations, but with the pure motive of serving them and taking the message of love and peace in their midst. If you do that, you will find a ready response."

Subbalakshmi had already found a much readier response than she had expected. When Gandhi visited Cuddalore on 8 February, 1934, her school for the slum children of the neighbourhood was already a success.

She had started it without money, and without a building. Instead, it was in a palm grove, shaded by the trees and with great quantities of clean, golden river sand spread to make a floor. Students from the training school plaited mats to be used as seats. It was not necessary to coax and beg the potters and toddy tappers to send their children. When the sand was first spread, the children, most of them naked or with no more covering than bit of dirty rag around their loins, had come to watch what was going on. They were invited to stay. Some were too shy and ran off. Those who remained found it such fun that next day their playmates joined them.

Sister and the older students told them stories. Reading and writing and arithmetic were taught by making drawings in the sand with pointed sticks. Then, as the children began to understand symbols and to be able to make them for themselves, their parents would spare a few coppers for exercise books and pencils.

Charitable people helped, too. The collector and his wife, an English couple, gave all the assistance they could. They helped Sister to organize a social centre where the mothers of the slum children could come for a little relaxation and be taught elementary principles of hygiene and childcare. Soon, fathers came along as well. Sister admired the work of the potters, and as she got to be on friendly terms with them, made suggestions for new designs.

She was too busy to be homesick. The vidyalaya still needed her direction and nobody could imagine the Sarada Ladies' Union with any other secretary. In fact, the long holidays made it possible to carry on these responsibilities without too much difficulty. But in Madras she was greatly missed. When, at the end of her first year, Subbalakshmi went home for the Christmas holidays Chitti was very unwell, and confined to bed. She was as cheerful as ever, eager to hear about what Subbalakshmi had been doing, and to report on everything that had happened at the Ice House and the vidyalaya. She took part, too, in the New Year celebrations, when Subramania Iyer's children and grandchildren and their uncles and aunts and cousins held what they called their annual conference.

The turn of the year, when the weather was as its coolest and most beautiful, was the conference season, and every year several of the learned societies of India would hold their annual session in Madras. The family conferences had started as a kind of parody of these meetings. They were held for fun, but they were serious too. The members of the family, not only the older people but the boys and girls who were growing up, would make speeches, sometimes about topics of current interest, sometimes about literature or philosophy or religion. Then, in the afternoons and evenings, they would play games or perform short plays or give concerts. The house which Subramania and Visalakshi had built for themselves had a big upstairs hall, roomy enough to hold as many of their friends as they cared to ask.

One morning, as everyone was getting ready for the conference session to open, a widow was seen coming down the lane. The edge of her sari was drawn tightly over head and she held one corner up to her eyes, wiping away tears.

One of Sister's nephews went out to ask what she wanted.

"Is this," the stranger asked in a voice torn by sobs, "where the great lady Sister Subbalakshmi is staying?"

"Yes."

"Please take me to her."

It was hardly the right time, but everybody in the family knew that Sister would never allow anyone in trouble to be turned away. The stranger, leaning forward with shoulders trembling, was led into the room where Sister was.

They were left together. A minute later there was a shout of laughter. The family rushed into the room to see that the stranger had lifted the sari and revealed himself as an old family friend who had been trying to enter into the spirit of the conference by playing a practical joke.

Sister was not sure that she was amused. Chitti was. But she was also in great pain. Her right leg was terribly swollen. She had a fever which defied every attempt to bring her temperature back to normal.

It was impossible to believe that she would not get better. When Sister returned to her official duties in January, she did not even guess that she was saying goodbye to her darling Chitti for the last time. The news of Chitti's approaching end came in a telegram which arrived at Cuddalore on 25 January, 1935. Subbalakshmi, who perhaps owed more to Chitti than to anyone else in the world, set off for Madras at once. When she arrived her aunt, the splendid, indispensable Valambal, was already dead.

It seemed impossible to imagine life without her. Yet life had to go on. There was work to be done. The vidyalaya was crowded to capacity. More money would have to be raised to enable it to keep on growing. The Ladies' Club would need more attention than ever now that Chitti was not there to help. And Cuddalore, when Subbalakshmi went back to it, still had many problems which needed to be solved.

Perhaps it was Subbalakshmi's mother who missed Chitti most. They had lived together, worked together and studied together for so many years that it seemed natural that after Valambal's death Visalakshi should also begin to fade. When summer came and Subbalakshmi returned to Madras once more, her mother, who for some time had been suffering from diabetes, was so weak that there could be no question of anyone going away for the usual summer holiday. As May gave way to

June to July, it was evident that she was sinking. On 22 July, Subbalakshmi wrote in her diary, "At about 8:30 in the morning the great and noble soul became one with Ishwara. Most unbearable. God help us."

It was so unbearable that now work, besides being a duty, was a refuge. The collector of Cuddalore and his wife had become friends in whose home Subbalakshmi was always welcome. She had made other friends too. Yet she felt lonely, and longed for the company of people whom she had known all her life.

Letters came. Some were from the girls who had made up Chitti's family at Adi Cottage, some from those who had entered the Widow's Home when it was in T P Koil Street, and others from girls whose liberation from widowhood had begun in the Ice House.

Chitti had been the dear aunt of all these girls. She had loved them and petted them and allowed them little indulgences which Sister herself would never have permitted. Chitti, no less than Sister, had encouraged them to study and had helped to develop their beliefs and ideas. Now many of these girls were women, and the ambitions which Chitti and Subbalakshmi and her mother and Mrs Drysdale and Miss Prager had nursed for them were being realized. Parvathi and Chellam and a number of others were teaching in high schools. Gita, who had joined the Women's Medical Service, had done postgraduate work in Britain in both medicine and surgery. Now she had, as Sister loved to say, most of the letters of the alphabet after her name, and was head of one of the Lady Dufferin hospitals for women. Her sister, who had taken a degree in Madras University, had taught for a time, and was now happily married to the right man. Alamelu, who had looked like sergeant major and had left three small children behind her when she came to the Ice House, was employed on board ship, looking after the welfare of women and children who were emigrating to Burma. The older Saraswati was an inspector of schools. Saraswati Deshpande, who had joined the Indian National Congress and in 1930 had gone to prison, was now educating the daughters of the ruler of one of the princely states. Then there was Kamala, who, after going to Queen Mary's College and taking a degree, had married again and was now, with her husband's encouragement, spending all her spare time doing social work.

It was wonderful to read letters from writers such as these. There were very many of them. By this time, too, many of the girls who had joined the Sarada Vidyalaya six years ago, when it first opened, had gone out into the world to lead their own lives. One of them sent Sister a short autobiography, illustrated with comical pen and ink sketches of the child she had been.

She was not one of the widows. She had been married when she was a very tiny child, and her earliest recollection was of the day when a letter had come from her husband's family to say that they had decided to make other arrangements for their son's future and that the marriage must be considered to be at an end.

"I remember," she wrote, "how my father stormed, while my mother looked on helplessly, seeing me as an unfortunate and useless child."

A year or so later, both her parents died. She went to live with an uncle, and it was he who eventually took her to the vidyalaya in Madras. "The unkempt and awful village girl," she continued, "gradually vanished, and I was changed into a happy-go-lucky child who found a real home in the institution." Then, as she was growing up, "there came a letter from that strange youth, my husband. The result was a shy meeting and a joyful ending."

Not all the letters which Sister received came from her former pupils. One was from a Madrasi lady who described how, some years before, when she had been visiting relatives in Kumbakonam, she was approached by a young brahmin widow who lived in a neighbouring house. Did the stranger, the girl asked, know the famous lady Sister Subbalakshmi?

Yes, she did.

"I am anxious," the girl had continued, "to run away from my father's roof, where I have been working for the past six years under the watchful and cruel supervision of my chitti – my father's second wife – and her widowed elder sister, who are two devils incarnate."

Her father, she had continued, was a clerk earning about rupees forty per month, and was perpetually henpecked by his wife and sister-in-law, who pretended that it was they who did all the work of the house.

"At about four o'clock every morning," said the girl, "the elder devil would rise from her cosy bed to empty her bladder, and before returning to the bed would kick me – lying on the floor with a plank for my pillow – in the loins, telling me to get up and begin the work of the day. I must clean and wash all the vessels, sweep and clean the kitchen floor and the house front with cowdung mixture, and light the fires for the bathroom and for the coffee kettle and milk. By 6:00 am the sisters would be ready to mix three good cups of coffee, taking care I don't get a taste of it stealthily."

The sisters would then serve the father's morning meal while his daughter was forced to pretend to read a book – under the threat that if she ever complained of how she was being treated she would be bundled up and thrown into the backyard as a suicide – and, she added, she had been beaten often enough when her father was out of the house to realize that the threat was to be taken seriously.

She toiled all day, wretched and more than half-starved, until night came and she was allowed, at about ten o'clock, to lie down for a few hours.

"And," she finished, "as my stepmother has not had any baby until now, they have arranged to take a trip to Rameshwaram, and I have been told that the occasion will be availed of for me to have my head shaved, in order that I may be more fit to take part in all the orthodox ceremonies of the household." She could, she said, endure no more. The tears were running down her cheeks, and she could not say another word.

She was taken to the Sarada Vidyalaya and accepted as a pupil. Four years passed before the lady from whom she had begged help saw her again. By that time, the young widow was headmistress of an elementary school. The children liked her, and she was respected by their parents. As she talked of all that had happened as a result of the stranger's intercession on her behalf, tears were again streaming from her eyes. "But this time," the letter to Sister ended, "they were coming from the outer corners of her fine eyes. Tears of grief and of joy appear to have different places of exit."

It was letters such as these which made Subbalakshmi feel that she ought to go back to Madras. Now that her mother and Chitti and Lady Sadasiva Iyer were no longer there, she was needed more than ever before. Nothing, she was sure, was more urgently necessary than to extend the work which was already being done for young widows, abandoned wives and for the girls who would be the mothers of the next generation.

All of these, as they grew up, would help to change the outlook of the people among whom they moved and would, quietly and unostentatiously, begin to transform society. They would not achieve results either easily or quickly. Some of the vidyalaya girls had, when they first started teaching, been ostracized by the respectable people of the villages in which they were employed. The young teachers had endured their criticisms and, without exception, stuck to their jobs. Sometimes it took them months, but often only a few weeks, to break down resistance and to win over their critics by their modesty and their popularity with their pupils. As this began to happen, the schools in which they taught filled rapidly. Slowly, the young teachers found themselves absorbed into the life of the villages, sharing responsibility for the future.

Hundreds, thousands more of them were needed. The number of parents who understood the importance of educating their daughters was increasing fast. Although several new high schools had been established in Madras city, it was impossible to satisfy the growing demand. By 1936, the Sarada Vidyalaya had more than three hundred pupils in its various sections. If it had been possible to provide additional accommodation there would have been many more. Somehow, Sister told herself, the accommodation would have to be found.

She applied for a year's leave of absence from her official duties and, as soon as it was granted, hurried back to Madras.

"By this time," she told me, "I realized what a mistake I had made when I rejected the offer of the gentleman who had suggested that we should build in Mambalam. So I went to see him and asked if the site was still available. It was, but the cost of drainage had turned out to be so high that he could not afford to let us have it as a gift. He suggested a price. It seemed reasonable, and I agreed at once."

When the land had been paid for, the education committee of the Ladies' Union still had a substantial sum in hand but not nearly enough, even if it were doubled by a matching grant from the government, to provide all the buildings that would be needed. A big effort would have to be made to raise more money. Times were hard. Building costs were rising. On a realistic estimate it would, Sister and the committee members realized, take years to accumulate enough funds to enable them to carry out their scheme. Meanwhile, still another temporary home would have to be found for the vidyalaya.

Sister found one without much difficulty. "It was," she told me, "a pleasant place, though not as big as we would have wished. The staff and the girls settled down very happily, and it was when they had been there about two years that the miracle happened."

"The miracle?"

She laughed. "Really, it seemed like a miracle. I had never hoped for, or imagined anything of the sort."

The year was 1938. Subbalakshmi, at the end of her leave, had returned to Cuddalore and had then, after some months, been sent to take charge of a big secondary and training school at Rajamundry. Now, by what seemed a great piece of good fortune, she had been asked to resume her duties at the Lady Willingdon Training College and was once more living in the family colony in Edward Elliot's Road, a bare half mile from the college.

"One evening," she told me, "I received a surprise visit from an old friend of our family, Mr Ramanujachariar, who had founded the Ramakrishna Mission Boys' Home next to Vivekananda College. He was a very fine man, a wonderful organizer, and at that time was secretary of the Madras branch of the Ramakrishna Mission."

The Mission, as everybody in India knows, is a great educational and charitable foundation which owes its inspiration to Swami Vivekananda, the disciple of the nineteenth century Bengali saint Ramakrishna Paramahansa, and Mr Ramanujachariar had come to Sister to suggest that the Mission should take over the vidyalaya.

She was smiling broadly as she said, "I was never more surprised in my life – and I simply jumped at the offer. I knew that I could not go on forever, and although the members of my committee were very good and enthusiastic, I used to worry sometimes about what would happen when I had gone. Well, when Mr Ramanujachariar saw how delighted I was at the proposal he said, Of course, there will be conditions. Can you guess what he meant?"

"That you would continue to be the secretary of the committee?"

"No. I think we simply took that for granted. But I may tell you that I couldn't guess what he meant either, so I simply answered that there would be conditions on our side too. He asked what they would be. I replied that the most important was that we must keep the name Sarada." She was still smiling as she went on, "Well, when I said that I saw that he was looking at me in a very cunning way. I had guessed and it turned out that I was right, that he was going to make exactly the same condition. You see, for us in the Ladies' Union, when we speak of Sarada we are thinking first of all of the Goddess Saraswati, and of the worship of learning. When the members of the Ramakrishna Mission speak of Sarada, their first thought is of the Holy Mother, the saint Sarada who was the wife of Ramakrishna." She chuckled happily. "So, you see, we were both satisfied."

"And the members of the Ladies' Union agreed?"

"Of course. It did not mean severing our connection with the vidyalaya, but it did mean that the organization was greatly strengthened. We knew that the new buildings, when they went up, would be really everything we had hoped to make them, big and well-planned, and that the management would succeed in keeping alive the spirit which we had tried to create. Oh, yes, all the ladies were just as happy about it as I was. And do you know what we did with the money we had collected?"

"What?"

"We kept a few thousand rupees to spend on other activities – work we were planning to do which doesn't belong to this story." She was looking at me, bright eyed, amused, her silvery hair lit, like a halo, by the last light of the setting sun. "The land we had bought and the big round sum we had managed to save in all these years we decided to give as a dowry."

"A dowry!"

"Yes, a dowry for the education of all the girls who were

studying at the vidyalaya and who would study there in the future. So you see, after all those years of struggle there was a truly happy ending."

"An ending?" I repeated.

She seemed not to hear.

"Wasn't it," I insisted, "really a beginning?"

"Why yes," she acknowledged, "of course it was. But surely you don't want me to tell you about everything we have managed to do in the last twenty five years?"

"Why not?"

"Because there is so much to tell that you couldn't possibly put it all into a book. Besides, as I said just now, it is quite another story."

Looking Forward

THE GOLDEN JUBILEE – the fiftieth anniversary – of the Sarada Ladies' Union was celebrated at the Sarada Vidyalaya Training School in Mambalam on 21 January, 1962.

Just a week earlier, men, women and children all over South India had celebrated Pongal, their traditional harvest festival, decorating their houses with tender green leaves and plumes of sugarcane. Now, as the taxi drove along a broad avenue arched by enormous rain trees, I looked out to see cattle strolling along with their horns freshly painted, some red, some green, and with gaily coloured beads strung around their necks. Most of the people walking in the streets seemed to be wearing new clothes, the men in crisp white shirts with matching trousers or dhotis, the women in bright saris, and the little girls in traditional anklelength skirts with fitted jackets above.

The taxi turned a corner. On our right was the gateway which led into the spacious grounds of the Ramakrishna Mission Sarada Vidyalaya High School. A week or two earlier I had talked with the headmistress, Miss C Subbalakshmi, who had been widowed when she was a little girl of eleven and had, soon afterwards, been taken by her parents to the Widows' Home in T P Koil Street to be educated. Now she herself had more than eighteen hundred girls in her care. About ninety per cent of them, she had told me, continued their education after leaving school. An educated girl could usually, if she wanted to, get a job, and the parents of boys often, by no means always, preferred to choose university graduates as brides for their sons. In Madras city alone, there were five women's colleges, each with some hundreds of students, affiliated to Madras University, and there were many girl students at the Presidency College, in training colleges and in specialized institutions such as the Medical College.

The taxi turned again and, a couple of minutes later, drew up outside the Sarada Vidyalaya Training School where, on weekdays, about three hundred girls and young women were preparing to become elementary school teachers.

A group of students stood outside the hall in which the meeting was to be held. One held a tray of posies, inviting the guests, as they arrived, to take their choice. Another clasped a silver bowl filled with yellow sandal paste. Near the door, a third girl was holding a big silver container, shaped like a sugar sifter, lifting it to sprinkle the new arrivals with rosewater as they slipped off their sandals and mounted the steps into the hall.

The hall was already crowded. All round me were women and young girls, mothers and daughters, grandmothers and grandchildren, many whose memories might possibly have stretched back for forty years or more, and a few who were old enough to remember the first meeting of the Ladies' Union.

I looked up, through the chinks of space between the grey heads immediately in front of me, towards the stage. A row of chairs, a table and a microphone were waiting for the minister of the Madras government who was to preside and for the speakers who were to follow him. Girls who were to receive prizes were already seated, cross-legged on the floor, their faces placid, unexpectant; and on the other side of the stage stood a ceramic image of the Lord Krishna as a boy, his blue face glinting with mischief above the garland of fresh pink roses that hung around his neck.

Down below, Sister Subbalakshmi, dressed in cream coloured silk, was bustling about, receiving guests, completely in command. Then her silvery head bobbed out of sight, and a moment later she was ushering the speakers on to the platform. Suddenly the whole audience was standing, waiting to listen to the group of girls who had appeared at the front of the platform to sing the opening prayer.

I was still staring, trying to recognize among the rows of bent heads those of Sister Subbalakshmi's pupils whom I already knew. I thought I could spot Meenambal who, after graduating from Queen Mary's College, had spent the whole of her working life teaching in the vidyalaya and, during many of these years, acting as Sister's secretary. The gay chatterbox Rukmini was in the front row. She had retired from teaching, and I knew that she was managing, on her small pension, to support her widowed mother. I looked for Parvathi, but if she was there I failed to spot her. She had retired too, after serving for some years as headmistress of the Lady Willingdon High School which, at the time when she left it, had more than seventeen hundred pupils on the rolls. Chellam, the younger Chellam, was headmistress of Lady Sivaswami Iyer High School in Mylapore, and Dharmambal, whom I had met only once, was headmistress of the Madras Seva Sadan High School in Chetpet. "So four of us," Parvathi had once pointed out to me, "who entered the Widows' Home when there were scarcely more than a hundred girls in the high school section at Triplicane, have been managing high schools with a total of between six and seven thousand pupils – and you would have to multiply these figures by many times if you wanted to try to measure Sister Subbalakshmi's achievements in terms of arithmetic."

Shanti, Shanti, Shanti, the girls were singing – peace, peace, peace. The rustle of silk ran through the hall like the echo of a breeze as the audience sat down again. I tried to listen to the opening speech, and found that I couldn't. I was trying to picture Miss Lynch, who had died in London just ten years ago, when she was in her eighty fifth year. "Mrs Drysdale," Miss Prager had written to Sister, "was a great woman, a great Indian nationalist, and a great worker – and we three were together in the early days of work, of fight, of progress. Now you and I are left – and I wish I could see you once more in this earthly life before we too, pass on ..."

Sister, I knew, had invited Miss Prager to leave her home in Coventry and to come back to Madras and settle down in the vidyalaya and teach English to the students. It had not been possible for Miss Prager to do so, but neither she nor Sister had given up hoping that someday she would come and make her home in the place where both of them felt that she really belonged.

Now another speaker was standing behind the microphone.

The committee members of the Sarada Ladies' Union, she was saying, had wanted to celebrate the completion of Sister Subbalakshmi's fifty years' work as secretary of the organization by erecting a statue of her in the forecourt of the Vidyalaya Training School. Sister had come to hear of the project and had vetoed it with such firmness that it would have been useless to try to persuade her to change her mind. The money collected could, she had pointed out, be put to much better use, either by endowing scholarships or helping poor students in other ways. The portrait of her which had been unveiled eight years earlier would remain as a sufficient reminder of her physical existence.

Her real memorial, intangible yet far more lasting, would be in the continuing achievements of the organizations which she had founded. These achievements had, during the last decade or so, been widely recognized. She had served as a member of the Madras Legislative Council. She had, since her retirement from government service, taken a leading part in the activities of the Women's Indian Association. She had been awarded one of the highest decorations which the Indian Republic bestows on distinguished citizens for service to the community. But such honours, pleasing though they might be, were not important to her. She had never craved for fame or public recognition, and she had never cared more than she did now for the future of the girls and young women who needed help in order to realize their full potentialities and to be of service to the community.

I knew that this was true. Sister had told me a little, though not as much as I would have liked to hear, about the work she had done and the new institutions which she had helped to found during the twenty four years since the Ramakrishna Mission had relieved her of many of the responsibilities for the development of the vidyalaya. I knew that during the difficult years of the Second World War she and her sisters had run a school in the family colony, and that it had since been successfully established in a suburb which was particularly lacking in educational facilities. I knew, too, that during the past few years several of her former pupils had, with her help and encouragement, opened schools in different parts of the city, and that one of them, Vidya Mandir, was already a big, flourishing institution, famous for its introduction of modern methods of teaching. It was well-known, besides, that for many years Sister had devoted a great deal of her time to finding employment for needy women and girls. Many widows who had been left with young families and without the means to bring them up had been helped by Sister to place their children where they would be well cared for while they themselves practised their domestic skills in other people's homes. Sister's own cook, the girl who had served me with sweet and spicy dishes on my first visit, had recently left, and it was only when I asked what had become of her that I learned that Sister had been coaching her for two hours every day for the past year to enable her to enter the Sarada Vidyalaya Training School, where she was now preparing to become a teacher.

In fact, Sister Subbalakshmi, well on her way to her seventy sixth birthday, was still so active that I was sure that I would never, however hard I tried, succeed in tracking down all her activities. Next day, when the celebrations were over and I went to see her, I told her so.

When I went into her room, she was sitting at her desk,

head bent, making lists of people in different parts of the world to whom copies of the Sarada Ladies' Union Golden Jubilee Souvenir were to be sent. The Souvenir was a volume of about a hundred and thirty pages, containing essays and articles by well-known men and women, all of whom had been asked to write on some aspects of the ideal and practice of service to others.

I sat down with my back to the window. Sister turned around and, after we had chatted for a few minutes, handed me my copy of the Souvenir. As she did so, I felt the touch of small fingers on my scalp and then a violent tug at a bunch of hair at the back of my head. I turned. Sister's greatniece, seven year old Gayatri, was standing just outside the window, with one bare arm pushed through the bars.

"Can't you see," Sister told her, "that we are busy just now? You can come and play when we've finished."

Gayatri, tousle haired, merry faced, gave me a small, secret grin, half-threat, half-promise. Then she ran off to join her little brother.

A visitor arrived. Could Sister, she asked as soon as a few formal politenesses had been exchanged, recommend a cook, someone who would appreciate a good home and who could be trusted? Sister could, and did. Then, as goodbyes were being said, another visitor entered. She had not come to ask for help, but to offer it. She wanted to endow a prize for girls who were studying Sanskrit. While she and Sister discussed details I moved my chair back a pace or two and began to turn over the pages of the Souvenir.

Soon I was absorbed in an article which dealt with the education of girls and women under India's Third Five Year

Plan. Although the number of schools in the country had more than doubled during the fifteen years since India had achieved independence, the country was still a long way from achieving the aim of providing free and compulsory education for everybody. The more modest aim now, the writer explained, was to try to ensure that by 1965-66 all children between the ages of six and eleven should attend school. Already four out of every five boys in this age group were going to school, but only one girl in every five was receiving even primary education. About sixty per cent of these children left school without having attained permanent literacy, so that even today more than three quarters of the people of India, boys, girls and adults, were unable to read and write. Equality of educational opportunity between boys and girls was still a dream. Although the number of girls' high schools and colleges had increased enormously since 1927, when the Women's Indian Association had held its first conference on the subject, only one girl in twenty received any secondary education, while the proportion of boys in secondary schools was approximately one in five. The work which Sister Subbalakshmi and Miss Lynch and Miss Prager and the other women of their generation had flung themselves into with such pioneering ardour had produced remarkable results. Many of their pupils, and men and women in other parts of India too, had been fired with ambitions as burning and selfless as their own. Now the fire seemed to be smouldering. An India in which every child would have a chance to acquire the knowledge and intellectual discipline that is needed by those who are to be responsible citizens of the world was still a long, long way from present realities.

I closed the book and stood up.

"You are not going?" Sister asked.

"Yes, I must."

"You need not hurry away. I shall be free in a few minutes."

"No. I must go now. Really." I was still thinking about the future, and I didn't want to. The facts I had just read were too depressing. I wanted to run away from them, to read history and to think about the past.

Sister could still, as always, command obedience. I was compelled to remain. I sat back, staring out of the window. Gayatri had forgotten me, and she and her brother were tossing a ball at each other, utterly absorbed. I watched them, noticing, as I had often noticed before, the fleeting yet unmistakable resemblance between the small child outside and the ageing woman who sat a yard or so away from me, earnestly discussing plans for the future.

The future, I saw, was in both their hands. Gayatri's battles would perhaps, in their different way, be as hard, but certainly no harder, than those which Subbalakshmi had fought throughout her life – and Gayatri, when her time came, would enjoy battling, and would fight with the happy, unshakeable confidence that is needed to win.

A Child Widow's Story was first published by Victor Gollancz Limited in 1966.

Biographical Notes

Dr Monica Felton had been in active public service, serving on the London County Council, the Hertfordshire County Council and on various town-planning committees in Britain before she came to India in 1956. She spent the last fourteen years of her life in Chennai working on various books till her death in 1970. She is also the author of *I Meet Rajaji*, a moving biography of Shri Rajagopalachari based on a series of meetings between her and Rajaji, besides a novel *To All the Living* and a book about her journey to North Korea titled *Why I Went*.